fire doesn't burn

THE
SEAGULL
LIBRARY OF
GERMAN
LITERATURE

RALF ROTHMANN

fire doesn't burn

TRANSLATED BY MIKE MITCHELL

LONDON NEW YORK CALCUTTA

This publication has been supported by a grant
from the Goethe-Institut India

Seagull Books, 2019

First published as *Feuer brennt nicht* by Ralf Rothmann

First published in English translation by Seagull Books, 2011

ISBN 978 0 8574 2 722 9

British Library Cataloguing-in-Publication Data
A catalogue record for this book is available from the British Library

Typeset by Seagull Books, Calcutta, India

Printed and bound by WordsWorth India, New Delhi, India

fire doesn't burn

1
early years

However routine or unimportant the journey may be, however dreary the station, however full the compartment with noisy children, clumsy suitcase-carriers and panting last-minute arrivals who've just made the train: when all the announcements have been made, all the doors closed and everyone is waiting for the train to start, there is often a moment of quiet which seems to be about more than the unspoken 'At last!' or the distance between here and there, a moment which is like a mysterious pause, a pause for breath before the future, which makes most people, even the bad-tempered or impatient ones, look humble for a brief moment.

We know nothing when someone dies, not much, we're faced with an enigma and it's better to say nothing if you want to avoid obscure-sounding pronouncements. True, we've become accustomed to saying that the deceased will live on inside us, in our thoughts. But at some point we too will be forgotten, and what then? Only one thing is certain—no one in the world can erase a life, whether a long or a short one, pretend as if it had never happened. It did take place, once and for all, it had and is still having an effect on the past, present and future state of the mysteries. And just as nature, the physical realm, knows no death, only endless transformation, there will be an equivalent in the metaphysical realm. Now, at this moment, countless people are closing their eyes for the last time and at the same moment countless others are opening them for the first time and, if you disregard everything personal, you can get the impression that the whole of existence, all this fuss about growing and dying, is nothing more than a blink, a wink, in an all-encompassing indifference. Will that be a comfort?

The journey seems endless. It's hot, the air over the maze of rails is shimmering. Poplar seeds float round in the compartment. An old carriage of the urban railway with wooden seats, the kind of thing that disappeared from West Berlin ages ago—the fire extinguishers wobbling, the open windows rattling in the frames, doors slamming shut with a loud crash. The stations have unfamiliar names—Ostkreuz, Wuhlheide, Rummelsburg. Horses are dozing in the sun outside the long, graffiti-sprayed stables of the trotting course in Karlshorst. It's getting greener and greener, the people hardly speak and look out of the windows with faces you wouldn't credit with a great sense of humour. Many of the men are wearing shirts with faded patterns, unbelievable ones, such as you see on sofas in cheap furniture stores. The women with straw-coloured hair, cheap jewellery and cement-coloured complexions which grow a little greyer, their lips thinner, when they realize you're looking at them. Although they stared their fill when he and Alina got into the carriage, a look in their direction is clearly unwelcome, not even one that's meant to be friendly. A woman, having got out in Köpenick, turns to have one last look at them and when Wolf nods to her, she shakes her head and walks off, offended, in her sandals from the other German state.

Even more poplar seeds, without the trees being visible. Not a soul on the platform in Hirschgarten. Sparrows pick moss out of the gaps between the concrete slabs that have been patterned to look like cobbles and Alina takes a mouthful of water out of a plastic bottle. He secretly observes her reflection in the carriage window, the quivering, blurry silhouette. She's sitting upright, her hands relaxed in her lap, sometimes turning the ring on her little finger and, since she's pale and bleary, her blue eyes look darker than usual. There are fine lines running from the corners of her eyes to her temples but, although she's thirty-six, her forehead's still smooth. Recently she's had her red hair, which used to be curly, cut short, making her face look slightly plumper. With her round chin, thin lips and straight nose curving in slightly just before the bridge she has something of an art nouveau beauty such as you see in old prints or bookplates. But their decorative earnestness and high-flown fatalism are not her thing at all. She has too much of a sense of humour for that. She's breathing deeply, lips parted, and, as always when she notices him looking at her, her face brightens in a smile that's almost an automatic reflex. The train stops, for some reason or other it doesn't go on, and the silence continues to intensify. Poplar seeds are swirling round like furious flurries of snow.

They'd made the decision at the end of the previous year, towards Christmas. They were fed up with the district where they'd been living. In the Berlin air, the harmless touch of bronchitis he'd brought back from a book-launch tour in October, the result of standing round on draughty stations, turned into pneumonia with a high temperature that dragged on and on. He lay in bed, exhausted, sipping tea and trying to read while Alina was decorating a few pine branches with bows, candles and glass balls. The magic of Christmas is a must.

Despite keeping the windows closed, there's always a smell of smoke and exhaust fumes. The frames are rotten, the panes wobble when delivery vans drive up the road. The druggies in the rooms above them quarrel, swearing at one another in croaky voices. There's a Spaniard or a South American among them, he shouts, 'Te mato!' then again, more shrilly, 'Te mato!' Something crashes onto the floor and down below, Lola, the janitor's dog, barks. He seldom takes her with him when he goes out to the bar, a damp vault in the basement. At night they can hear the click of the billiard balls in the chimney and the bass of the jukebox makes their bed vibrate.

The house is enough to drive you crazy, even though it has a lovely view. You can see the swans on the Landwehrkanal and the sky stretches all the way to the cranes above Potsdamer Platz. It's dirty and it stinks to high heaven, especially when Wolf comes back from trips round nice clean West Germany, where he's been staying in his publisher's house or the Frankfurter Hof, when he pushes open the heavy front door and climbs the stairs between dented letterboxes and dried-out potted palms to the fourth floor, it feels like an insult. Crown corks crunch under his feet, fragments of broken light bulbs.

And Alina suffers from strange sneezing fits, she's probably allergic to the fumes from the rubbish in the courtyard and of course they know it can't go on like that, have known for years. After the Wall came down, the balance between the various districts shifted, almost imperceptibly at first, just as dentures change after new crowns or bridges and what was previously considered a smile is now an undisguised baring of the teeth. The motley bohemian crew which had occupied Kreuzberg along the canal bank fled from the new rents to Friedrichshain, gangs from Neukölln are prowling round Hasenheide and the Südstern underground station has become a meeting place for drug-dealers and junkies. They stand outside it in groups with their Rottweilers and such, muzzles hanging loosely from their collars and, when she comes back from an evening course or after giving private tuition, Wolf has to go and meet his partner off the train.

She's afraid, hardly goes out at night any more, and he often feels uneasy too. But he's more worried by the idea of a different area, of a new, perhaps less free, life. For the building, however awful it is and however depressing he finds the drunken and scruffy tenants, has one great advantage. They live there together yet separate. They have two flats on the same floor. It came about years ago, without them having to make any great effort even though it was a time when housing was short and rents extortionate. Alina was already living there and he circumvented the waiting list for the neighbouring flat, that had suddenly become available, by writing to the person in charge, a polished appeal to her romantic side, and enclosing a signed book with the letter—the first time he got a flat because he was a writer. Before that he'd been refused one or two for the same reason.

Next door to one another, apart yet close enough to share, that was their idea from the very beginning. A life together without the magic and attraction being worn away by too much closeness and familiarity—there it seemed possible. They have two kitchens, two bathrooms, two wide beds and one hope, and that for the last seventeen years. Often, they don't see one another for days, sometimes he puts the meal he's cooked for her in a pot outside her door. They slip notes to one another through the letterbox, poems, nonsense, marzipan, and say good night to one another by knocking on the wall and when they speak to one another on the phone and Wolf can hear that Alina has some music on, he still hears it softly after he's hung up.

Her flat is at the back and is brighter and quieter. Moreover, her windows are watertight and the heating works and it's late on Christmas Eve when they squat down on the carpet and spread out the street map, a tattered thing from before the Wall came down, the Eastern section is still as good as new. 'Where shall we go, my angel?' So far he's lived in Steglitz and in various streets in Schöneberg, she spent her first years in Berlin in Wedding and naturally you don't go back. The very thought of such a step seems to reverse his circulation and makes his heart beat on his back. To Friedenau or Charlottenburg then, where there are large apartments with high ceilings and parquet floors? Or even Dahlem? But the familiar Western districts, especially the middle-class ones, seem out of the way and faded since the dawn of the new age—stacks of small pudding bowls at the flea market come to mind, enamel signs for the bathroom, dark sideboards in Berlin rooms and bald pipe-smokers in leather waistcoats. And in the new districts they might consider—Berlin Mitte, Friedrichshain and Prenzlauer Berg—you can't move for lifestyle and logos, youth has become a profession there, success a religion and they're living on much too thin ice, they can hear it quietly creaking when they close their laptops. So move away from the city? There's no question of that either. You can't love it, certainly not, but it's still the best place for someone who doesn't really belong anywhere.

Because she wants to smoke one of her roll-ups, Alina opens the upper window. It's snowing, the flakes are falling through the light from the window into the backyard where the branches of an oak tree scrape against the wall when it's windy—you can see the marks in the crumbling plaster, a pattern of half-moon scratches. She closes her eyes, moves her index finger round and round, then brings it down on the street map, in the very bottom right-hand corner. Twisting streets, almost lanes, a village layout on the north bank of the Müggelsee. There's an observatory and a tunnel under River Spree, which is called the Dahme after a bend, the Forum Köpenick, a shopping centre, is close by and Schönefeld Airport reassuringly far away, and Alina strikes the match and says, 'That's where we'll live.' The flame is reflected in the windowpanes, double glazed, and a few snowflakes swirl round the room and melt on her red hair.

Writing about yourself in the first person seldom works without pretence. The 'I' can show you up in a bad light and the intention of being brutally honest, even shamelessly so, always gets toned down during the process and weaknesses are transformed into good qualities. That leaves the third person, a thin disguise, perhaps even with a 'speaking' name. It's like a child imagining it can't be seen if it keeps its eyes closed or puts its hands over its face. It's like a naked person, trapped with no way out, exposed to all eyes and any derision. The third person is a lowering of the eyelids.

Walking round Friedrichshagen, they like the two-storey, early-nineteenth-century house at first sight—white areas of plaster between sections of yellow brick, large windows, balconies on pillars and a glassed-in verandah on the ground floor, now a doctor's waiting room. In the shade of trees that are still bare, the proportions are on a pleasingly human scale and it is Alina who discovers the little notice behind the ornamental ironwork of the door. 'Attic Apartment to Let.' She grabs his sleeve and drags him into the courtyard. The landlady, a woman of around sixty, is in the garden and welcomes them with a friendly, almost beaming, smile. With shiny court shoes and a dark suit without even the suggestion of a waist, she's wearing pink rubber gloves with the price tag still attached and her permanently waved hair is so stiff with spray that it reminds you of a meringue. Her well-groomed appearance clearly says 'keep your distance', an almost American 'be on the safe side', and no detail about them escapes her sharp eye. She puts the hoe down and says she's sorry she can't show them the rooms today, after all it is Sunday and the current tenants would be taken by surprise. But they arrange to talk on the telephone. 'You're a writer? Well, this is the right place, then. Strindberg once lived next door.'

During the next few days, they keep going back to the district to see if the house really is the right one. For above all, they want it to be quiet. From that point of view, an attic apartment is better than any other storey—no noise of footsteps from above. And to judge by their curtains, the other tenants seem to be solid middle class, no rappers or punk rockers. You can hardly hear the railway, the goods trains for just an hour or two in the evening and the aeroplanes that turn above the district to start their approach to Tegel fly very high when it's clear. Anyway, they're going to close that air-port. But the street is a rat run for many motor-ists avoiding a set of lights with a long red phase and on the cobbles all tyres sound like studded tyres. The same rasping noise can be heard from nearby Furstenwalder Damm, constantly, and the lorries crash and clatter over the humps. But Alina tells Wolf there's hope they per-haps won't be able to hear it in the apart-ment. Anyway, it's still quieter than in Kreuzberg with the roar of the Südstern junction.

A phobia about noise is an occupational disease. You can hear the fleas on the fleas coughing. Yet for a long time noise meant nothing to him. At the rock festivals of his youth he slept under the stage on occasion and even as a thirty-year-old he would begin the day with Iggy Pop's 'Dum Dum Boys' at full blast. It never occurred to him to choose a flat according to whether it was noisy or quiet, he was just happy that he had one at all. It was only when he began to write prose that noise suddenly got on his nerves. Noises were so sharp-edged, it felt like having his skin scraped off and he made the banal discovery that language which goes beyond the everyday cannot be had without quiet. For that isn't simply an absence of noise, it's the translation of truth into the acoustic sphere, he has to listen to it to hear what wants to be rendered in his writing, and since then the search for conditions in which he can work, for quiet hotels or islands with no traffic, has consumed almost as much energy as the work itself. On the other hand, he's dubious about the desire to write something in peace and quiet. The important pieces of writing don't care whether the space round is noisy or quiet—something that wants to take shape will do so under almost any circumstances.

Two weeks pass before they can view the apartment. Although it's a cold, almost frosty, morning at the end of March, all the windows are wide open and they keep their coats on while the landlady takes them round. There are three rooms, a bathroom, a second lavatory and walk-in cupboards and the fully fitted kitchen with its ceramic hob and polished extractor hood under old beams looks almost luxurious. But Wolf, who once worked as a bricklayer, can see at a glance that the restoration work was done on the cheap, with corresponding materials. Underneath the carpets is chipboard and the gable walls have been covered with plasterboard, which is often a sign of hidden damp or even mould. In addition, he thinks he can smell the chimney that's blocked with soot and, given the streaks on the frames, it's questionable whether the velux windows are watertight as well. But when he asks the woman about it, she shakes her head. 'I don't know anything about that, you'll have to ask my husband, he's an architect. We have three houses ~~we rent~~ out. He converted them all and no one's complained yet.'

The mention of her husband's profession calms his concerns and after a glance at the look in Alina's eyes, he doesn't want to be a wet blanket. She's enthusiastic about the rooms and secretly gives him a pinch as they follow the woman through the glass door out onto the roof terrace. There's a dusting of hoar frost over the courtyards and extensive gardens below them, the delicate crystals on the fences and bushes and cabbage stalks glitter in the pale sun. Somewhere on the edge of the woods a tram rings, a flock of pigeons circles above the dovecote and a horse snorts in an open shed. 'This is where we're going to live,' she whispers when the land-lady leans over the balustrade and shouts some-thing down to the first floor, where her son lives. 'Or not?' she asks, almost anxiously, and once again he admires the braveness and determination to face the future in her expression and wonders for a melancholy moment what he has had to offer her all these years apart from his moods and neuroses and ageing skin. He's had nothing to offer to this marvellous woman and as he finally nods and puts an arm round her shoul-ders, a Lufthansa plane thunders past over the roof.

Memory, even and especially deliberate recollection, is seldom true—it creates the illusion that something is behind us and is over and done with. But as our hori-zon broadens, so does our suspicion that time is not something that moves. Rather, all time is at the same time, which is probably correct for the very reason that it is beyond our understanding. Who knows, perhaps at this moment the Middle Ages are happening somewhere in the dream-deeps, the ancient world, a future in machines made of mental power and light. At this moment a midge bite makes me itch, while Plotinus scratches himself and someone transfers his software to me with a wink. However that may be, memory is certainly not the means of making a work of art out of one's own life. For that it lacks completeness.

It's different with love. It began hesitantly with them, almost a classic example—the author and the bookseller. He had just published his first book and been awarded a year's bursary in the Sauerland for his poems and a short story. It included a flat in a villa which also housed the town's registry office—marble staircases, spacious rooms, large, oval windows with a view of hills and forests. It rains and snows a lot here, almost uninterruptedly, there are always wisps of cloud among the tops of the huge pine trees and the only bright spot is the main shopping street down in the valley. But the stream of glowing light is deceptive. The people dress in grey or beige, or both. Even their shoes are grey or beige. And naturally he takes the discontent on most of their faces personally. He's getting vast amounts of taxpayers' money for a few poems which don't even rhyme and they have to count their coppers in the cheap stores. A man, a blue-collar worker, pushes his shopping trolley against his heels, several times. He should move forward, nearer to the checkout, and when he eventually does so, though under protest, the other says, 'There you are, you can do it.'

He puts on a show of being brooding and industrious, talks about his first novel, when in fact he's just lying on the sofa staring at the grey sky, for months. Not much is expected of him. He has to read from his work now and then, at the local Rotary Club, for example, in the lending library, in the cultural centre of the neighbouring town, a former watermill with the clatter of the wheel. Despite that, his depression is often so paralyzing that he finds it difficult to raise his teacup to his lips. Since childhood writing has been a delight, despite the effort it takes. Being a writer, on the other hand, is hardly bearable, at least in public. That he's supposed to have something to say beyond his writings he finds unreasonable and when he can only stammer a few words, it tends to encourage his own suspicion that he's not a proper writer. The brewery-owner points out a questionable use of the genitive, the high-school teacher's read everything anyway and his wife asks if he knows that poem by Schiller that begins 'Higher you too aspired . . .' while her husband mutters something about Hölderlin. They watch with interest as he signs his book and promptly his fingers tense up so that he doesn't finish his signature. If, however, he tries to avoid that by beginning with a flourish, with large first letters, he doesn't have enough space to finish. The mill-wheel clatters and the organizer looks at his watch. He runs a mail-order bookshop next door with a considerable theological section that also includes devotional objects. He doesn't sell much contemporary literature, gardening books go best. There's an audience of seven and he has another appointment, so he introduces him to the trainee at the table with the books for sale. 'She'll take you home afterwards.' She gives him a nod, seems embarrassed, but her hand is warm and soft and pleasantly dry. She wears her full red hair tied at the back, in her soft voice there's something that reminds him of meadow-grass and asked about her unusual first name she mentions a Latvian great-grandmother. She has a well-thumbed copy of his poetry book with her and when she asks in for a dedication, he writes, 'All the better for seeing you.'

The reading's held on the first floor, in an absurdly large hall. She dims the light and sits down in the front row, the only person in it, the cash-box on the seat beside her. A white-haired couple have brought a dog, a huge, shaggy dog that lies down beside the radiator. There's no microphone, fighting against the emptiness brings him out in a sweat, his glasses steam up. 'Louder, please,' one of the audience shouts from the back and he clutches the pages and reads more quickly to get it over with. Since he's depriving the words of breath, the magic's lost and even the funny bits are lame. But when the dog yawns now and then, giggles can be heard, a snort of laughter. When the applause finally comes, hesitant, thin and yet with an echo that makes the hall seem even higher, the animal jumps up, barking, and can't get to the exit quickly enough.

Later, over wine with a gallery owner, the manager of the cultural centre and the pharmacist, the fair maiden is mostly silent, playing with her car keys and looking dreamily out of the windows, bulls'-eye windows. In vain he tries to see what her figure's like under her fleecy pullover and wide jeans, probably dungarees, at least they have a ruler pocket. Her shoes look sensible, too, and she's not wearing any jewellery, the holes in her ears are empty. Her curly hair glows with a halo from the candles on the window ledge, the skin of her neck is disturbingly white and Wolf, whom the pharmacist has just told he's a 'Goethe fan' and goes to Weimar every year, takes her hand, her restless fingers, and quietly asks her if she's bored and would rather go home? But she shakes her head, a lock of hair falls down over her forehead and her smile seems to him both hesitant and mocking at the same time. A disturbing smile, since she actually only moves one corner of her mouth, she raises her upper lip a little and her canine teeth can be seen in the flickering light, their shining enamel. She gently withdraws her hand.

She seems to show no interest in the writer in his thirties and to be too chaste for him anyway. It's been snowing outside and it remains cold for a long time in her car, which is very small and very rickety. She says little, her eyes fixed on the road. She has to concentrate on the steep curves in the forest and on the bridges where the wind polishes the ice until it's like glass. However, he does learn that she has an exam soon but doesn't want to continue working as a bookseller. She'd like to study German, art history and theatre studies in

Cologne. She's already booked a room in the hall of residence. He places his hand so that hers has to touch it when she changes gear. But somehow she manages to avoid it, her tongue sticks out between her lips when she turns into the parking space at the registry office. The magnolia tree's still bare. 'My fiance's also at the university in Cologne,' she says. 'Studying management. He's going to take over his parents' travel bureau.'

So that's clear, but Wolf doesn't get out straight away, the heating's started working. He pretends to be interested, he'd like to ask her in, for a coffee or a brandy. He's afraid of the dreary hotel feeling after such events, the hour between cold sheets, but he can't find words that would be better than explicit. He picks at a sticker on the dashboard, a white dove on a blue background, and when he offers to show her the rooms in the villa, the listed stucco with lots of fruits, putti, roses, that smile reappears, now with a clearly suggestive touch. 'I know the rooms,' she says and she puts the car into reverse, 'my father restored them.' Although he stays outside the house, watching her turn the car, Alina ignores him as she drives past. She's wiping the condensation off the windscreen with the back of her hand and concentrating on the road.

At the time he didn't think he was without a sense of humour but he certainly lacked the playful note that is possible, sometimes even necessary, between the sexes. At the end of the 1970s and the beginning of the 80s, when it became clear to him that he was attractive to women despite his shyness—he never had to do much, only return their looks steadily—people became intimate more quickly when they got to know one another and that has probably left him with a lack of empathy and patience. The whole business of courting a woman isn't his thing at all, his pride stands in the way of that and, anyway, he finds it difficult to respect a woman for whom the carry-on of the mating ritual is important. The idea that she should show him the cold shoulder with an enticing smile, in order to ensure that his intentions are serious, to check his strength, stamina and the quality of his genes, seems too zoological to him. He dreams of mute recognition beyond all the jabber, of the one look that says every-thing. He dreams of someone with whom he can be silent.

The winter lasts a long time in that area, the ground-floor windows disappear beneath the snow, but now it's thawing again, the buds are getting fuller and shine as if they'd been glazed, and he begins to work, at last. Something drives him over the pages, a new confidence that must have something to do with the season, the change in the sun's orbit. He sits naked at his table in the morning brightness and, just as when reading some books you fall into an almost cosy trance in which you only vaguely sense and understand precisely what you're reading—you surrender to the flow of the language, its timbre, trusting that the words will somehow help you, do something for you—that's what happens when he writes now. All his plans and outlines are forgotten, most of his notes crumpled up and, as he abandons himself to the rhythmic and poetic logic of the sentences, the smell of the pencils, the soft hiss of their points on the paper, he fills page after page with a story of which he hadn't thought of a single word beforehand. Yes, spring is writing for him, it's making a fool of him with superfluous adjectives and making the buds burst and the telephone ring as if in the distance. Presumably, someone's calling the registry office. But then it gets louder and rings in the hall—Alina.

He's still got a little comma on his chin, chives from his hastily prepared omelette, he sees it in the mirror on the hall cupboard. The oral examination for her bookselling course is coming up, she says, and she's decided to present a paper on him and his work and would like to arrange a meeting, as soon as possible. He suggests an Italian restaurant in the main shopping street that's usually empty in the evenings, a plaster grotto full of aquariums where she's already waiting when he arrives. The tumblers are blue and the wine glasses have frosted-glass stems, slim statuettes. They eat noodles and agree to use the familiar *du*. She has a tape recorder with her, no bigger than a cigarette packet, and while she sips her cola and asks him about his writing and life as an author, he looks at her face again and it makes a different impression on him than a few weeks ago—as if it had been redrawn by a serious decision that is aimed at his innermost being. He's astonished that he doesn't harden his heart against this, possibly that's because of her pale skin, the complexion of redheads which he can't imagine concealing anything bad. He's more and more moved, especially by the clear skin round her palely freckled forehead and her blue eyes. There is something here coming towards him which doesn't necessarily have anything to do with her, a person's aura could not be more pure. In a crowd or just in a photo—even one of those grainy ones from the time when neither of them were yet born—he would recognize that part quicker than his own face.

As she's interviewing him he feels more and more cramped in his role of author, its ridiculous respectability which makes him think of tweed jackets, damp, slightly steaming ones—the author trap, he thinks. Until recently, he's had lots of jobs, physically demanding ones, and the membrane between poet and prole is still too thin and lets too much through for him to consider himself one or the other. So, once again he takes Alina's fingers and asks her about her eyelashes. How does she manage to avoid leaving the little lumps in them most other women have, not a single one? And she gives an embarrassed smile and switches the recorder off. Yes that's a kind of art, she says, a tedious one every morning. But she doesn't like their natural colour, the red that's a little lighter than her hair, in summer it's almost blond. 'My boyfriend says that without make-up I look like an albino.'

This time she leaves her hand in his a little longer and later on she drinks some wine. The buttons on the cuffs of her white blouse, dark garnets, clink against her glass and, as they chat, he's more and more taken with her attentiveness, the calm trust it contains, it gives his words precisely the light, the clear definition they generally lack, nonsense doesn't even reach the surface. Her understanding, which twines round his words, makes her say things which have a gentle strength that seems to straighten something out inside him and, for one unbelievable moment, he has the feeling that their respective secrets cancel one another out and there's nothing wrong about him any more, not even his worst mistake. Even though their conversation concerns more or less everyday matters, its innermost echo plumbs depths between them in which they've always known one another and have never been separated. And when they fall silent and look at the fish in the aquarium, this mute accord, which manages without words unquestioningly, enfolds them like an invisible, velvet-lined case. Wolf orders another schnapps.

On the way back to the villa—she walks through the town with him as a matter of course, sometimes the whole width of the street is between them, the moonlight shining on the wet tarmac—he asks her about her boyfriend but she doesn't say much to that, naturally. He doesn't want to talk about his girlfriend either, that's quite another story, and they stop underneath the magnolia, now in full bloom and illuminated by a streetlamp. A few of the rooms in the registry office are used for further-education classes in the evenings, for a tango course, as it seems. They can't see the dancers, only their shadows on the wall which continue to move when the bandoneon stops playing. Clouds are scudding across the sky, hiding the moon, and in the silence they can hear the hard petals falling on the grass, on the street.

They're both slightly drunk. When it becomes clear to him that they would spend the night together, he takes just the amount he needs so as not to come too quickly. In the flat, Alina takes his lapel, her hair tickles his face and he's a little disappointed at her way of kissing. He would have liked her lips to be softer and more mobile, more experienced as well, a bit depraved. He would also have liked to feel her hand between his legs. But she has childishly moist lips and still keeps her eyes closed when he breaks away from her. Then she takes a deep breath and asks if she can use the telephone.

It's in the bedroom and she rings home to say she'll be out for the night. Although he can't under-stand a word, he notices the change in her voice—as if a gold thread had been removed from it. The shadow of the familiar, the everyday, falls over her, it's not just a daughter's agreed obedience but also the curt determination not to listen to any advice or warnings, not this time. Although obviously the attempt is still made, after all they live in a small town in the Sauerland, she's engaged, and the way she replaces the receiver with a frown gives the atmos-phere a momentary chill. Wolf uncorks a bottle of burgundy. 'Careful,' he cries as she sinks down onto the sofa, 'the backrest's loose.'

'Who cares,' she says, dropping her cufflinks into an empty wine glass, 'the whole world's loose.' They kiss again and while he's lighting a few candles, she slips her jeans and panties off in one go and he tries in vain to clear the hoarseness that's taken hold of his throat. The nondescript, or perhaps slightly unfinished, aspect of her beauty, as it appeared to him when she was dressed, is erased by the sight of her mature figure. She hasn't much pubic hair, just a slim flame, her nipples are pale, almost pink, and he is all the more moved by what is rubbing against his hand and readily opening out because Alina has no idea how magnificent she is, how radiant in her youth. He tells her that as he undoes his belt and kicks off his shoes, and she clasps her hands behind her head and looks down at herself with an ironic grin, as if to say: if you want to think that's the body of a goddess, that's OK by me. Let's do something nice with it.

Wolf is vigorous during the night, almost rough, as if he needs to find out how much it's him personally she wants. But Alina, keeping her lids shut tight and clasping him with all her limbs as if seeking something to cling on to, to stop her being swept away in the current, Alina is crying tears of pleasure and wants it harder and eventually the condom bursts. 'Doesn't matter,' she pants, 'doesn't matter at all. I'm OK.' But her heart is pounding and later, when they're lying side by side, all sweaty, sharing a cigarette, she dries his prick with a tissue, smiling and saying, 'He's still crying.'

The next morning she walks round the flat naked, holding a cup of coffee in both hands. She treads hesitantly, as if the floorboards weren't to be trusted. She's very discreet in the way she looks round, ignoring the chaotic desk as if it were something very personal, and sometimes she points out of the window, across the town, crying, 'Over there, that was my school,' or, 'On that slope I broke my nose sledding.' She holds her shoulders slightly stiffly, they're exceptional, of classical symmetry, and, like many cautious or not very self-confident people, she pushes her hips forward slightly, so that her bottom looks flatter than it is, making a hint of a stomach, a Florentine curve. But from behind, she looks boyish, with powerful calves, and her shining hair, sticking out in all directions, a mane of fine copper wire, makes her skin look even whiter, delicate, almost transparent. Everything about her says, 'Protect me,' and, to his own astonishment, for a brief moment, he feels he has the strength to do that.

She's interested in the stalls that are being set up in the market square outside the building, the spring fair, and so as not to be seen through the window, she puts her lower arms on the sill and rests her chin on her hands, and now the curve of her bottom sticks out behind, her ribs stand out, and he quietly slips over to her. 'Stay like that,' he whispers, goes down on his knees and breathes in deeply the faint smell of amber between her thighs.

The bursary continues for two more months and in that time they hardly see one another more than once a week, mostly on Thursdays. That's when she's officially doing keep-fit exercises, because of a mild curvature of the spine, followed by a massage. She doesn't want to present her parents or her fiance with a fait accompli which is perhaps no such thing. She parks her car behind the registry office, between rubbish bins and bushes, and draws the curtains over the big window as soon as she's in the flat—one of her aunts lives nearby. But she always comes as if she has something to celebrate, with wine or champagne or chocolates, and she can hardly wait for them to clear the table and for him to take off her pullover or dress. She likes nice lingerie, she buys suspender belts out of her trainee's wages.

In bed, she makes it easy for him. Although there can hardly be recognized standards in that respect, he's always felt he is a mediocre lover. Leaving aside the fact that he detests it when people talk about a well-ordered or balanced sex life, as if it were a hygienic necessity, it happens again and again that he's been alone for too long and gets too charged up, so that he lacks caution or sensitivity or stamina at the decisive moment. But Alina doesn't give marks, she takes him as he is and sometimes comes for the first time after a few seconds. She loves his impetuousness and clearly doesn't sense much of his diffidence which is definitely related to her youthfulness, the almost unreal smooth-ness of her skin makes clear to him for the first time in his life what has gone for good. In the darkness especially, or in the light of a candle burning behind a bouquet of flowers, he's afraid of her hands, her gentle exploration, as if it would expose him, so that he rolls on top of her like a brute. But he has to laugh on their last evening when she says, 'Do you know what struck me about you first of all? Should I be honest? Your fantastic mouth. No, your arse!'

Their farewell is unsentimental. Hope is a beautiful word but it's not right here. To go to university in Berlin must remain an unfulfilled wish for the moment, all the places are taken. They drink a glass of wine and each promises the other they'll give up smoking. Finally he gives her a chain, fine gold with a single pearl, and accompanies her to the door, to her car. As she drives away, she tears off a twig of lilac blossom with her side mirror and he sees that she's crying. But she sticks her tongue out at him and drives round the corner. On the day he leaves, he sees her in the shopping street, through a shop window. She is looking at the shelves of a gentleman's outfitter's, getting the assistant to show her some handkerchiefs, finely woven articles, and, although he waves, she doesn't see him. For a brief moment, he wonders whether he should go to her, then his taxi comes.

There are moments after a reading which are some of the saddest, dreariest for an author, especially if it's been a good event, with friendly applause and lots of books sold. The audience has left, the bookseller's counting his takings and the author signs a few more copies for the shop window, the trainee takes them out of the transparent covers for him. And, while he's wondering how he can get out of the usual invitation to dinner in some restaurant with heavy, leather-bound menus and typical dishes of the region, he looks up and sees that a few of the audience have stayed behind, possibly friends or acquaintances of the bookseller, for they're making themselves useful. They straighten out the display tables and gather up glasses, ashtrays and bowls of peanuts. Some nod to him or give him a shy smile, others talk quietly and the author, who's writing his name again and again, suddenly has the awful feeling that everything was in vain. That he wasn't able to give people what they desire in their heart of hearts, never will be able to, despite all his art, and that he's therefore just a miserable clown, one of those men who dazzle the audience out of vanity in order to keep their own blindness hidden. For each of these con-sumers of culture has left their quiet house, left their apartment with its cat and the blue picture postcards behind the spice rack, each was hoping for a promise fulfilled, something that would take them soaring up into the clouds—and now they hide their disappointment by helping to stack the chairs.

He thinks of Alina, back in Cologne, he wishes she were waiting for him in a hotel room, with only a sheet draped round her, and a pornographic film running on the video. But he doesn't even have her telephone number, if she has one. She's the one who occasionally rings him, from a telephone box outside the student residence, and on Sundays he can hear bells in the background, the whole city seems to be echoing with them. Then they talk uninhibitedly, cheerful chatter with no reservations, he's not usually like that and he's astonished at himself after he's hung up, he's almost always in a lighter mood as he sits down at his table and writing is easy for a while. But it still doesn't occur to him that that can have anything to do with her, not even after it's become more difficult again.

Where was he yesterday? The publisher arranges the engagements, the author has to fulfil them. By now he knows his little book by heart, he could close his eyes while reading and decide whether he'll go and have a pizza afterwards or, rather, a steak. More fruit would be better, less chocolate. And the next day, the same, for weeks on end, and he makes a detour to his hometown and stands by his parents' grave for a while, with the taxi's meter still running.

During those years, there's something eerie about the journey from Kreuzberg to Wedding. After Kochstraße, the underground leaves West Berlin and runs under the Eastern part of the city and before they reach Reinickendorfer Straße they have to crawl through six stations which have been mothballed, closed to the inhabitants, unchanged since the end of the war. Gothic script riddled with bullet holes, crumbling staircases, bricked-up entrances, here and there a slogan or a poster. 'Anti-Communism and Anti-Sovietism are the Causes of the Tense International Situation' or 'The German Democratic Republic Stands for the Preservation of Peace between Nations.' There are only occasional bulbs or fluorescent tubes and their light seems greyer than usual, making the faces of the soldiers on guard, mostly there are two, look waxen, like masks.

In the winter they wear fur hats with a red star and earmuffs and you can see their breath. But they don't react when exuberant tourists wave to them or drunks bawl something through the narrow upper windows of the train or even throw out a banana. Arms shouldered, they stand there, silent, among the pillars and girders, scrutinizing each carriage, and the young ones look sad, helpless in their authority, and the older ones angry from repressed longing. One can well believe that one or other of the officers, brows furrowed over a steely look, is thinking 'Just you wait', the desire for revenge, when one of those shiny yellow, triumphantly bright trains runs through his underground republic—like a pain in old veins.

After a few months by the Rhine, Alina has managed to exchange places with a student from Wedding and has also taken over her flat for the time being, one room, kitchen, no shower. If you've just come to West Berlin, you can hardly find a more desolate area. Rats, metal doors, overflowing rubbish bins. The cramped backyards stink of damp walls and smoke, the neighbours' dogs keep shitting in the stairwell and she uses the indoor swimming pool two streets away and walks round the block with wet hair on frosty winter days. As planned, she's studying German, art history and theatre studies and to finance it—her parents can't give her much—she has an occasional job in an engineering works, stamping pieces of sheet metal, piecework. Or, during vacations, she goes to West Germany, the Krefeld area, and spends twelve hours a day stuffing gherkins into jars. 'With no gloves,' she says, showing him her wrinkled fingers. 'And there's no soap in the toilet.'

She has friends in Berlin, people from the Sauerland, and lives her own life without him playing much part in it. He is now actually working on his first novel and, because he lacks confidence in his talent, he makes a big thing of discipline. They only see one another at weekends, mostly in Kreuzberg, in his quiet attic flat. They fill the fridge and only reemerge on Monday. Or he goes to her place to burn the corrected sheets of his first version in her tiled stove and then cook a meal for her. For a long time he had casual work in pubs and big kitchens, so cooking at the stove's no problem, and, since he's doing it for just a smile, for the delight on her face, some things turn out well, although they never seem as good to him as to her, living as she does mainly on kebabs and apples. Moreover, cooking is more than just a necessary activity for him. Even if hardly anything ever tastes as good as it did when he was a child, when his parents brought peas and rhubarb in from the garden, and the board on which fresh mushrooms are chopped has a stronger smell afterwards than the mushrooms themselves—the attention food and its preparation demands calms him down and brings order to his mind, simply because there are no doubts about the point of the activity.

That Alina came to Berlin because of him is never expressly stated, yet it's obvious. Her engagement was broken off. But she doesn't seem to expect him to change anything about his own life. She comes across half the city to be with him in a black box dress with nothing on underneath. She points at the wall, at his slim shadow with the horn and turns on the bedside lamp so that it looks even bigger. He likes the brazen submissiveness with which she opens her drawn-up knees as soon as he comes to the edge of the bed. He loves to rub his cheek against her hard, yet elastic, nipples and then to lean over her as if he's doing a press-up, his arms straight out, his body tensed from his toes to his shoulders, while she milks him, slowly, very slowly and with a matter-of-fact curiosity. At first she uses just her fingertips, then her fist, and, as with no woman before, he enjoys the feeling of the semen he has saved up for days only for her spurting out of him with full force—and that she pants with pleasure at the power he gives her. Then placing her arms round his neck and pulling him gently, whispering, down to her.

It's only in this that the difference in age between them can be felt. For Alina, in whose school photo on the wall the teachers have long hair and the kids are wearing brightly coloured pullovers with horizontal stripes, sex is as natural as breathing or drinking water. She's not shameless, she can blush when he comes across her naked in his bathroom. But, just as she never thinks ill of others, never curses anyone or has a bad word to say about them—and not because that's her conscious approach but because it's her nature—it would never occur to her to feel guilty about a desire for happiness for which her body is merely a lovely means. Wolf's driving force, on the other hand, comes from the taboo which gives it a certain vehemence and flexibility but seldom helps him to transcend the limits of his body. Thanks to the Catholic Church and its hypocritical education at school and in the youth club, he's truly messed up and ready for almost anything. But ultimately, however disgusting he finds the word, he just makes love. Alina is love.

Sex—a chronicle of inhibitions. For ages it's been the main thing in his life, his real blessing, and that's why he's fouled it up so often. It awoke in the 1960s, fresh from the catechism and with the cassocks of finger-wagging priests looming over him, almost at the same time as his delight at the songs of the Beatles and the Rolling Stones, and when he disappeared into the bushes at the edge of the small town with a girl for the first time, he was just thirteen. His idea of what was to happen next was based on the vague articles in the magazine *Bravo*, the dirty jokes of his classmates, who had obviously all done it already, and a few porno-graphic photos. He was so afraid of being found that he only took off the minimum of clothing, his trousers were hanging round his knees and he was trembling all over and couldn't even find the hole of the sixteen-year-old girl who did it with lots of boys. When he breathlessly begged her to help him, for God's sake, she just turned her head away and said, in a bored tone, 'No.'

A humiliation with grass and semen stains, that was his first time. And for a long time it was the beginning of endless feelings of guilt, simply because he was horny. Sexual morality in those years had something to do with hairspray, the stiff hairstyles, with painted eye-brows and cocktail dresses, cocktail chairs and cocktail sausages in households where they never had cocktails, with ribbed underpants and elastane passion-killers, with unfulfilled desires and a thin-lipped whisper in the dark: 'I don't do that kind of thing.'

It was better for a while in the flowery 1970s and not just because he was earning money and could go to a brothel if necessary. He tried out a few things in the smoky dens of the subculture without ever really belonging. His girlfriend, whom previous lovers had called Flash-fire, or Flash for short, because she came in a real spray, wanted him to call her Flash, too, and then soon went over to feminism. And suddenly his prick was a problem again, suddenly it didn't give her the orgasm it had been giving her for so long. He should think over his lovemaking, and he made the mistake of reading more feminist literature than any woman. For it didn't help. However sensitive he was, he remained a man and would never understand women the way they wanted to be understood. And when he did understand them like that, it turned out that they wanted to be understood differently. They were always one smile ahead of him.

Then came the 1980s. If the hairstyles and clothes of the previous decade, with long hair, bell sleeves and flared trousers, had had the form of a cone, everything broadening out organically from the top of the head, that was now inverted. Shoes were pointed, trousers narrow at the ankles, and shoulders so immensely padded that you looked like a wedge. Even your face, from the chin to the hair sticking up and out radially, echoed the shape. You locked yourself in the loo in the Jungle or Slumberland or whatever the departure lounges to happiness were called, wiped the snow off your nose, always cut stuff, and had a quick, hard knee-trembler. And once, when he wanted to lick the woman, she pulled him up by the ears and said, 'No, not that. That's too intimate.' And the next weekend, in the same place, among all the dancers with their sharp-edged silhouettes and jerky movements, they were already ignoring one another.

When the novel's finished, he invites Alina to go on a trip with him and she chooses Amsterdam, where she's never been before. He, on the other hand, often went there during his younger days in West Germany because of the easily available joints and the concerts in the Paradiso—and was repeatedly driven back home by the cold, damp wind in the narrow brick lanes. He can only stand being close to the sea in the south. Moreover, he finds the ubiquitous crime a strain and when he says, 'Forget Amsterdam,' she nods, sadly, but then she says that would be a good title for a book. At that he gives her a kiss and books a room in a hotel on Prinzengracht.

In the meantime, she's moved from the run-down area in Wedding to Kreuzberg, by the Südstern. By chance, they now live only two streets away from one another and use the same shops and cafes. This at first seems to be a problem for her. She's afraid of appearing to put pressure on him, though she probably just wants Wolf to tell her she's not putting pressure on him. But, if anything, he's glad she's close by, at least for the moment. He types out each page of the final version fifteen or twenty times, for he takes the most minor error, even just a comma, as an indication that there's something wrong with the whole text. Which mostly turns out to be true. It's only later that he realizes that this method of working is also a sign that there's something wrong with him. For weeks on end, he doesn't get more than four hours' sleep a night, drinks pots and pots of coffee and suffers from such nervous tension, is so fragile, that he often feels a cigarette butt flicked away could knock him over. But in the evenings, during the cheap but good meals at the Indian or the Turkish restaurant and the following walk along the canal, he enjoys Alina's contented humming at his side and her smell comforts him and her smile gives him strength.

She doesn't seem bothered by his unpredictability during these weeks, the sudden outbursts, moods or even nastiness of a man whose demands on himself are driving him to the wall. She makes sure he doesn't run out of provisions, makes him hot milk with honey and, while he stands there at the window sipping it, corrects the pages he's just finished and almost incidentally comes up with solutions to problems that had brought him to the brink of despair. To be clear, to express himself clearly without yielding to the terrorism of explicitness—that's his ideal at that stage, and his desperate attempts to achieve that make some things turn out obscure. 'That's wrong,' she says at one point, indicating a passage just before the end. 'Fire doesn't burn! Fire flickers, or glows or smokes. It's something else that burns . . .' He feels himself go pale with shame.

So the trip, by way of thanks. After he's taken the page proofs to the post office, he finds a rabbit in the grass, a little, white soft toy that probably fell out of a pram. He feels weary as he walks through the warmth of the afternoon, still with Tipp-Ex on his hands and the rhythm of the last sentences in his head. For a moment, he thinks of buying a rose but then he drops the idea. Their plan is to eat in Alina's flat and then take the night train via Hamburg and Bremen. The unrest in East Germany is increasing, lots of people are leaving the crumbling state across the Hungarian border to Austria, the garden of the West German embassy in Prague looks like a refugee camp but the trains on the cross-border line are still running. They listen to the news and music and, while he chops the vegetables, Alina parades up and down in the clothes she's going to wear in Amsterdam. For the first time she's painted her nails red, dark red, a little clumsily still. He hasn't seen the shoes before either, sandal court shoes that don't quite cover her toes at the end, the cramped gaps between them arouse him like the cleft in a low-cut dress. This first holiday together seems to mean more to her than he realizes. She chatters all the time, already on her second glass of wine, and her cheeks are flushed when she suddenly wants him to tell her exactly what his feelings for her are. His hands full of onion peel, he steps on the pedal of the waste-bin. 'Sorry? I can't hear,' he says, 'the violins are too loud.'

Then he takes the white rabbit out of his holdall and lobs it to her. After dinner, there's still plenty of time but Alina takes his hand out of her hair and makes some tea. As she does so, she tells him about her new part-time job, starting next month, just round the corner. He recognizes the name of the shop, formerly a left-wing bookshop, its window display used to have homemade posters from the 1970s larded with plastic carnations, endless calls for action full of exclamation marks. Now it's a chain selling standard stock, the managers notorious for their American treatment of staff. But Alina's happy to have the job, she'll be working two days a week and will finally have more time for her studies, for the master's degree she wants to get over and done with. And she even makes a gesture, as if she were throwing something over her shoulder.

Once more he's astonished at how casually she manages her day-to-day existence. She obviously never imagines she might find herself without essentials such as a roof over her head, work and food, and since she doesn't feel an urgent need for anything either, everything seems simply to drop into her lap. More quickly than he did during his first weeks in Berlin, she saw this restless frenzy, subsidized left, right and centre, for what it was—furious activity leading nowhere, a strain on the nerves but not on much else. Hardly anything in the life within the walls seems to be of truly vital importance, not even its dark side. But now she clearly seems sad, or at least depressed, something unspoken has turned her aura grey and she doesn't look up when he asks her about it.

She fondles the soft toy in her lap and he can hear the change of key in her silence. His heart begins to race, he closes his eyes briefly and, because his chronic lack of realism has sensitized him to anything that might endanger his dreamer's existence, has made him a virtuoso of foreboding, he's not surprised when she tells him she's missed her period. He just nods, looks out of the window, staring into the distance, and takes a sip of tea—that is, hides behind the gold rim of his cup. Alina plucks out a few of the rabbit's hairs. The inaudible crackle of a new, for him harsh, reality crystallizing round her last statement abruptly falls silent when she goes on to talk about a false alarm. It was just one month she missed, now everything seems back to normal again . . .

But he can sense there's something else weighing on her mind. She's fiddling with her jewellery, pushing the pearl on the chain this way and that and blinking all the time. And then she takes a deep breath. However, when he examined her the day before, the gynaecologist did say that it was about time she began thinking about children, now, in her mid-twenties. Such things were usually a signal. And so . . . She swallows hard, he can hear the gulp in her throat, and when he gets up to open the window, a little too abruptly perhaps, something seems to sag inside her, at least she suddenly starts speaking much more quietly, almost whispering: that's why she'd like to know what he thinks about it and whether he could imagine them.

At that moment he's moved by her more than he'd admit and he doesn't want to disappoint her. But he doesn't want to give her false hopes either, just because it suits her hormone level. True, to expect a healthy woman to abandon all her hopes and not have a child would be as inhuman as to expect a man never to sleep with a woman again. But his problem is that he doesn't see the world the way it is but the way he feels it ought to be—a free existence full of grace and adventure, and who can imagine that in a three-room flat with a playpen or a terraced house with fixed holidays?

He's caught unawares when Alina quietly reminds him that life doesn't have the free space of a margin and that its logic can be different from that of love poems, that it contains a demand for responsibility, for a future, and he thinks he has a right to get angry when she goes on to tell him about the next-door flat which will soon be available . . . Now of all times! 'I can't manage it before my skiing holiday,' he hears someone shout in the street and the radio announcer tells them their well-earned weekend begins here on Culture Radio with Chopin's Scherzo no. 1 in B minor, op. 20. Something's being set up here, that's what he suspects and he feels as if he's forgotten to read the small print, those secret clauses in which the tight geometry of what is likely is ready to pounce. He has a strangely grey taste in his mouth, all at once the trip has been ruined and he tosses the tickets on the bed, picks up his bag and leaves Alina alone with her tears.

Hardly is he in his flat than the telephone rings but he ignores it. He puts his clothes back in the wardrobe, clears his desk and tears notes and different versions of his manuscript into little pieces. Then he peels an apple and listens to the radio again, news of the unrest in the GDR.

Like most of his acquaintances in those days, he's never really been aware of the state on the other side of the Wall, even though the television tower with its reflecting sphere, reddish on summer evenings, was visible. He's been to East Berlin only once in fifteen years and he was so horrified at the dreariness of the treeless streets, the stench of the ridiculous cars and the careworn expression on the faces of the people disappearing into houses with bullet-scarred facades that it simply made his romantic socialism, which was based on the assumption that liberty, equality and fraternity cannot exist without beauty, all the more romantic. It had to be a temporary error, surely, and because he found no opportunity to spend the twenty marks you had to exchange, he went into a bookshop on Alexanderplatz. Inside, he immediately felt better, even though he quickly realized that was because of the customers, mostly people from the West, for at that time the opportunity to buy good books in cloth binding cheaply—Gorky, Brecht, a complete Dostoyevsky for less than a dinner at the Robbengatter—was for many the only reason to go to East Berlin. And Wolf, too, was amazed at the well-filled shelves full of classics which didn't need consumer glossiness and whose binding and layout therefore appealed to him as a human being more than in the West. A Shakespearean sonnet, set in crooked type he could feel under his fingertips, or Goethe's poems, poorly printed on woody paper, suddenly moved him again and he spent hours rummaging round on the various floors—even though he eventually only bought a little book by Max Frisch.

The woman at the cash desk, wearing a woollen skirt and a white, poorly ironed blouse, entered the amount into the till. She was at least twice as old as he was, had no jewellery on her hands which were reddened from too much washing, no smell at all and a face that seemed to deny itself any expression—perhaps that was why he found her mysterious—but she didn't respond to his smile. She was wearing stockings that had disappeared in the West, brown with a seam like something from a liquorice wheel and had tied her hair in a bun and, while she was taking his money, it occurred to him that he could buy some-thing else. He pointed to the gallery with shelves full of international literature. 'Would I find Proust there as well?'

He hadn't meant it to sound mocking or provocative, after all, he'd seen countless volumes of Hemingway, Faulkner, Sartre and Malraux. He was simply a young man who'd long wanted to read *In Search of Lost Time* but couldn't afford the expensive, hardback Western edition in its slipcase and had now spotted an opportunity. He had so many East German marks left. The woman looked up, pushed a loose strand of hair behind her ear. She was wearing lipstick, a dull red, and he noticed a handkerchief with crocheted edging in the sleeve of her blouse. 'Proust?' she asked quietly, as if she hadn't heard properly, but her face remained expressionless.

Wolf put his change, the tinny coins, in his pocket, while she looked him up and down. Her face showed profound disappointment, which had clearly become habitual, and apart from the fact that nothing could ever make up for that, she refused to be mocked into the bargain. Even her complexion looked offended, her flabby cheeks quivered as she shook her head. But the expression in her big eyes, inflamed round the lids, was alert and knowing. Then she seemed to realize that he was indeed naive, this guy with the long hair and leather jacket, an innocent in the bitterly cold war, and clicked her tongue like a teacher at something an incorrigibly stupid pupil had said. 'There's no Proust here,' she said, turning to the next customer.

But when he went out into the street and the smoke from his cigarette drifted over the window, she looked up again from her ivory-coloured keyboard, with its end-of-work cover ready beside it, and the lines of her face now seemed softer, almost relaxed. He thought he could see quiet understanding in her look, perhaps even sympathy, and there was the ghost of a smile playing round her sad lips, where the red was already fading at the corners. And then she moved her head in such a way that it could have been taken for a nod, for a secret acknowledgement.

'God, you don't have to get all hurt like that.' Alina's sniffling and he jams the receiver between his shoulder and his ear to core his apple. Her voice, usually so bright, full of verve, sounds strangely dull, as if over-shadowed by the silence with which he makes him-self seem unapproachable. 'I don't want a child at the moment,' she goes on. 'I know how important your independence is for you. I just want to know if you could imagine it as a *possibility*.'

There's something wrong with his perception of the whole situation. Just as biting into a summer apple can sound as if you were treading on fresh snow, there's a chilly crunch to her words about what he assumes is in her mind, and he sits on the edge of the desk and stares out at the flocks of crows crisscrossing the purple twilight. 'There's a lot of things I can imagine . . .' he says through his teeth, and it sounds colder than he intends, he's just trying to gain time. But the pause he leaves must whisper '. . . but not with you' in her ear, even though that's not what he's thinking. On the other hand, he makes no attempt to correct that impression. He observes his silhouette in the dirty window, his motionless features which make him look more grown-up than he feels, and flicks a few paper clips into the waste-paper basket. Then Alina clears her throat and says she's going to Amsterdam despite all this, without him if necessary. She waits for a moment, during which he's winding the lead round his finger and, when he doesn't reply, she hangs up. No goodbye.

What has happened, for Christ's sake? That his resentment, looked at in the clear light of day, is inverted shame, shame not so much at his panic reaction as soon as life makes a demand on him but, rather, at the fact that Alina was witness to his alarm, is something he can hardly bring himself to admit, much less his cowardice. As he tries to convince himself that his stomachache proves he was right (in fact they're caused by the onions), he tears up a few last passions captured on paper and looks at Alina's picture beside his typewriter, the crumpled black-and-white photo with the glare of light on her forehead. He'd used flash even though it was bright in the room.

And he suddenly remembers that sometimes she puts on her make-up before phoning him, that she first checks the fit of a new dress in his expression, not in the mirror, that she feels 'lilacky' in May and, unlike him, always sees the truly poetic things, the furry underside of a leaf, the tea-smell of some horses on the bridle paths in the woods, someone glancing at their watch with a host in their mouth. And as he recalls that one of her dreams is about a room just for beautiful chairs and that, until her last birthday, she still thought the sound inside a shell was the murmur of the waves that had somehow been preserved and that the German word for purse, *Portemonnaie*, came from *port de monnaie*, harbour for money, he chokes with remorse, picks up the timetable and looks through it. His fingers tremble as he does so.

All out of date, yesterday's trains, only something impossible can help him now. He has to withdraw from the present, away from the guilt, the pain and the tears, and he calls the railway inquiry office and learns that there's still a train that leaves before the night express, with that he'd be in Amsterdam around six in the morning, an hour before her. And he packs his bag for a second time and finds the rabbit in the side pocket.

The big yellow tiles on the wall of Zoo Station. The melancholy of the low-ceilinged hall. The tub with frankfurters, the half slice of toast. For a long time now he's dreamt of writing a story that begins: 'When there were still platform tickets . . .' It must have been some time when he was a child. The Deutsche Reichsbahn carriages are surprisingly empty, he has a compartment to himself. The wall covering and the undivided benches are typical GDR and there's a photo of the Thuringian Forest over the headrest. Nothing has changed in the station on the other side of the Wall. Moonlight gleams on the sliding windows of the tower and the uniformed men with little attaché cases buckled on over their stomach watch in silence as the train enters the station. In the sidings at the back are low loaders full of tanks covered with tarpaulins, only the barrels sticking out. Moths flutter against the tall lamps and the powder drifts down off their wings.

The men, left hand dangling casually by their trouser seam, right arm resting on the aluminium rim of their case full of stamps and receipts, nod to the engine-driver and climb aboard. A few go straight to the restaurant car or chat up the—female—ticket-collector but the one who opens the door to Wolf's compartment is strict about doing his duty. Without a word of greeting, he examines the luggage rack, crouches down a little to look under the seats and then demands, 'Travel documents, please.' Everything as usual. He too doesn't smell of sweat or deodorant or aftershave, his light-blue shirt has been starched, his fingernails are spotless, his wedding ring is where it ought to be. Outside the windows the lightless repub-lic. After he's checked the number of Wolf's passport against the ones on his wanted list, he puts a much-used piece of carbon paper—it's almost transparent from all the names on it—underneath the transit certificate and fills it in, all official. But when he places it in his passport, takes a step into the compartment and holds them out to him, there's a thin smile on his face, a somewhat melancholy and, for a brief moment, amused expression, as if he knew that all he was doing was putting a stamp on thin air. Then he says, 'Have a good journey.'

Amsterdam Central is aglow with morning sunshine as the train comes in to a cacophony of recorded and live announcements mixed with the flap of pigeons' wings. On the platforms, countless people who have to go to work, a mute stream moving to the buzz and click of the ticket machines, you're only in the way, and when he comes out of the flower shop, Wolf waits behind a board announcing future strikes.

As the air brakes hiss and the pantographs are drawn in, his heart is pounding with excitement, he's even sweating a bit and, at the same time, his feet are cold and, although the carriage she gets out of is five or six from the end of the platform, he sees Alina immediately. Someone hands her her suitcase and the hair she pushed back with one hand falls back down over her forehead as she nods her thanks. She's pale, with rings under her eyes and she sees him behind the board after only a few steps, with no signs of surprise. She's holding her blue raincoat closed over her breast and pulling her suitcase through the crowd. He comes out from behind his cover, his impassive gaze fixed on her. He keeps getting jostled, but he stays there, the ironic rose in his hand.

There's something in her face that makes him think of a child, a good, peaceable child to whom something nasty has been done simply because she's lovely or upper class and whom the ugliness of the deed just makes even lovelier, more superior, despite her tears. She looks hurt and, at the same time, as if transfigured by the astonishing discovery of a deeper layer of invulnerability appearing under the hurt. 'Why're you here to meet me?' she asks softly, as the letters and numbers on the indicator board rattle above them and, although he's understood, it sounds to him like 'What are you doing to me?' and the gentleness of her voice almost breaks his heart.

She looks as if she's not slept during the whole journey, just cried—which is what she did, as she later tells him—and the sides of her nose are chafed and red from blowing it all the time. He cautiously kisses her on the forehead, on her eyelids with the now colourless lashes, on her still incredulous lips, touching as he does so the furrow they used to call 'snot-gutter' when he was a little boy and which, so the story went, comes from an angel, from the finger with which it closes our lips before we're born, before we go to the other side. And then he feels the roots of all the hairs on the back of her neck as he thinks of the later reverberations of this moment, which he finds so moving because, among other things, it is already intensified by memory, because in some distant future one of them is just remembering it.

'Come to bed,' he whispers.

2

american mysticism

Untruth begins with the determination to produce a work of art, with arrangement, but at first you don't notice. Over the years, however, weariness sets in, weariness with fiction, revulsion at all the imagining, narration, scene-painting, retarding and omitting. There's something obliging, whorish, false about it and, after over a dozen books, he thinks he knows that it's all over, this storytelling palaver, it's just not possible any more. Every idea seems shallow before he writes it, every subject served up ad nauseam on television, what's the point of a new twist? To continue making things up today means to be lost to the truth and the only thing drearier than an expert is his satisfaction at his expertise. But once you seriously begin thinking about giving up for good, you're heading straight for the worst of all traps. It wouldn't just be the end of all future prospects, it would destroy everything you've achieved so far. Anyone who can stop should never have begun.

On the south-eastern outskirts of Berlin, shortly before the border with Brandenburg, it's almost rural. Greenhouses under wind-blown pines, allotments, the Erpe valley. A stream in the tall grass, its curving, willow-lined banks kept in shape by a network of twigs, a single horse-rider beyond the rushes. Even more poplar seeds are swirling round, much too early for the time of year, the whole rattling railway carriage is full of them, you have to pick the spores off your lips, out of your hair. They gather in gossamer threads, long flakes that roll under the seats, and the flurries only die down when the train slows down as it comes into a station. Once more Wolf observes Alina's reflection in the window, her silhouette with the pearl earring, and she gives a vague smile and strokes his hand. 'We can do it, can't we?'

What can he say? The boxes are packed, the van's loaded and is probably already parked outside the house. After a sleepless night full of doubts, which grew into despair on the bare mattress, and after hours of discussion before daybreak in the course of which he put them both through such mental and emotional torment that she ran sobbing to the bathroom, he's just tired. He's never lived together with a woman in the same rooms for any length of time, no more than Alina has with a man. Every attempt went badly wrong,so that he no longer believes he can learn, not now that he's approaching fifty. On the other hand, it's clear they can't afford two flats in Friedrichshagen—the district's in demand from young, well-heeled families and the prices reflect that. If they want to get out of Kreuzberg, then they have to move in together and there's something humiliating about the financial constraint—with the amusing touch that it reminds him of the early 1980s, when there was hardly any affordable property in West Berlin and couples living together who wanted to separate, simply found it impossible . . .

So far money hasn't been a problem. It comes naturally to them not to demand more of their circumstances than the bare essentials so they've never known really hard times. And if elegance is reduction to the essentials in their most beautiful form, then you could even call their life elegant. He remains an unsuccessful author—sufficiently unsuccessful to keep the wolf from the door, true, and he can rely on his publisher—and Alina teaches German as a foreign language in private schools, where the pay is equally measly. But so far they've always had precisely as much money as they needed—they were mobile and could feel free and now he sees that freedom as endangered. But Alina, who's a millionaire when it comes to confidence, who's chronically optimistic, laughs at him, believing as always that life knows better than he does, he who's wondering about taking on commissioned pieces, getting a job as a publisher's editor. 'Just accept your good fortune,' she tells him the day before they're to move. 'If you were ever to do something just for money, I couldn't love you any more.'

Then the bell rang and the matter was settled. It was Mr Schmischuh, a sinewy man with a goatee and long hair, a hippie who's been transporting furniture with his men since 1968, in his van decorated with flowers, and they made coffee and sandwiches in the bare kitchen. As they ate, he told them the story of the academic couple the previous week. A new, more spacious apartment at last, and in Grünewald as well! They'd spent days packing, consigning decades to crates, pausing all the time because there was a story about this glass or that letter. But when they parked outside the new house, a breathtakingly beautiful, late-nineteenth-century villa, the wife suddenly refused to get out of the car. There were tears in her eyes, she couldn't speak for almost a whole hour, and the man was silent too, staring out at the rain. Finally they'd all driven back, without explanation or comments. They drove back to their old familiar—if cramped—home and unpacked everything again . . .

He probably meant to encourage them. With his experience, he knows what it's like when people break out in a cold sweat as they hesitate at the last moment. He doesn't just transport furniture and household goods, he transports mistakes as well, no problem. 'Fortunately, there's *me*!' is what's on his visiting card. Coffee mug in one hand, cheese roll in the other, he strolled round the two flats, examined the sparse furniture, the rolled-up carpets and the boxes full of books and said, in his Berlin accent, 'Nah, we'll get the lot in one load.' In the days when people everywhere were suddenly dancing the tango, a sentence had drifted into Wolf's mind from somewhere or other and he'd noted it down: 'You don't have to be perfect, it's OK to make a mistake, a wrong move, but do it with conviction.'

It's almost midday and Alina's still fast asleep. She's got red marks on her arms from carrying the boxes. On a saucer beside the bed is her jewellery, a chain with an aquamarine. Soft music can he heard from their neighbour on the same floor, Bach toccatas. The sun's shining through the orange blind on the mansard window, the beams are creaking in the heat. Every time a truck drives down the street or a train along the railway embankment, the surface of the water in the glass on the chair trembles and the tips of the pot plants scribble the slightly irregular cardiogram of the hour on the air.

As she usually does when it's too bright for her, Alina is sleeping with one arm over her eyes. One leg is sticking out from under the blanket, the nail varnish on her toes is flaking off. Her calves are powerful, her skin white, like alabaster, she often feels ashamed of it, she never goes out without wearing stockings. A few short reddish hairs can be seen in her groin and her breasts stand out under the nightie with the threadlike straps and satin trimming, they've hardly changed in all the years, they're delicate and heavy at the same time, perfectly formed. She wheezes softly and when she turns over on her stomach and bends one knee her skimpy panties slip down. There are a few light, scar-like stripes on the sides of her bottom but, unlike most other full-bosomed women when they're approaching forty, she has broad hips and round buttocks. He slips his hand under the material and carefully feels the shaven skin between her thighs and her cunt, the smoothness here is different from elsewhere on her body, a soft relic of childhood. He presses up against her and gives her a gentle bite on the ear.

'Welcome to our new home,' he whispers, his voice hoarse after his deep sleep, his lips dry. She yawns and stretches, fumbling for his prick as she does so, which isn't stiff yet, as occasionally happens now. It worries him sometimes. Up to now he could rely on his erection, a clock hand that was usually even fast, and his problem tended to be to conceal his arousal—strength at the wrong time is also weakness. But now he finds his member keeps going limp and, so that Alina won't think she's not seductive enough, he moves away from her hand and kisses her where she likes it best, taking care not to scratch her with his stubble, not yet. She breathes deeply and pushes her bottom towards him, at the same time stuffing a little cushion under her belly, then a bigger one, and the professionalism of the gesture brings him to full arousal.

But she's not moist enough yet, he can tell when he tries to penetrate her with his thumb, so he lets a glittering, crystal-white drop of spittle dribble down between her thighs and rubs it with the tip of his penis. He begins slowly, very slowly, ignoring the panting and slight jiggling she often gets into immediately after his first thrusts. His attempts to move in rhythm with her are often thwarted by her wild frenzy and he calms her by lying on her with his whole weight and keeping his head at such an angle that she can't smell his morning breath. He clasps her breasts.

Birds are squabbling on the roof. The toccatas have fallen silent. Alina comes with a deep groan, splaying all ten fingers, but then immediately starts moving again and he enjoys delaying the end. That's hardly been difficult at all since he's learnt to breathe deeply and clench then release his pelvic muscles. Even on the odd occasions when he sleeps with other women, he rarely comes too soon, so he no longer has to fake it or tense up. The embarrassing or sobering side is elsewhere now. Still, it's a gratifying if curious fact, given his age, that despite the reduction in his virility, his orgasms have become more overwhelming. Since he has no idea yet what the acoustics of their new flat are like, he suppresses his cry and, with a quiet, 'My God,' nestles his face in Alina's neck. Then they go back to sleep again.

Later, when she's in the bathroom, he uses the second lavatory, enjoying a sense of luxury. But already during breakfast—the kitchen with the view out onto the roof terrace seems more spacious than it actually is, apart from the fitted units there's only room for a small, square table and two chairs—he feels constricted by the idea that from now on they'll be sitting this close together every morning. Alina has no make-up on, her face is slightly puffy, her tousled hair needs washing and she has a faint smell of sour milk, as is often the case with redheads. She's wearing a slightly tatty velvet leisure suit and different-coloured socks. Moreover, she eats her toast in a way he's always found astonishing, given her small mouth—one bite and it's half gone. But what he used to find amusing is suddenly off-putting and already he's resisting the idea that her munching with bulging cheeks while staring dreamily out into the gardens is a sign that things are bound to go wrong. He puts some music on, a John Cale CD. For years, the vigour and humanity of this voice has helped him overcome his own narrowness of heart. 'Fear is a man's best friend.'

Then they discuss who's going to have which room once more and Alina insists she's more than happy with the two smaller ones, one to sleep in, one to work in. After all, she says, with his desk and all his books he needs the big one, the living room, and she'd even been wondering whether two beds were really necessary, he could always sleep in hers. But when he looks at her, not uttering a word, she quickly raises her hands, 'OK, OK, it was only a suggestion.' They also needed to think about furniture for the flat where hardly any of the walls are at right angles. Almost none of their furniture really fits, some items are already stored in the cellar. They ought to have shelves and cupboards built into the acute angles and it would give them a bit more space if they could have a glass roof over half the absurdly large roof terrace, a conservatory as a dining room. But in the end they haven't got the money for all that. He doesn't want to ask his publisher for some before the manuscript he's promised for the summer is ready and, while Alina furnishes the flat as well as she can, doing small repairs here and there or some painting, he settles down among the still-full boxes and types out the final version on his computer.

In the evenings they go out together to explore their new district. The station building, with all its pointed arches and battlements and cast-iron pillars from the days of the Kaiser is next to the spa gardens. People used to drive out here for relaxation and when you go along cobbled streets called Linden Avenue or Chestnut Avenue or Breest Promenade and look between the stuccoed houses into the gardens, with everything in bloom you can hardly believe you're still in the city. Apart from a relatively limited estate from the communist days and a high-rise building opposite the church, there are only a few large buildings. The oppressive massiveness of Berlin is almost entirely missing, most of the houses, built round the turn of the century and under preservation orders, embody the humanity that must have informed architecture before modern functionalism arrived. Many of them, even the new buildings carefully inserted in the rows, have chest-high metal fences, traditional wrought-iron work. Here and there art nouveau decoration can be seen. The woods around look as if they're endless, spruce plantations and mixed woodland full of old trees, and on the first night on their terrace they realize that in all their years in the centre of the city they've never seen such a clear, starry sky. On the second, beneath a full moon, they hear a cuckoo call.

Whichever way they look, the area appeals to them, even if some of the things about it make them feel slightly uneasy. At the beginning at least, the quietness gives them the feeling the streets have something to hide. The Weberschiffchen, a spacious restaurant with an open fire and oak panelling, is empty. There's only a policeman sitting on the ledge of the Italian ice-cream-parlour window, spooning the ice out of a tub, and the yellow tram, already brightly lit, hurtles through the town, empty. Flowers, lovingly cared for, on every balcony but hardly a human being anywhere . . . Although it's warm and summery and light stays till late, already at seven the curtains are drawn and the blinds down. In places, there's a flicker of the television through the gaps.

Lots of old people live here, citizens of the vanished state, and they rarely smile, hardly ever say hello and still call the supermarket the *Kaufhalle*. They're often carrying a prescription or a doctor's referral note in their hand and it's not unusual for Wolf and Alina to find the eerie lack of expression in their faces oppressive, if not even threatening. It looks as if in the GDR people couldn't show when things were going well, when they were cheerful and full of the joys of life, it aroused suspicion. But to make it clear that things were bad, that you were suffering in and through the state, was equally suspicious. Consequently, the people of the old and middle generation adopted this cement-grey fixity of expression, a thin-lipped mask. Added to that is the lack of discretion, the unconcealed stares and, when the two of them stroll along Bölschestraße in the centre and Alina, in her bright, free manner, laughs at one of his stupid remarks or jokes, people often stop or turn round to look at them.

Hawthorn and chestnut trees overhang the twisty pavements, the unevenness of which takes some getting used to, grass is growing in some of the roof gutters, and on their walks they're almost always drawn towards the lake, the magnet of their souls, as Alina calls it. In the tunnel deep below the green water of the Spree, turned to gold by the setting sun, it is so chilly at night you can see your breath and when they come out of one of the pubs along the bank and can hear nothing but their own steps on the glistening tarmac, they can hardly believe their luck. A hedgehog scurries under a parked car, an owl hoots and each road seems to have a moon of its own.

But those are just illustrations. The real attraction of the area, which is part of Köpenick, has a less poetic basis—Friedrichshagen is simply a beautiful district which has not yet been taken over by the rich. As well as the old, there are an increasing number of young people living there who clearly come from the West and for whom the discovery of the place is a welcome reason finally to leave their bohemian days behind. Most of them trundle their statistical two children round the streets behind the plastic windows of their bicycle trailers and those who haven't yet got any have 'family planning' written all over their faces. It's certainly a good place to bring up the next generation. There are birthing centres and day nurseries, private and state schools, any number of second-hand shops for baby clothes, relatively little traffic and lots of ponds where swans are fed—the kids feed them bread and the old folks crusts. The cafes and restaurants are reasonable and, in contrast to the city centre, you can rely on it being quiet at night. After eleven, all the windows are dark.

Alina orders two bicycles by mail order, smart aluminium jobs on which they intend to explore the surrounding area, the woods as far as Erkner and Grünau. It wouldn't be that far to Buckow or even the Oderbruch either. But on the day they're delivered, they see an accident in Ahornallee. A woman driving a Trabant has driven into a young cyclist who's now squatting on the edge of the pavement, holding his bleeding head. Passers-by hand him tissues but he just looks at them uncomprehendingly. The car, with its synthetic bodywork, is chugging away to itself in neutral, its exhaust bathing the scene in a delicate, breathtakingly foul-smelling blue and, back home, Wolf rings up the mail-order firm to have the bicycles, which are still in their packaging in the hall, taken back immediately.

The subsequent argument with Alina releases all the nervous tension of the last few weeks. His sensitive stomach rebels. The fluffy animal still swaying under the rear-view mirror of the two-stroke car, the blood on the cobbles, the bent spokes—he reads the world like a book, in which he sees signs everywhere, usually of disaster, which she, with her cheerful pragmatism, finds amusing, especially since she's developed a remarkable ability to prove the contrary to him. However, she quickly becomes depressed when her sunny outlook fails to convince him and he persists in his gloomy view. And her quiet sadness, which brings out her profile so beautifully, like the sadness one feels when confronted with someone who is ruining their life by doing something particularly stupid, makes him aggressive.

His awareness, developed over the years, that arguing has assumed a clarifying, almost hygienic, function between them, after which they treat one another more tenderly again, does nothing to change his astringent pleasure at making her cry while they're arguing. He finds this power monstrous, a gift of the devil—and compensation for the fact that he doesn't command that sad logic-chopping with which she manages, before he knows what's happening, to twist most points at issue, so that he ends up taking the blame. It's only because she's crying that she refuses to give in. She's convinced that if she doesn't stand up for herself she'll lose his respect, not to mention her self-respect, and she clearly gets as much enjoyment out of having the last word as she does out of applying the finishing touch with the nail-varnish brush.

For all that, this theatre of acrimony is not without its funny side. They discover that at one point when they're about to hit one another. Chins raised, teeth gritted and eyes glaring, they freeze for a moment in disbelief before slowly letting their fists drop and concealing a grin from one another by going at it hammer and tongs again. And the very next day the argument turns out to be almost nothing, a storm in the microwave, and by the day after that they don't know what exactly was the reason for his fury and her tears, the shouting and slamming doors, and when Wolf finally goes to her, he's not even sure whether he has to apologize to Alina. He just can't bear the strained atmosphere between them any more, it just seems to make the flat feel more cramped, and the bleakness of being right is just as bitter as being clearly in the wrong. But she beats him to it, puts her arms round him, presses her forehead against his and whispers a plea for forgiveness.

In the end, it's less the disagreeable scenes that make you unhappy or ill than the determination—be it out of lethargy or weakness—to become accustomed to it. However much they like their new environment, what Wolf vaguely suspected when they viewed the house becomes a certainty after a few weeks. The end of May is warm, almost hot, and the roof turns out to be insufficiently insulated. It's like living in an oven and they simply have to leave the windows open so that the traffic noise, all the louder since a bypass has been closed, pours in. Mould appears under the paint in the bathroom, the blocked fireplaces have a stronger and stronger smell of gas and Wolf can't sleep, keeps getting headaches, and Alina has inflamed eyes. Their landlady can't explain it. After all, a family with a baby lived there before them and had no complaints. The building biologist from West Berlin they ring about it refuses to come out to see them. It's always the same in the East, he says, especially in converted attic storeys. For apartments that were renovated just after the collapse of the communist state, they still used all kinds of stocks of materials from the GDR or Poland—wood soaked in formaldehyde, asbestos insulation panels, corrosive adhesives and cheap varnish. 'Move away,' he advises them, pointing out the possibility of allergies, damage to the nerves and even cancer. 'The only solution is to torch it.'

But they can't believe they've made a mistake, they still hesitate. The move took too much energy out of them. Anyway, the manuscript has to be finished, the publisher's already rung up to enquire what stage he's reached and to ask for a suggestion for the cover. So they decide to stick it out for the moment. In order to purify the air in the rooms, they place pieces of rock crystal everywhere, spider plants and silver vines, and if it's too hot, they sit in their vests out on the waxed stairs where it's cool and Wolf continues typing on his laptop and Alina leafs through magazines or stares dreamily out of the multicoloured windows until it begins to get dark and flocks of crows head for their dormitory trees.

But one day when they come back from a walk in the Hirschgartendreieck, a nearby park, they can smell smoke in their flat, cigarette smoke, and for one terrible moment they think there's been a break-in. But the lock on the door's undamaged, so it must have blown in from the balconies all round. But when they close the windows, it makes no difference. On the contrary, as the hours pass, the smoke gets worse, now there's no doubt that it comes from the flat below. Often enough, the smell of coffee or cleaning materials has come through the floorboards and sometimes they can even smell when the young mother changes the baby's nappies. But anyone who's lived in a Kreuzberg tenement is used to worse. Wolf remembers the rats sprayed all kinds of colours belonging to the punk girl next door. They'd eaten their way through the plasterboard . . .

Cigarette smoke, however, is unacceptable. It's already causing him shortage of breath because he gets so worked up about it for, like many converts, he's come to find cigarettes and their smell nauseating. Again he rings up their landlady, whose cool politeness immediately strikes him as disdainful, an unspoken 'Not him again.' This new phenomenon is, apparently, another mystery to her. But when Wolf doesn't allow himself to be put off and even threatens to reduce the rent, for a moment he hears nothing but the whine of a fax machine in the background and thinks he can even smell nicotine on the receiver. Then the woman clears her throat and says, in an aggressively friendly tone, that her son, who works in bridge construction, is back from a job and he smokes, though not in the flat, because of the baby. At most he has the odd one in the evening when the little darling's asleep. You can't blame a hard-working young man for that, can you? Live and let live, no? 'Moreover, young man, you will remember that when we signed the contract I specifically asked you and your wife if you smoked . . .'

Wolf was flabbergasted. She had indeed asked that question and, even though he thought it was none of her business, it seemed to him a natural one for a house owner who was concerned about the state of her rooms and floors. Her claim that she was not only sounding them out to see whether Alina and he would object to cigarette smoke but, at the same time, informing them they would smell it in the flat, takes his breath away. Moreover, he's deeply hurt that she clearly thinks him such a dimwit that he won't notice her subterfuge and that turns her little piece of chicanery into the embryo of a monster. He recalls Alina recently asking how it was that citizens of the GDR, a socialist state supposedly disapproving of private property, could come into possession of three large houses with over forty flats, and he sees the television pictures after the Wall came down—masses of outraged people storming and partly wrecking the central offices of the Stasi, vociferously demanding their files. He'd assumed they were people who'd been spied on or harassed by the state, what else? But, in fact, the majority were spies panicking, concerned they'd be unmasked, 'unofficial collaborators', who were now fearful of their neighbours, colleagues or spouses and wanted to quickly erase as much as possible of their traces, of the notes that would give them away.

The telephone call ends on a frosty note. The woman talks of a superior apartment in a superior situation and says she cannot understand how anyone could keep on finding fault, she's never had anything like it before. In a block of flats, tenants have to show consideration for others. Wolf, who doesn't have a lawyer, hangs up after telling her she'll be hearing from his lawyer and, as always when he doesn't know what to do, feels as thick as two pairs of socks. But shortly afterwards, when the electricity bill's due and they see from the list inside the box with the meter that they're the twelfth tenants in eleven years, they give notice for the flat from the end of the month. Alina cries but she's relieved and switches her computer on to look for another one, definitely in Friedrichshagen. Wolf sits down to work on his manuscript again.

Anyone who understands his times stops looking for victories. The tattered, yellowing notebooks, some over twenty-five years old, smell of dog's hair.

The ultimate dulling of our responses, live on screen. Endless horror after a short commercial break. The flare of flashlights across the screen, in the light of the infrared cameras these people look paler than they can be, women and children driven out of their beds, stumbling over the utensils soldiers pull out of their cupboards. Green points of light glow in the eyes of the bound men squatting in trucks just before they get sacks and bags put over their heads. They don't believe an old man, lying in bloodstained clothes among overturned chairs, is dead and shoot him again in front of the cameras. The body rears up under the impact of the bullets. 'I did my job,' the soldier says.

In the summer, Wolf receives an invitation to the New York Goethe-Institut. Together with other German authors, he would express his views on the September 11th attack and the threat posed by terrorism. How can literature respond? is the question. He's offered an astonishing fee and well remembers the sentimental liking for the Chelsea Hotel and its run-down charm he expressed ten years ago. But he turns it down. Whatever he had to say, it would scarcely be original if he used normal syntax and definitely not politically correct if he were to say what he really feels when he sees the television pictures. Moreover, he's not very keen on going to the country, never has been, not even in the early 1980s when having lived for a while in New York was de rigueur for anyone who wanted to make their mark on the literary scene.

Despite that, he has been there several times, for weeks or months, for his work. Initially quite prepared to believe the Americans have a secret, a special power, in his very first nights on foreign soil he was woken from his sleep by horrible dreams full of orgies of violence in which he cut off heads and genitals, tore out hearts and drank blood. And the fact that the land of the free consisted entirely of slaves to television, who can only think in dollars and can hardly move for bureaucracy, didn't exactly fit in with the cliche of highways through wide prairies beneath a blue sky. His application for the social security card he needed for his brief time as a college professor turned into a grotesque farce in a labyrinth full of plastic plants behind which you were given a further stamp and sent on to the next door, to the next building, for two whole days until you ended up back with the first official. And all these functionaries with permanent smiles on their faces were deadly serious.

His feelings there were a mixture of fear and amusement, as if you were permanently being bawled out by someone you couldn't take seriously. All the skyscrapers were saying 'Me! Me! Me!' all the time. And everything else was jeering, 'Not you! Not you!' That American society is prudish is a commonplace which is not necessarily true of all Americans. In the college where he was teaching—though that's overstating it, he talked once a week to a dozen students about German literature, in German, and was given recipes for cheesecake and banana bread—there was a secretary available to him. In a notice covered in signatures and stamps over her desk, he could read what female employees were to regard as 'sexual harassment at work' and immediately report to the authorities—jokes that fell into that category, any kind of touching, an equivocal look in the eye or at other parts of the body, putting your tongue in your cheek, repeatedly licking your lips while talking, scratching yourself below the belt or a handshake lasting longer than necessary. The woman there clearly had difficulty squeezing her bosom into her tight blouse and there-fore wore it somewhat more unbuttoned than usual. He was looking at a face with make-up that could not be more provocative and when he asked if his three-day beard was permitted, she gave a beaming smile and said: as an exception, since his English was so poor.

She was called Peach and was a student but, since her parents couldn't afford the three thousand dollars a month in fees, she had to work in the administration, leaving her youth behind. And she was well off there, poorer students cleaned the lavatories. The pressure at the elite college was immense, anyone who didn't get top grades damaged its reputation and therefore its market value. Moreover, any semester that had to be repeated would ruin her family. To save money, Peach didn't live in the student residences nor ate in the expensive canteen. She'd rented a house with five other girls on the outskirts of the town, a draughty wooden shack with the white paint peeling off. She heated ravioli in the tin and helped him improve his accent, for a fee. They read the translation of his book together. 'We only think of sex,' she admitted to him one evening while they were having a drink, 'and we talk about it, every minute of the day. But of course you can forget the boys here.'

He massaged her neck and her shoulders, which were hard as wood, while she zapped the channels, and when he expressed surprise that there was nothing but violence on all of them, shots, dead bodies, wrecked cars, twenty-four hours a day without anyone being concerned, while the whole nation was up in arms when breasts that were bare or just covered with thin material could be seen, or the president, like every executive in the world, was screwing his secretary, she just shrugged her shoulders. 'Don't ask me,' she said, undoing the buttons on his jeans. 'That's American mysticism. When I was four, my parents were arrested. They'd let me swim in the sea naked. Anyway, Clinton really is a swine.'

Even if he had to laugh because he could feel the breath from those last words on his foreskin, the moment shed light on something his longing for a secret had blurred—in this country, where people think they're clever because they have power behind them, and whose almost desperate patriotism betrays a profound homelessness, even the depths are on the sur-face. America—that's brute matter at its most brutal, meaning pain, and all the countless convolutions of the brain put together go to make the shining dome beneath which power is working to corrode our brains. If everything to do with sex is made taboo and anything risqué or erotic is blacked out or replaced with pips, the obvious effect is that people think of nothing but sex, day in, day out. And anyone who thinks of it all the time, who is forced to think of it out of pure frustration, the only release being aggression, loses interest in other areas of life, lets things take their course and politicians and generals do their worst. And, in the cool expression of the young soldier, who says he's just doing, and always will do, what his president ordered, before emptying his magazine in a dead body, you can see precisely the same defiant narrow-mindedness and breathtaking remorselessness that strikes you the moment you get into a taxi at Kennedy Airport.

Often the only ray of hope is the humour of the blacks. 'Germany?' the driver asked him once. 'What time is it in Germany now?'

'About six,' Wolf replied.

At that the man laughed and shook his head. 'So early? You guys really are crazy, man.'

Books protect. Life, when it's written about in a way one can relate to, loses its murky, threatening quality for a short time. The reason a reader can feel snug and safe with a book is not least because it holds in check the things that frighten or disturb him. Bound in the author's formulations, they no longer have any power over him, at least not for as long as he's reading. Only happiness feels uneasy in a book, happiness has to flee. A deer with no fear of man always has something of Disneyland about it.

It's a comfort that life is more wonderful than any literature. During their exploration of the district, they noticed a couple of new developments, not far from Goldmann Park with its immense plane trees, and Wolf, who liked the tasteful duplex houses with front gardens on the cobbled street lined with oak and chestnut trees, casually remarked, 'I'd like to have moved in there.'

Later, when they've sent in their notice and Alina waves him over to the computer, there's just one flat in the whole district which is the right size. The advert says: 'Ecological design and construction, only non-smokers need apply.' They ring up and arrange to view it. Since they're still not very familiar with the area, they take the street map and suddenly find themselves in the part of Friedrichshagen where Alina put her finger when they began looking. Not only that, they're outside the ochre new house with the dark-stained shutters that appealed to Wolf a few weeks ago. It's a three-room flat, small but very distinctive, the evening light gives the oiled parquet floor a velvety shimmer. The heating's concealed behind the walls, which are plastered with clay and between which the air moves differently, more pleasantly, and the internal oak staircase, a spiral up to the attic, gives the cleverly designed house a particular tension, as if it were a house within the house. It has a narrow balcony with a view between the trees in the avenue and another, higher one on the south side from which one can see over roofs, sheds and turrets to the lake, and the owners—he's almost ashamed at the relief he feels—are from the West. They have the ground floor, a couple of Alina's age, originally from the Frankfurt area.

The rent is right for such an apartment, perhaps even a bit lower, but still more than that for their toxic attic flat and this makes Wolf slightly uncertain. He hates the idea of living beyond his means, it would inhibit him in his life and in his work, make them feel less genuine, of that he is convinced. On the other hand, it could give his destiny a nudge—hasn't he found more than once that everything really important goes according to his wishes? Despite that, he keeps humming and hawing in a way he would find disappointingly petty in a figure in a novel, not worth getting worked up about, and that leaves him with the grudgingly accepted comfort that ultimately his concerns are a kind of dark optimism, the fuse for a blaze of joy at the successful outcome.

They sign the lease and once more the floral van stops outside and Mr Schmischuh is inspecting the flat, hardly surprised that there are fewer things to be transported this time. While his men are struggling with the furniture and crates, he carries a Japanese paper lamp out to the van and takes a bite of his roll. 'As my grandmother always says, moving twice is like being bombed out once.'

Work on his novel becomes foreseeable, his nerves begin to twitch. As mostly happens, there are some good signs—the epigraph he's been trying to find for ages turns up, episodes that refused to take shape assume their final form almost automatically, a female acquaintance he hasn't seen for fifteen years and whom he described, more or less, in the last chapter, rings up one evening. At the same time, however, his body makes its presence felt—the usual back pain, stinging eyes, his stomach. Not that he's ill, he's never been really ill, his good genes, enjoyment of exercise and, last but not least, his hypochondriac nature have clearly saved him from that. But not being ill used to feel more light-hearted. Or, to be more precise, he took less notice of the fact that he was healthy. Moreover, the time when one of his temporary jobs was as an orderly in a university hospital has left him with—alongside the memory of a mild case of hepatitis—a superficial smattering of medical knowledge, the result being that he still sees every ache or itch as the first symptom of some disease, naturally of the worst possible one with the most complicated course imaginable. One of his easier exercises is to keep telling himself he has a temperature until the mercury in the thermometer actually does rise.

Hypochondria as a heightening of your self-esteem. An imaginary pain makes your self somehow bigger. But even if it's just the funny side of suffering, its teasing, so to speak, seen through the refracted light of your middle years sudden shooting pains, a surprising dizziness, angina seem more and more like the anticipatory rumble of a catastrophe that you can't see simply because it's already right over your head. True, he does secretly believe that it's his fear of being helpless, dependent on others, that has up to now protected him against more serious illness, but at the same time he suspects that it will probably be an illness which will heal this ungodly fear. After all, does not every illness contain the sense of other levels, is not every one preparatory? That often became clear on the intensive-care wards, in the soft-grey hour before dawn, when pains and death throes seemed to pause awhile, the nurses and staff on night duty had nodded off and even the bleeping and ticking of the machines seemed quieter, the space was filled with a strange lightness, the infusions glittering like crystal, it was almost serene, as if the horrors belonged to this world alone. As if something like grace were possible.

The aeroplanes up in the sky, the rattling urban railway, the goods trains making the former marshy ground vibrate slightly—the metabolism of the city. Squirrels in Goldmann Park, white sails on the lake. Birds call in the bushes and when it's not too hot he works on the south-facing balcony and looks out over the gardens with old, in some cases huge, trees and foundations for new houses being dug. The patches where people grow vegetables, even tobacco, are connected by narrow paths, overgrown with elder, and the rag-and-bone-man's bell can be heard again in the high archways of the freshly restored town houses. All round are new beginnings, through many windows you can see piles of packing cases, young families are having breakfast on the resurfaced terrace and, while he's polishing his sentences, Alina's arranging the flat. As she's doing that, she makes sure he always has some mineral water, fruit juice or freshly made tea and this new experience is like a gift—the cheerful determination and strength and confidence of a woman who is setting up a home for herself and her beloved for the years to come. She makes plans, discusses things with the electricians and the plumber, after work she looks round the furniture stores, brings catalogues and fabric samples home. She buys light-coloured beech or cherrywood cupboards and shelves that go with the parquet floor, huge but light cane chairs and a big sofa in dark-brown, grained leather. She doesn't want any carpets, just a kelim in subdued colours here and there. She cooks evening meals for him, since he needs every minute, and he loves her limited repertoire—risotto or quiche with salad again and again, 'Classic Minestrone' from the tin again and again. She puts flowers in his room and plates of peeled fruit, gets tubs of ice from the Italian ice-cream parlour and shuts his notebook when she thinks it's time he took a walk and for that he feels almost humbly grateful. That writing is hard physical labour—even that sentence is going grey at the temples.

Her energy seems inexhaustible because she doesn't see what she does as expending energy. She does what has to be done and she's already fallen asleep while he's still complaining about feeling tired and exhausted. But when he wakes up beside her one morning, she looks worryingly fragile and pale, almost white, with tiny drops of sweat on her nose and clutching the corner of a pillow. He can still see the child on the school photo in her, especially when she's asleep. She sighs softly, huddles up a bit and, although there's no reason for con-cern, he instinctively thinks, stay with me, girl, don't die on me. An absurd thought which alarms and annoys him at the same time. He slaps his forehead with the ball of his thumb, gets up quietly and makes some coffee.

Not often, mostly during periods when he feels profound affection for her, he's suddenly struck with fear for her health and her life, then he secretly looks to see how warm her coat is, examines the soles and lining of her winter boots and checks their supply of vitamin tablets. He makes sure her cellphone's always charged, shouts to her from the balcony not to cross the road when the lights are on red again and pulls her back, furious, when she stands too close to the edge of the platform or the pavement. If, when she's out, he finds a hair in his suitcase or in a book she's read before him, it's a painful reminder that the day could come when she's not with him any more—and, to his surprise, it also brings a smile of satisfaction that he cannot now imagine once more being free of his concern for the woman, free for everything living together shuts you away from.

When he comes back with the breakfast tray, Alina is awake and smiling sadly. Her eyes are moist and, at first, she doesn't reply to his question, just stares, motionless, into space. He sits on the edge of the bed, pours milk into her coffee and waits, and after clearing her throat and swallowing, she tells him—some sugar trickles down on the floor—that she actually dreamt of her death. Her mother, she said, had come with the news that she was to die in six weeks time, on a Thursday. '"What, so soon?" I said. "But I have to look after my husband. Can it not be put off?" But she just shook her head, so I thought, OK, then. I'll just come as a familiar spirit to help you.'

He exhales audibly. For the first time she's said 'my husband' and that imbues her girlish nature with an earnestness that delights him—as if with these three syllables they had become, after years of physical maturity, emotionally mature. But when he asks her if they should get married, she laughs again and wipes her eyes with the back of her hand. 'No, no, my friend, let's forget that. I know you. Hardly have you signed something than you want to tear it up.'

She takes a drink. He shakes his head but secretly he's pleased with her answer. Even though he naturally assumes he's going to spend the rest of his life with Alina, with a contract it would only be worth half as much. Love with an official stamp, that's like a poem with no poetry.

He goes back to his work and one day he hears something strange with the rustling and crackling of packets and bags that usually accompanies her, a silence with a different tinge on the landing. Sometimes she brings students back and gives them a private lesson, mostly without charge, but she doesn't whisper to them and, as he puts his pencil down and rubs out words that had been sitting ready in his head for too long to sound alive on the page, the key turns in the door and there's a dog on the doormat.

One of Alina's colleagues has got an exchange post in Venezuela, just for a year, and her father, who was going to look after it, has suddenly fallen ill. Webster, a four-year-old mixture of Labrador and pointer, is, despite his proud silhouette, a gentle, well-trained dog with dark amber eyes and a short, brown coat that shimmers like finely ground coffee, and when he pushes his head inside the door for the first time, the room stuffed full of books and piles of paper, the old guitar in the corner, is changed for ever.

He radiates a quiet, almost childlike sense of wisdom, an aura of strength and sadness, and while Alina's hanging up her jacket in the hall, the dog goes down flat on his belly and crawls towards him, slowly and in short bursts. His claws make a soft scratching noise, his tail swishes over the floor and bits of fluff swirl up from under the cupboard. He smells of the woods, of damp earth and grass, his muscles twitch under his coat and when Wolf leans down and lets him sniff his fingers and cautiously places the back of his hand between his ears, he pushes his forehead up towards him and briefly closes his eyes. Then he leaps up, dribbling a little urine in his excitement, and whirls round and round, barking. It's a surprisingly high and young sound, which echoes in the body of the guitar, and Alina leans against the doorpost and says, 'Great, now off you go to the butcher's, the pair of you.'

Whatever comes about when former lovers appear on the edge of the screen, it is overshadowed by melancholy. The number on the display is the same but the voice has changed. Charlotte has reached fifty as well. In contrast to earlier times—when a feminism based on psychology and, therefore, somewhat self-righteous, along with the fierce determination to be successful in her career gave it a somewhat sharp-edged, at times slightly squawking, sound—her voice now has a darker, warmer tone, grounded in experience. For a good fifteen years, he's been switching on to her undertones, her nuances of meaning, as soon as she rings up. But, on this day, she sounds astonishingly relaxed, with no sourness, and although there is a touch of reproach in her drawn-out 'Well?' an unspoken 'Why haven't you got in touch for so long?', it has a more transparent quality now, like gauze over a very sensitive spot.

They met in the middle of the 1980s, when he and Alina had fallen out—a brief separation for some almost forgotten reason right at the beginning of their relationship. Charlotte, the sister of the Munich radio presenter with whom he'd had a 'night-talk' about books and who'd invited him for a meal afterwards, was already sitting at the big table, talking to other writers, and, although it was approaching midnight and he knew that his stomach would make him pay for it, he ate the substantial meal with dessert and coffee. It had more or less become a custom with him after events because he hardly had to talk while eating, he would just nod or shake his head as he chewed, secretly looking forward to his hotel room and the TV beside his bed.

Despite the teardrop earrings and padded shoulders that current fashion dictates, despite the tight leather skirt and dangerously high-heeled bootees, Charlotte's elegance has little to do with her accessories. Her black hair, cut by a good hairdresser, is very fine and her narrow face with big eyes expresses intelligence and sensitivity, her unadorned hands, by contrast, strength. Her raised chin seems always to be hovering a little above whatever's going on. The most striking thing about her, though, is her posture—her straight back, her very narrow waist, almost as if it's laced up, and the self-assured way her bottom sticks out. She has broad thighs and muscular calves that make her stockings shimmer, and there's decisiveness and direction in the way she walks, emphasizing her hips—she brings him a serviette from the bar. 'You can fuck me, if you want,' her somewhat mocking smile seems to be saying, 'but you have to be good.'

That evening, Wolf hardly speaks to her but he's also careful not to appear to deliberately ignore her. She's a psychologist with a special interest in communication studies, she's just finished her PhD and is looking for an academic career, a chair in gender research. A declaration commonly heard at the time—'Naturally, that's a challenge for us women'—does nothing to make her any less disturbing but when she laughs out loud at some joke, he's relieved to see the metal edges of some very ordinary crowns. When they say goodbye outside the inn, she puts on a rather histrionic doleful look and the pressure of her hand is softer than its strength suggests. Then she goes, well aware that he's watching her. She makes a clatter with her high heels.

When he sends a card to the presenter, brief thanks for the successful programme, he adds greetings to his sister and gets a letter from her by return of post, a light-blue envelope with nothing in it but a visiting card. But he doesn't respond, not to her first telephone call either, though he listens to it without lifting the receiver. When she rings again, he's as brusque as possible. But one day she comes to Berlin to visit a girl friend, or so she says. He arranges a rendezvous with her in a grotty bar in Kreuzberg where she looks out of place in her pinstriped suit with brass buttons and is so nervous she knocks her glass over. The waiter, who stinks of sweat, looks distinctly displeased and drops a cloth for the spilt beer onto the table. Charlotte gives an embarrassed laugh and says, 'I'm always doing that.' Much later, she tells him she was already drunk.

That evening, the conversation between them never really gets going. There's a crackle of lightning in the air between his stubble and her feminist lace, harmony takes an effort. He avoids expressing opinions, which would only lead to the opposite views being stated, very assertively even, and Charlotte puts on a show of sensitivity but, unlike Alina, it's understanding without intuition, it comes out of books and has been tried out in seminars and conferences, it's almost true but not quite. However, they're careful not to let differences become irreconcilable, after all, they want to go to bed together. And then he's surprised how arousing her waist feels above her hips, a kind of golden groove, and how yielding her kisses are under the chestnut tree outside his house. She has a soft response to every movement of his lips and, for a moment, he feels clumsy, like an ungainly man whom a woman leads secretly in a dance, allowing him to believe that he's a good dancer.

He urges her into the vestibule. 'Actually this is all too quick for me,' she says, but then they're already in his flat, in the light from the courtyard lamp, and he unbuttons her blouse and carefully, as if they were soft dough, lifts her breasts out of the cups of her bra. The fact that she's not very clean that evening, that her cunt, with the grey labia turned in from the tightness of her panties, have a slightly ripe smell under her expensive skirt, really turns him on, especially since he imagines that this gives him the right to shag her more violently and to come quickly. He looks pale beside her all-over-sunbed tan but they suit one another perfectly and, when he slaps her on the bottom, she gives a few contented groans.

The things she says to spur him on sound false, as if she's taken them from some sex film, and he can clearly sense that she's putting up with, rather than enjoying, him. He clenches his teeth and he scratches her back, leaving weals, and sticks his thumb up her arse. He's going in and out like a fiddler's elbow but with every thrust he's farther from a climax, which, given her smiling forbearance, he can already see as a failure. Eventually he becomes suspicious, thinks how old she is and can't believe she's happy to open her legs for him without wanting anything more in return than his stupid poet's prick. As he pulls it out air escapes in an obscene fart. But her experience, which shows in the way she doesn't find it embarrassing, as many other women would, that she simply ignores it, makes affection well up inside him. He strokes her cheek tenderly.

'What's wrong?' she asks, breathless. 'Can't you come?'

He crumples up a pillow and wipes his chest with it. 'What about you?'

She doesn't answer right away, gnaws at her lower lip and stares at the ceiling. She's shaved her armpits, not usual in those days, and, when she takes off her glasses between the tips of her fingers, he has a furtive glance at her watch. Gently she pushes him down and now, as he rubs his face against her pubic hair and kisses and licks her, she opens up more than just her body. Moaning with pleasure, as if she were sinking into a warm bath, she bends her head back, her powerful throat, bends her knees and becomes so moist that a large damp patch appears on the sheet. At the same time, her clitoris swells and pushes out, he can almost handle it like a tiny penis and he's astonished at how wide and hard he can feel it under her skin. All the while, Charlotte is lying there, almost rapt, as if she were listening to something far, far away, bites her thumb or strokes his back with her foot and after a good half hour, when his tongue is tired and hurts at the root, he's just blowing at her. Then he digs his fingernails into her nipples, with their dark aureola, and she gives his hair a violent tug and comes.

Her orgasm is something he's never seen before. It begins with whimpering, almost like a child, and she pushes her pelvis forward more quickly and holds him, his head, so tightly to her that his lips can't move and his tongue has hardly any room for manoeuvre. She rubs herself against his front teeth and then she cries out, pushes him away, turns her back on him and doubles up. He tries to cuddle up against her but she pushes his arms away and begins to tremble, goose pimples appear on her breasts and thighs and her breathing sounds like shivering, as if she were cold. She keeps pulling her stomach in, so far that it makes a deep hollow, the navel hardly visible any more, and her lower ribs stick out. Her hands grope and, looking for something to hold on to, squash his fingers, her eyelids twitch and, finally, she turns round and seems to relax. She even smiles, licks one of the corners of her mouth and Wolf pushes a strand of hair out of her face and is about to get up when a new wave of shudders runs through her and she begins to hit out at him with all her strength. Her spine arched, baring her teeth but not looking at him, she punches his hips and thighs and, at the last moment, he manages to catch hold of her wrists and stop her hitting him in a more sensitive spot. There's a convulsive power in her arms, like stored-up electricity, and, while she's moaning, as if she were being burnt up from inside, and even kicking out at him, she's probably not aware of him at all. She closes her eyes and is as alone as a naked person can be, blackish tears drop onto the pillow. And then she cuddles up to him, falling asleep as she does so, snoring softly.

A few days later they meet in a cafe by the Südstern and they're back where they started out. They're both on their guard, as if they sensed that the pleasure they can give one another could just as well be pain. They drink coffee with brandy. Charlotte, in whose vocabulary the words 'performance' and 'success' appear as naturally as he avoids them, talks about her work, a study on women's new freedom and the depression that causes. He doodles plants and caricatures on a paper napkin. Being tied no longer to clearly defined structures and conventions makes people increasingly unsure of themselves, she explains. A permanent relationship, yes or no, move in together, yes or no, children or work . . . All the decisions that have to be made eventually lead to stress and profound weariness, especially in women, so that their hysterical disposition turns into a depressive tendency with all the typical side effects—compulsive pill-taking, alcoholism and frigidity. Hysteria, defined as a specifically female illness at the end of the nineteenth century, will, she says, be replaced by depression at the end of the twentieth.

That makes sense, no question, and at that time it's new for a man who doesn't read scientific literature. But he finds her lecturing tone inhibiting and irritating. She wants to impress him with her padded shoulders, her PhD. She crosses her legs, keeping her shins parallel and her expensively styled hair reminds him of the chat-show presenters and news readers on TV who all seem to have the same hairstyle and point the same faces, full of self-assurance and devoid of feeling, at the cameras, the corners of their mouths stretched in prim smiles, as if a person's life had no dark corners, no irresistible urges, no filth, as if any problem could be solved with common sense and a clean panti-liner. He says aggressively, 'You're sitting there on your hole wanting to be screwed and you behave as if you wanted something quite different. Feminism's brought women nothing but trouble.'

She remains silent for a while, which is intended as a rebuke, and blows the smoke slowly out through her nose. 'That was stupid,' she says eventually and he has the bittersweet taste of guilt on his tongue and stares at the floor where the tip of her toe is going up and down.

But then he crumples up the napkin and puts his pencil back in his pocket. '*You* have to be clever and smart,' he says, getting up. 'After all, you want to get on. I can be as stupid as I like, as long as, in my wisdom, I stick to poetry.' It sounds good, even if you can tell it's one of his stock phrases. A final word if ever there was one, putting a full stop to something he refuses to leave open any longer. Putting a banknote on the table, he goes out.

However, he just cannot convince himself that he's put her behind him, once and for all. After his annoyance at Charlotte's readiness for a fight—irritating because it's all too manifest—has faded, he's left with a feeling of disquiet, which he finds difficult not to mistake for that of being in love, when he thinks of the morning when they woke up in the same position in which they'd gone to sleep—his knees against the back of her knees, his stomach against her back, his hand on her soft breast. And the casual way she moistened her fingers and felt between her thighs to slip his penis in, her slow, almost sleepy movements and his quiet orgasm, during which she kept tensing the muscles of her vagina, gave him the feeling of something cosy, almost as if he were sleeping with a sister.

She doesn't give up that afternoon either. Lying on the sofa in his flat, he hears her coming up the stairs. It must be her, he knows the steps of the others who live in the tenement and none of them wears stiletto heels. Instinctively, he holds his breath when he knows she's at the door. He hears her clear her throat, smells her perfume and, although he's expecting it, starts when the bell rings. It echoes round the bare rooms.

The thin door, not much more than a painted board covered in scrapes and scratches from break-ins before his time, has a letterbox through which you can see into the flat but Charlotte doesn't think of using it. She rummages through her handbag, with a clatter of keys and cosmetics, then the stairs going up creak, just one step. Thinking he's not at home, she's presumably sat down to wait. That surprises him, it doesn't fit in with her pride, but he forces himself to stay there on the sofa. Cigarette smoke comes through the gaps, now and then there's a rustle of paper. Clearly she's reading and he thinks himself strong in his motionlessness, his definitive renunciation, so he doesn't have to feel he's being cowardly. After every page she turns, the silence in the room gets more profound and, eventually, he falls asleep, waking only when it's almost dark in the courtyard.

He raises his head and sniffs, nothing comes from the stairs but the usual brackish smell of the cellar, the ivy on the outside wall rustles in the wind. Cautiously, he takes off the chain and opens the door, just a crack.

The stairs are empty. There are three fag ends outside his door, one still has lipstick on it.

Since then, over fifteen years ago, they haven't seen one another. Sometimes, when one of his books had a review in a national newspaper, she would ring up, usually from Hamburg where she's been living for some time. After the initial pleasantries, their conversations would quickly take on the mildly challenging tone they used to protect themselves, to keep their distance from one another. She would point out typographic errors or stylistic infelicities while he would avoid telling her that he's seen her on TV now and then, she's occasionally interviewed as a specialist on the psychological aspects of the new media. Once, when he was writer-in-residence in Kyoto for a few weeks, he interrupted his solitary masturbation on the sofa to phone her. She was alone in her office, having to spend the Sunday working because of some deadline or other, and said the things he wanted to hear, words that were no longer obscene but still had that effect. And she was obviously not at all aroused by the fact that she was making him—staring at the clock tower of the conservatory on the other side of the world—come just by the sound of her voice. 'Clean yourself up,' she said severely and hung up.

By now, she's a professor and is not only working at the university but also as adviser to TV channels and various companies and, a month ago, she was appointed to the chair she's longed for in Berlin. She ignores his congratulations, he can hear the clatter of her keyboard while she's speaking. Lots to do, lots to do, some of it still in Hamburg, she's commuting back and forth like mad, she tells him, but soon she'll have an apartment in the central district of Berlin, a little hideaway, and it would be nice if they could meet, perhaps one weekend?

Wind, a summer wind, making the meadows shine and the shadows of the trees seem to be moving. Splinters of glass glitter on the path and Webster shoots out of one thicket and disappears into the next, churns up the ground that has already been churned up by the pigs, keeps his head stuck in a hollow tree for a long time and starts when a sail on the lake flaps noisily, barks at the swans until they hiss at him and falls silent in the echoing underpass where the patter of his paws on the cement floor sounds eerie, like the pulse in the empty heart of the Spree.

Wolf loves going for walks with him, wandering through the woods, the surrounding marshy meadows. At the same time, he regards the animal with an almost reverent awe and not just because of his strength. He feels Webster is superior also by being completely satisfied with what creation has destined for him, by not wanting to be anything other than a dog—and that leads him to suspect that Webster is perhaps something quite different, a prehistoric hieroglyph, undecipherable. For some obscure reason, he feels the dog has greater claim on the present than he has and the insecurity, self-doubt and inferiority complexes he often feels wrapped up in, as if in damp blankets, seem pathetic when faced with that look, that noble silhouette. His head slightly raised, his slim breast curving out, he can sit for hours by the balcony door, watching the birds in the lime tree, his ears and nostrils twitching, and, when he calls him or claps his hands, he always reacts with a slight delay, as if he had to fix something in his mind first, he pants softly and it sounds like a sigh. He warms his feet when he's sitting at his desk or puts his head on his knee when he's watching TV but, when they go out, it's always the dog that determines the direction they're taking and he senses it clearly if Wolf insists on going the opposite way, out of obstinacy, to assert his authority. Then he gives him a brief glance and trots past him in a way that almost makes his master feel that he's given a brief shake of the head, that Webster feels sorry for him.

But, most of the time, it's Alina who looks after him, he follows her quite naturally, as if they've been together for ever. She talks quietly to him, almost tenderly, sometimes she just clicks her fingers to call him. She even takes him to the school, a private language school on Hermannplatz, he sleeps beside the radiator in the classroom or, if she has Muslim students, under the desk in her office. Sometimes he carries her bag or a magazine in his mouth and when Wolf, standing on the balcony, sees her coming down the avenue, he often feels he can sense some bond between them, even though they're often quite far apart, from which he feels shut out.

To be jealous of a dog—he ignores the raw edge of this feeling simply because there's something poetic about it. He often enough feels guilty about the fact that Alina, originally of a calm and dreamy nature, has adapted to his rapid character, his weak man's impatience, his constant 'I want it *now*!' even in her speech rhythms and can often hear his misgivings or desires before he's expressed them. But he's a little uneasy when he now sees her slowly find herself again, merging back into her old outline at the side of that animal and appearing nobler and more energetic in the way she cares for it, which is distinctive because it expresses more than their togetherness. Her casual, almost ambling gait when Webster stays behind, the calm, anticipatory earnestness with which she watches him when he forges ahead into the park, the quiet, relaxed concentration with which she sits on a bench, reading, while he's sniffing round in the bushes—when she is with the dog, Alina gives the impression of being looked after and protected more clearly than she ever does when he's at her side.

He does pride himself on the fact that he's hardly ever been jealous, not even of the good-looking male language students she gives private lessons to, but, if he's honest, he has to admit he's never been put to the test. There are signs that the time has now come, he can tell from the fact that one day he can't stand the intimate silence between her and the dog any longer. When he asks Alina, in a deliberately offhand tone, how she feels about having a baby now that the flat's furnished, she gives an embarrassed smile and shakes her head. Perhaps she blushes as well, he can't tell in the evening light. She opens a tin. All those years ago, she says, when it almost made them split up, it would probably have been OK. But not any longer. When, astonished by this, he asks what she means, after all, she's not forty yet, she hardly seems to be listening. She scrapes the dog's food out into its bowl and says, 'Anyway, people can tell what kind of family is right for them, can't they? And we're a family of two.'

Shortly afterwards, a letter from a well-known foundation arrives. The scholarship she applied for about a year ago has been granted, at last she can begin on her thesis: The Influence of Meister Eckhart on German Romantic Literature.

Steel neckties. Houses in screaming colours on the edge of the woods. Pale barbecue sausage whirls. The longer they live in the district, the more deep-seated his secret reservations towards these people with their permanently grumpy look become, he calls them aborigines and the irony is only superficial. There is something dully threatening about them, at least at first sight, and Wolf has long since given up believing in the cliche that it's caused by a feeling of disadvantage or insecurity towards Germans from the West or defiant resignation at the speed with which history is striding on. The lifestyle of some of the winners from the fall of communism suggests they don't want to bother with the West German version of capitalism. They make their garden fences higher, rev up their Harley-Davidson until the windowpanes rattle and head off straight for LA with oiled muscles. They give their wives and daughters cosmetic surgery as Christmas present, block the streets with four-by-fours with tinted windows, have countless security cameras fixed to their lurid yellow houses which they roof with purple tiles.

Inwardly, the East remains grey. Much of the fallow land has an acid smell. The doctors' waiting rooms, especially the consultants', are overcrowded, people are standing in the corridors. And, even though at first Wolf and Alina have hardly any contact with the people, their experiences with their first landlords, who set lawyers on them and whom they had to pay an outrageous sum to cancel the contract, the jeering of the youth hanging round in the park when he goes jogging there, simply because he's jogging, the botched work of the clockmaker who wasn't up to dealing with the automatic movement of his clock but refused to admit to it, the dark looks Alina often gets when she's preparing her classes on the train, 'German as a Foreign Language' or 'German for Foreign Students' is on the covers of her books—all of this means Wolf keeps having to make an effort not to work himself up into a bitter, almost pleasurable, hatred of the Easterners. The very fact that it could so easily happen makes it clear to him that it would be unfair. On the other hand, forty years of the dictatorship of the proletariat is no excuse for not being polite.

A steel necktie. The waiter at the Weberschiffchen wears one, with a small knot. The three or four polished metal plates fixed to the fabric with studs glint in the candlelight when he comes into the restaurant and takes the chair out of Wolf's hand with a, 'Now then, what d'you think you're doing?' It's not just wobbly, it's dangerously twisted and the man shakes his head. Bony face, thin lips, hair brushed back flat. 'You tell me that and I'll get you another. You can't do just as you like in here.'

Wolf forces himself to remain calm and friendly. The man's arrogant manner is clearly a reflex action from the past, when he was lord of the scarce tables with the power to allocate or refuse. Now the place is empty and they order fish, marinaded pike from the lake, Alina would like saute potatoes to go with it. The wine comes from Saxony and as dessert there's crème fraiche with freshly picked berries which do actually come from the forest. At least they find a beetle in it, one with a bluish shell that lost two legs when the fruit was stirred in. Wolf wipes it clean with his napkin and places it where it can be seen on the edge of his plate. But the waiter ignores it, merely twists his lips in contempt, as if they were just as petty-minded as he'd thought, and asks if they want coffee. When they say no, he brings the bill without being asked. He can knock off and it's not even nine yet.

He scrapes the crumbs off the next table with a beer mat, it sounds like a cane swishing through the air, and Wolf taps the bill with his finger. 'It says an extra portion of saute potatoes here,' he says.

The waiter's eyes narrow. 'And? You ate some, didn't you?'

Wolf takes a deep breath and Alina grasps his hand and shakes her head; her voice is calm: 'But I wanted them *instead* of the boiled potatoes.'

'I know, I'm not deaf.'

Her jaw drops and she stares at him. She's not just speechless, as she usually is at a piece of effrontery, she looks sad, which clearly provokes him. His jawbones twitch. 'The dish is on the menu with boiled potatoes. Printed in capital letters. If you want a different kind of potatoes to accompany it, there's an additional charge. I should think that's obvious.'

Wolf puts the sum on the table, without a tip, he's determined not to come down to the same level. 'Additional, that's the word. Spoken in italics. How come we didn't get any boiled potatoes, then?'

'Because you wanted saute potatoes. What's all this about? How was I supposed to get them on the plate?'

'Oh, yes, of course,' he says and gets up. For a moment, he's tempted to ask for the potatoes in a doggy bag, for Webster. He tries to catch the waiter's eye but he's avoiding him, busying himself in putting out the candles. As she buttons up her jacket, Alina looks at the room with its crystal chandeliers, its crooked chairs, its sooty fireplace, as if it's somewhere she's never going to come to again. They're almost at the door when she goes back to the table and puts some coins as a tip on top of the bill.

The fact that the world in this part of Berlin seems to be more petty-minded than the districts they're familiar with would perhaps be less striking if it weren't for the perceptible lack of genuine intellectual and creative activity. The decades during which the East part of the city was bled dry of its intelligentsia have left their mark most noticeably on its outer suburbs. The fashionable film director, tousle-haired and in a leather jacket, who makes jolly films about the GDR and its slightly dim-witted but basically good-natured secret police and prison officers, the be-earringed poet who writes topical poems to order and reads his lyrical homespun straight from his laptop to the cameras, the wordy tobacconist who self-publishes memories of the defunct state in which not everything was bad—*It's my Turn to Speak*!—the water-colourist, she calls herself a 'qualified artist' and sells ornamental 'oscillograms' between the fish and honey stalls at the weekly market. That's the sum total of the bohemian scene. The local politicians only appear during elections when they spend an hour or so standing at the trestle table covered in leaflets and definitely regret the fact that hardly any foreigners—and no coloured ones at all—come to their beautiful Köpenick and the fact that the far-right German National Democratic Party has set up its headquarters nearby. But what can one do?—it's a free country.

In all areas of life, people there seem to concern themselves solely with material things—even in the church, before the service begins, there's a report on the amount of the collection and what it was spent on. So they're happy to discover the odd eccentric. The house on the corner, a crumbling villa with young birches growing on the roof, has enough room for three families. The pillars on the porch are squint, there are curtains on the high arched windows of the first floor but they're presumably there only for show, the rooms are empty. It's only in the basement that there's a light now and then, a standard lamp with a faded shade. A dilapidated sofa and piles of books, paperbacks and newspapers can be seen on the floor. Kittens are romping among them and at times there's the glow of a cigarette from the even darker rear part of the room.

The inhabitant, a corpulent man of around sixty with a shock of grey hair, is rarely seen without the carrier bag that's customary here. Mostly there's the clink of empty bottles coming from it and although he never says hello or replies to their greeting, and even crosses to the other side of the street when he sees them coming, Wolf likes him from the very first. He doesn't seem to work, doesn't watch TV and never has any visitors. Because he mostly wears faded army-surplus shirts, they call him the Green Man and there's also something extraterrestrial about him in his crumbling cave, a mute ascetic in a neighbourhood full of Polyfilla addicts who are paying off their mortgage and take every opportunity to use things to express themselves and, every Saturday, switch on their sander, their hammer drill, their lawnmower, their lawn-edge trimmer and their electric hedge-cutter so as not to have to listen to the silence in their street, while the Green Man sits in his overgrown garden feeding bread and pumpkin seeds to the birds.

He presumably doesn't own the house, his whole being lacks the narrowness, the brow furrowed with reservations and worries that the ownership of property produces in the middle classes, he seems to have the kind of freedom that doesn't need space and his permanent, slightly amused look reminds you that wit and wisdom are related words. But perhaps they're wrong, perhaps he's just a simpleton, a temporary tenant the management somehow forgot? Or a man who never wanted the Wall to come down and has nothing but contempt for Westerners and their way of life? Whatever it is, it's the evening after they went to the restaurant when Alina, exasperated, wants to find out. As always, she's said hello to the man, who's repairing a bicycle and, as always, received no response. He didn't even look up from underneath the cherry trees and they've reached the steps to their door when she turns round, crosses the street and goes up to his fence. 'Excuse me,' she says, with just enough of a smile that it doesn't look as if she's trying to ingratiate herself. 'May I ask you something? Why do you never say hello to me?'

Slowly, the Green Man straightens up. 'Me? What d'you mean?' His voice sounds surprisingly young, his eyelids flutter as if he'd got something in his eye and he takes a handkerchief out of his pocket, only to put it in the other one. You could almost feel sorry for him and his lopsided grin, he scratches the back of his neck. But Alina stays there, looking at him calmly. For a moment, he seems to be searching for an answer, he has a somewhat vacant look, but then he suddenly stretches out his arm, pointing the screwdriver at Wolf standing in the doorway. The end is quivering. 'Well, him there . . . Your husband . . .' He takes a deep breath, sticking out his chest. 'He never says hello to me either.' He takes his bicycle and goes into the house.

3
only what is transient can blossom

'When I kill someone,' the young American soldier on television says, holding up his gun with both hands to the camera, 'when I pull the trigger and hit the target and see the swine fall, I feel as powerful as God.' Behind him, clouds of dust drift across the desert, smoke rises from wrecked aeroplanes and the barrels of burnt-out tanks point up to a sky so blue that it seems to be astonished at the self-assured swagger of an empty heart. For God does not feel powerful, Mr President, power and powerlessness have nothing to do with the absolute. But you'll only come to see that later, perhaps at the last moment, when the eyes of the men you've killed catch yours again. Until then, keep your gob shut. You can't ask their forgiveness anyway, there's no point in talking to them any more. But at least you could join them in their silence. Cut!

The shadows deepen in the *mezzo-relievo* of memory, the heights aren't bright enough. When was the first time he was unfaithful to Alina? The word is hardly right because no infidelity or affair ever changed his feelings for her. Even though he thinks she wouldn't make the distinction, if he asks his heart, or whatever you call the organ of truth, he was true to her from the very first moment. If, on the other hand, he asks his body, he comes up with quite a different answer.

So much is certain—when they still had separate flats and had more space to themselves, his affection was more exclusive, sexually as well. That he sometimes fancies other women, that he imagines slimmer or more bosomy ones when he masturbates or occasionally goes to a brothel is not, in his eyes, really being unfaithful—a furtive act brought on by the full moon or his hormones after which he goes back to her strengthened, despite his exertions, and finds her more attractive than before. That is what reassures him when occasional misgivings arise. So far, it has always been the case that she greets his renewed strength, his supple lyricism in the sack with cries of delight. It's playing away that brings home advantage.

He's a little late, building works on the railway, but he knows that Charlotte will arrive even later. She insists on making an entrance and that's OK. When she arrives at the Einstein, the manager in the double-breasted suit opens the internal glass door for her. She gives him a smile and also has a nod of greeting for the women behind the bar and a man reading the newspaper in the corner. Even though she's not been in the city long, she's obviously already a regular here. The waiter with the ponytail clicks his heels and says, in a Viennese drawl, 'Küß die Hand, Frau Professor!'

She gives him a beaming smile too and comes over to the little marble-topped table where he was placed. Her freshly tinted hair with the one strand of grey above the temple looks fuller with its permanent wave than it actually is, she's wearing a pink roll-neck sweater and a black trouser-suit with a fitted jacket. Initially, she says nothing to him but, chin raised, inspects the room and the mirrors, then points to a corner with her bulging briefcase that's worn along the sides. 'Let's sit over there, on the sofa. We're in a draught here.' The table's bigger and slightly hidden behind the black grand piano and Charlotte puts the 'Reserved' sign and the ashtray on the keys. She's still using the same perfume as fifteen years ago, a classic.

'You've got a dog? *You*?!' she finally says, holding the back of her hand out to Webster. He wags his tail and sniffs her sleeve. 'And such a lovely one. Do you feed him properly?' Wolf has brought Webster with him to legitimize his trip into town. Whatever happens this evening, it will have been a walk with Webster, he has the lead rolled up in his pocket. Charlotte takes his fingers and gives him a quick survey from head to toe, the aggressive pride in her posture is even greater and it's her bright-eyed, challenging look that reminds him that he's always assumed her eyes were blue. In fact, they're brown.

When they embrace, he thinks he can feel the hint of a promise in the way she nestles up to him. Her figure, both slight and compact, hasn't changed, not a bit, her waist is slim, her stomach flat and her behind curves out just enough to be noteworthy without anyone being tempted to call it fat. As they separate from their embrace, she absently strokes his biceps under the tweed of his jacket with her thumb and perhaps she felt something else with her hip, her expression is somehow forbearing, as if she's smiling to herself as she says, 'Later.' But first of all, she's hungry, first of all she wants to talk. And have a glass of wine, of course.

But as they sit on the upholstered corner-seat, her self-assurance gives way to an expression of girlish agitation. And her voice is quieter, a breathy whisper. 'My God, did I have to hurry,' she says, placing the backs of her fingers on her cheeks as if to conceal a flush. She's presumably trying to soften his first glance so that he doesn't become aware of the years that have passed the moment the waiter lights the candle.

But apart from her vigour of gesture and gait, her chic outfit, there's a touch of old age about her, despite her expert make-up. Her neck is slightly scrawny, the skin under her eyes sagging, her hair thinner. As Wolf guides the obedient dog under the table, he establishes, out of the corner of his eyes, that she looks decidedly more advanced in years than he does, which is not saying much, he's usually taken to be younger than he is. He's not overweight, he has a smooth complexion and the silver hairs that appear here and there are considerate enough to keep falling out to be replaced by new dark ones. But Charlotte, whose lip-print on her glass is more curvaceous than her mouth, could be getting on for sixty, a classy sixty of course, which causes him a moment of alarm. But then he finds the lustre of experience he imagines he can see in her even more arousing than youthfulness. He has a furtive glance at his watch.

Presumably sensing his thoughts, she tells him about her work and the masses of demanding tasks she has every day. All the committees in Germany, Austria and Switzerland she chairs, all the projects she's in charge of, the reports she writes, the discussions she has, and all that alongside the normal university business of lectures, seminars and supervision—slowly but surely she feels it's time to get away from it all. She's been in hospital three times recently—neurasthenia, circulatory collapse, intestinal obstruction. 'Once they shoved me into the washroom on my bed. And when I woke up in the tiled room, a nurse came in and said, thunder-struck, "God, I thought you were dead!"' Urs, her boyfriend for the last twelve years, a physics lecturer in Basel, hardly comes to see her any more because she can't get away from her computer. And Mark, her other boyfriend, a civil servant in the transport ministry, wife, two children, is always complaining that she only has time for sex on Sundays, one hour in the evening.

'What's intestinal obstruction?' asks Wolf, who's had more and more stomach trouble recently but gets annoyed at the way his ears prick up whenever the conversation gets round to illnesses. His fear has even begun to permeate language. If someone says absence, he hears it as abscess and if someone writes concert, he reads it as cancer. It feels like an old-age wart. 'What happens with that?'

The waiter brings Charlotte her salad and with her teeth—they're new, unobtrusive work, pearl grey—she pulls a piece of chicken off the skewer. 'Oh,' she says as she chews, 'your tummy swells up like a drum. You can't shit and you stink like a loo.'

He doesn't have anything to eat, just drinks water and coffee and, when she orders another glass of wine and talks about the way her life has been recently, he at first listens less to what she's saying than to her voice, to its tone colour, the echo of the years. And even though he knows better, he likes the erroneous idea that there's a possibility of something like harmony, or even happiness, between himself and Charlotte on the basis of their common age and similar experience. He has no friends, although there are some people or colleagues he would call that in their presence. Being too preoccupied with himself and his work, he lacks the time to cultivate friendships, which hardly anyone can comprehend, not even the most patient. Sooner or later, he gets letters full of subtext or a sharp telephone call.

Despite that, he keeps longing for an accord that isn't just an excuse to get drunk and which, as Charlotte casually sticks a piece of bread and butter in his mouth, they are cautiously approaching.

He feels cosy on the velvet bench and would most have liked to say nothing, just play with her fingers, her manicured hand, which he remembered as being more delicate and a little too big for his cock. But she's not a woman with whom one can remain silent. A thorough materialist, though that is masked by her intellectual manner, she would interpret his silence as a shortcoming, as a sign of a lack of vitality and as the beginning of boredom. The idea that it articulates something more profound she would dismiss at best as poetry, at worst as mysticism. Anyone who remains silent has nothing to say and is, therefore, uninteresting.

So he asks a question now and then and tries to pay attention, even if everything she tells him has an irritating veneer of self-importance. She completed her postdoctoral thesis in record time, only one woman before her had been quicker, her seminars attracted the highest number of students and her lectures to companies were always packed. Naturally, the sum total of research funds she had secured through laborious struggles exceeded anything that had gone before, her boyfriend in Basel was *the* authority as far as particle physics was concerned and, of course, the famous director general of the TV channel she was writing a report for did more than just chat her up. 'And you're easy on the eye as well,' he'd said at the first briefing.

The obviousness with which she puffs herself up slightly spoils his pleasure at her appearance in the mirror opposite, at their shared maturity in clothes that are not cheap and that look good on them, even though in him that is merely external. But the childish way Charlotte is showing off may be an overreaction from her awareness that they haven't much to say to one another and that they have nothing much in common apart from the naked language of their bodies—long, well-constructed sentences uttered almost entirely in their breathing. But she doesn't want to admit that, not yet. The academic that she is still has a concept of love as yearning which, despite its cloak of irony, derives from the pastel tones of women's magazines, the whiff of romance in the perfume supplements.

She gives Webster a piece of meat, letting him give her hand a thorough licking, and her apparently casual glances in the mirror tell Wolf how the rest of the evening is going to turn out. But first, she needs a third glass of wine and, later on, a gin as well. She asks about his work now and then, his books, and admits how proud she's often been when there's something about him in the papers or on the radio. That isn't just a ploy to see whether he reacts with vanity—a weak spot she would immediately have probed, with the kebab skewer. Just as she still wants her elderly parents and her brother and sister to be proud of her and what she's achieved, she needs to be proud of the people she associates with—that is the currency of her sadness. But, because for him, every vision is absorbed in the text and, after it's been printed, every text dissolves into thin air, so to speak, and he keeps finding himself faced with a new beginning, there can be no pride in what has been accomplished. If there were, he's so indolent that things would immediately come to a standstill. But she insists on seeing him as successful and when he waves her praise away and tells her what minimal editions his books are published in, she doesn't seem to be listening. She's smiling at an acquaintance who's just coming in, an art collector who's allegedly already had his eye on her. She spends a lot of time beaming that evening, bares her teeth even when the waiter just brings a straw or a man selling roses comes to their table. She shares out her smiles like little bags full of flowers which, however, makes her eyes look even more tired and herself even more lost, especially as she doesn't stop at that one gin.

And when she puts a hand on his thigh and accidentally on purpose touches him with her little finger on the place that is in the shadow of the table, Wolf suddenly feels inhibited by expectations he ascribes to her and which are about more than just bed and the imagination he shows in it. Perhaps he's wrong but there's something probing in her questions about his plans, his writing and life in the flat with Alina, whom she claims to admire because she's stuck it out with him for so long—she even wants to know how often they sleep together—that sounds as if she's quietly putting out feelers to see what might be available to her beyond this evening, which would mean her passion now should be interpreted as a gift or an investment. And when he diverts her away from himself and brings the conversation back to her career, her relationships, she says, 'Naturally I enjoy having two men, especially such attractive ones, but there's no security in it.'

The ice cubes in her gin clink on her teeth. Now her cheeks really are glowing and the more her make-up suffers from that, the more Wolf is aroused by her. He's listening less and less to what she's saying. As a chronic dreamer he's perfected a way of putting on a credible appearance of attentiveness, of giving more or less appropriate answers to questions he hasn't taken in, or at most just the intonation. And just as, despite his almost fifty years, a song is still more important, even essential, to him than any supposedly 'good' book and just as a song by Beth Gibbons or the Babyshambles can shield him from the darkness inside himself for weeks on end without him understanding a word, so it is with the voice of a woman he desires—the things he hears in it beyond speech strengthens him and demands a silent answer, at best a whispered one. Or obscene commands.

At some point she goes to the toilet and returns with fresh make-up and he's about to pick up his jacket when she goes over to the table of her acquaintance, a fat, bald-headed man, to discuss something with him. Her arms resting on the back of a chair, she sticks out her backside, on which the material of the trousers is slightly shiny, for everyone to see, leaving Wolf alone in the corner for almost a quarter of an hour. Slightly irritated, he waves the waiter over, pays the bill and asks for some water for the dog. There's a chrome bowl under the piano. He finds this crude way of emphasizing her worth rather cheap and, for a moment, as she sinks down on the sofa again, her seductive aura has gone. She seems to be thinking, her severe expression as she types something into her BlackBerry looks almost masculine, a thin-lipped old bachelor. Then she straightens up again, pulls her pullover down tight over her breasts and says with an amused glint in her eye, 'Yesterday I bought a small baguette and it was actually called a Singles French Stick.'

Her car's parked in Nollendorferplatz and on the way there they pass several women in short skirts or hot pants waiting on the kerb at remarkably regular intervals. Their high, patent-leather boots glitter in the headlights, the paving stones gleam like marble, the blue cigarette smoke coils up in the warm air and Wolf puts his arm round Charlotte's shoulders. Although a little shorter than he is, she's still too tall for him and takes longer steps in her high heels, and bouncier ones as well, so that they don't manage to walk together as a pair and it looks as if they're stumbling over uneven ground. It even looks slightly ridiculous in the shadow of the negotiable goddesses, who survey them idly out of the corner of their eyes and Wolf lets go of her. But he takes her hand and when they stop at a red light, she turns to him. The dog disappears in the bushes.

The air seems to have freshened her up, her look is as clear and keen as it ever was and when he draws her to him, she lifts her chin provocatively and narrows her eyes like a woman who knows that her kisses are precious and not to be given away casually, but because she smells of gin, he can't take it so seriously. A brightly lit train rattles over the steel bridge beneath the moon and he gives her neck a cautious nibble and holds her tighter, her incredibly slim waist, the axis of her suppleness. She's still fending him off, with a mocking smile, but when she can't lean back any further and he presses his chest against her, she's the one who nuzzles his lips, slowly, with imperious tenderness. Closing his eyes, he groans despite himself and thrusts his fingers into her hair in the abrupt fusion which seems to reduce the force of gravity on him and is satisfying, like the deep breath you take after dying in a dream, as if he were suffused with his own self. Calmly, Charlotte explores his mouth with her tongue, gently places her hand on his penis. Then the dog pushes in between them and she looks at her watch.

They can't go to her place, the rooms are being renovated. At the moment, the dean's putting her up in his guest room and the walls are thin, it would make a bad impression if the new professor . . . So, they go across the square to the Sachsenhof, an old hotel next to the Metropol Club with the night porter sitting by himself in the breakfast room full of rubber trees staring at the television. He gives them a brief glance as he goes behind the reception desk, a bony man with the pale face of a chain-smoking hotelier. There's nothing he hasn't seen before and when Wolf slightly over-emphasizes his posture and makes his voice sound a touch too casual, he gives a hardly perceptible grin. A room for the night—almost all the keys are still on their pigeonholes but he bends over the guest list, leafs through it and rubs things out, as if it's an extremely complicated, almost impossible task. Since he can sense they're in a hurry, he takes his time. Webster snuggles down on the mat, Charlotte feels the long shoot of a potted palm between her fingers and finally he nods, places three keys on the desk and says, 'Right. We've got a room with two beds, no bath, a shared shower. Then there's one with a double bed and a whirlpool, though the Internet connection's not working at the moment and one with a water-bed, though it's just an ordinary double bed, not king size. You can have a look if you like. It's fantastically comfortable but it ought to be heated an hour in advance. Oh yes . . .' He puts a fourth key on the desk, 'And then there's one with a normal double bed and bath on the first floor, if you're not bothered by the fact that it gives onto the courtyard.'

He points to the glass door at the back, the containers full of rubbish. 'No, we're not,' Wolf says, picking up the board with the registration form. His hidden erection, which is somehow stuck, hurts and he can't decide whether he should be amused or outraged because the man doesn't look him in the eye as he speaks and even now he looks at Charlotte as he says, 'But it hasn't got TV.'

But she wipes a hair off Wolf's lapel and replies with masterly casualness, 'Oh, we won't need that.'

He's pleased with her answer, feels relieved and less naked in his arousal. This magnificent woman will soon be licking his balls while the dry stick at the desk is sucking at his fag end. But he's sweating, too, and can scarcely believe that in this everyday scene, the kind he's seen in thousands of films—the clandestine couple, ready to commit adultery, checking in—he's started to tremble. Hardly noticeable at first, it's possibly even an illusion. But when both Charlotte and the night porter stare at the form, which still needs his signature, he feels himself go pale with embarrassment. There's a slight twitch, a little tremble of his hand, before the tiny ball of the pen touches the paper and another when it does, so that the first letter is scrawly and, in his imagination, it reflects more than just that one moment. Like the second-long flash in some USB sticks, telling you that several hundred pages of a book have been stored, it seems to compress the whole past and even though Charlotte will later say that she didn't notice it, that, on the contrary, he seemed incredibly blase and cool—on the one hand the trembling detracts from the impression of the masterful male he wanted to make and he still feels humiliated by it as their footsteps echo across the courtyard, on the other hand it makes it clear to him that what is happening here is more than just the one-night stand he at times regarded it as. As if his normally flowing signature had turned out shaky because there was one of Alina's hairs lying on the registration form.

He returns to their flat long after midnight but she's not asleep yet. She's sitting on the bed in her jeans and T-shirt, a glass of wine in her hand. All over the floor are books and torn-up or crumpled handwritten sheets and photocopies. She's staring into space, her eyes red, and Webster goes and lies down beside her without her pushing him off the blanket as she usually does. She fondles his throat, rubs her face against his coat, picks a nettle off his leg and when she looks up, the tears are back in her eyes. Since he hasn't had a wash and probably smells of what went on in the hotel room, Wolf stays in the doorway, a frown on his face. 'All that academic shit,' she says, glancing at the books. 'The stuff that's in it is dead. And what I write isn't any better, I have no talent, no talent for anything. My only talent is to love you.'

In a brick house on the other side of the road that was built shortly after they moved into the district, there lives one of the few couples in the neighbourhood without children—a tall man with a bald head and a walrus moustache and his stocky wife who braids her hair in a long plait that comes down almost to her hips. Their flat is across the road from them and the couple, who will be in their early forties, nod at them in a more-than-friendly manner when they come out onto their north-facing balcony. Hardly has she seen a shadow behind the window than the woman even waves, raising her arm and flapping her hand wildly, her glasses glinting in the sun, and when Wolf comments that they must be from the West, Alina laughs and says, 'Got it in one! From Britz. She spoke to me in the supermarket.'

The windows in the house, which is smothered in Russian vine—'ideal for covering an unsightly structure,' as the garden centre catalogue says—are so arranged that they can hardly avoid the couple's everyday life, unless they abandon their balcony. It's a perfectly normal life, possibly that of teachers or office workers—they breakfast at seven, each with their own section of the newspaper, and have dinner at half past seven, after that there's the flicker of a television or a computer is switched on and, at weekends or other free days, they set the table for lunch at precisely one o'clock, light a candle for coffee, open a bottle of wine a little later and are in bed by eleven.

They'd rather not see all this, of course not, but apart from the roller blind in the bedroom, there are no curtains across the road and, so, they're not spared the sight of what Wolf cannot see as other than ritualized dreariness—an impression that is only reinforced by the fact that the two seem to live out their lives together in relative silence, never laugh or smile, never embrace or even touch one another, to say nothing of kissing, and usually wear shapeless, nondescript clothes. 'Greylings' is his secret name for them, and although he knows it is conceivable that he's being unjust and that basically they're peaceable, hardworking fellow human beings who are concerned about paying off the mortgage on their home and occasionally even read a book, he cannot suppress a certain contempt. After all, they're acting out something that could happen between Alina and him, that one day they're so constantly *there*, they no longer see one another, live a life that's so uniform they hardly create any memories and have forgotten the magic that can occur between people because they've banished anything that's unforeseeable and unexpected from their life and made a lifestyle out of it.

At the same time, he's horrified at the way he dissociates himself from them, which says nothing about the couple but a lot—an embarrassing lot—about him. Why can't he just leave them be? Why must he turn everything into background cross-hatching? Doesn't he stand out distinctly enough at his age? He's just made up his mind to invite them to tea or a glass of beer when a leaflet appears in their letterbox with 'Warmest greetings from Helga and Günter', a reduced copy of the bright-yellow poster that's stuck up in the window opposite the next day. There are plans to set up a private kindergarten in the neighbouring property against which Mr and Mrs Greyling have protested to the local council both as far as building regulations are concerned and with regard to the level of noise it's likely to create—and that clearly in the assumption that all the local residents will be on their side. Wolf can't repress a grin. 'So, blockheads after all,' he says in relief, while Alina shakes her head and when he goes out onto the balcony shortly afterwards to brush the dog, he simply ignores the woman's greeting, the arm shooting up, the rapid wave with the palm facing forwards, as if she were wiping the outside mirror of her loneliness. He just brushes Webster who is going to stay with them now. His owner has fallen in love with the director of the language school in Venezuela, is pregnant and intends to go and live there. Alina's delighted. She buys Webster a new collar, a plainer one with no studs, and registers him with the authorities.

The ability to cope—now there's an expression. Even if the poetic approach to things of necessity creates a certain amount of inefficiency, everyday life still has to be dealt with and quite often leaves him baffled, especially compared to Alina. Things that are complicated problems for him she can do so casually that it leaves him abashed. The hem of her dress sways freely, she goes to answer the telephone without hesitation and when he asks her where she gets her untiring optimism, always getting down to things cheerfully, while for him the very thought of the day ahead and its demands often makes the duvet as heavy as concrete, she strokes his forehead and says, 'Life and your pleasure in it should determine the conditions, sweetheart. Not conditions your life.'

At first, it's hardly noticeable, like a tiny change in body posture or a little weight put on, but he's begun to become dependent on her efficiency. Of course, he appreciates the way she makes things easy for him, the care she takes, despite her work, to shield him from anything that would be detrimental to his writing and the undisturbed time he needs for it. He quietly enjoys the protective cover of her affection, especially in a place where people only seem to exist in pairs, with wedding rings, and every loner or outsider, especially every male one, is seen as a potential child-abuser the moment he encounters the groups of young mothers intoxicated with concern. To be accepted as solid and respectable in this terrarium of normality is something he ascribes to Alina's presence and he instinctively straightens up when Mrs Seidenkranz, to whom they both go every few weeks to have their hair done, shouts after him as he leaves the salon, 'And best wishes to your wife.' Especially in periods of intensive work, tormented by the fear of failure or the ticking of the clock, he has the feeling that without her he would have no grip on the uneven cobbles and would stumble at every dirty look. When she goes to spend a few days with her parents or with a woman friend in the Uckermark, he doesn't leave the house until he runs out of food.

But now, as she sticks bits of paper covered in footnotes or quotations all over the walls and mirrors, and lugs unbelievable piles of books home from the State Library, as she writes her thesis with quiet concentration, they're not just beside one another at night, as usual, they're together all day as well and, with that, have clearly crossed a boundary. What on the face of it looks like intimate closeness becomes oppressive distance, at least for him. Despite its two storeys, the flat seems more cramped, the bed narrower and he becomes more and more uncommunicative and organizes his day differently to avoid her. More and more he works until the early hours or watches television so that he doesn't have to go to bed together with her; he has breakfast with her less and less frequently in order to spare himself the sight of her sleepy face and her his ill-humour, his grey silence.

All the little details of living together—the smell of nail-varnish remover, the sight of the damp copies of *Elle*, *Vogue* and *Cosmopolitan* beside the bathroom scales, the letterbox jammed full of catalogues, Alina's countless pairs of shoes in the hall, all the personal-hygiene stuff in pink or light-green boxes—are making him more and more melancholy. More and more things are left unsaid and what is said always leaves a sour taste in the mouth. Her beauty doesn't move him any longer either or, more and more often, only after he's been away on business. Then his desire is intense but quickly sated, he pretends he's exhausted or stressed out, he buys a sofa bed so he can sleep in his study and, one evening, he notices that he feels embarrassed in front of his own partner and ties a towel round his waist before he comes out of the bathroom to get a pair of boxer shorts out of the linen cupboard they share.

After only a few months of this life together, they often look as if they've spent the whole day in stale air—and it's not uncommon for him to take it out on her with a new sharpness in his look, an extra dioptre of mercilessness. She always finds the rimless glasses he occasionally wears intimidating. Her hairs in his comb, the bra on the door-knob, the cotton buds soaked in mascara that missed the waste basket, too much or too little make-up, tousled or too well-groomed hair, poor or exaggeratedly upright posture—he cannot leave anything unremarked on. More pernickety than he really means to be, he keeps forcing her to explain or justify herself and doesn't even feel bad about it as long as she doesn't cry. For he thinks that the fact that he himself finds his behaviour loathsome, which he definitely does, excuses him. Thus he avoids having to change.

He picks pieces of fluff off the carpet or wipes the dust off the top of the doors, he puts banknotes in among the fruit in the bowl so that they smell better and the fact that Alina smiles at his idea of order and cleanliness just enough not to make him feel like an obsessional neurotic is part of her native tactfulness. She hardly looks up from her work. But when he criticizes the lack of toothpicks and the spice jars in the wrong order in the kitchen cupboard, it's finally too much for her and she tears her hair and screams, 'What d'you want, for Christ's sake? I have to live here too!' Her voice is shrill with desperation, the tears well up, her hands tremble and now he's profoundly shocked—'Live and let live,' that's another of those expressions—but instead of going over, putting his arms round her and saying he's sorry, he shuts himself in his room with a hip flask of schnapps.

It's impossible to live indefinitely with the oppressive feeling of having stayed in the country against one's better judgement, of having spent decades compromising with an inhuman system which muzzled people. It will curdle into a lump of bitter resignation, of bitter defiance and self-righteous coldness. One of the reasons, perhaps, why those who risked their lives and fled while the Wall was still standing or were allowed to emigrate after endless and degrading procedures or even imprisonment find they have nothing to say to those who stayed until the very end. As for Wolf's reservations about the people in East Germany, almost every personal encounter with one of the locals has washed them away and he keeps being amazed at the friendliness of those of whom, out of habit or appearances, he had assumed the opposite. For all that, he's often too fast for them, at least for some of the people here; overcoming their natural mistrust—presumably a relic of the surveillance and spying they were subjected to in the past—takes precisely the amount of time the Westerner asking the way in a hurry hasn't got. So he turns away, deciding that people here are withdrawn. In fact, however, they have retained a humanity which is not at all market-orientated and a readiness to look at other people positively. Their reaction is not one of unfriendliness, rather, one of delayed friendliness and then a warmth that is shaming.

It's only in shops and offices that the spirit of the former state seems ineradicable. As well as an inattentiveness, even sloppiness, which was natural because they had no fear of losing their jobs, officials and people in the service industries in the old communist state clearly also possessed a certain degree of arrogance that no one dared to criticize and that persists to this day. For example, the woman at the passport office, whom he couldn't understand because of the acoustics, says, when he asks her to repeat her instructions, 'Aren't I speaking German?' Or the surgery nurse who's going to take a blood sample without disinfecting his skin and, when he stands up in indignation, replies with a supercilious look, 'Why? The needle's sterile. I've been doing it like this for twenty-five years, so what can be wrong with it? Is there something wrong with your skin?'

The woman in the post office who's been going on for ages with a customer about knitting patterns closes the counter although there are two people still waiting. The cobbler who, when he takes back the pair of shoes he repaired not long ago and are already worn out, says in all seriousness, 'Well, if you must walk so much . . .'. And the man at the sausage stand who plonks two sausages down in front of him with greasy fingers and growls when he shakes his head, 'It's only cooking fat, squire. I'm making rissoles in the back. Or d'you think I'm repairing my car?' And when Wolf asks him why he doesn't wash his hands before serving him, that naturally makes him the know-all from the West whom the other customers in the queue give sidelong glances as they twist their cloth bags behind their backs.

'But people in the service industries were kings in the East,' says the hairdresser, Mrs Seidenkrantz, a delicate woman in her late forties who became allergic to the hair dyes and perming agents she had to work with after the Wall came down and now just cuts hair. Her diploma with the embossed coat of arms of the German Democratic Republic is on the wall beside the mirror. 'It's precisely those who earn least nowadays, the taxi-drivers and hairdressers, who got the most over here then. Don't imagine one of those gentlemen in his clapped-out taxi would have driven out to Schöneiche, where I live, he'd have had to drive back with no fare. Unless I could pay in Western currency . . . And my appointment book was fuller than old Honecker's. When I came home from the salon, there'd be a queue waiting at the door. I'd just have time to feed the cats, then I'd carry on working on my own account. The hair drier never cooled down. Or take my Aunt Gerda, a lavatory attendant at Friedrichstraße Station. Of her own free will, she spent years and years cleaning and scrubbing, fourteen to sixteen hours a day, and every night she came home with a shopping bag full of tips, half of them hard currency. When I offered her a job, clean and no stench, she just shook her head. She didn't want to change. She bought two houses and had her own yacht on Müggelsee—as a loo-cleaner.'

There's an amazing number of hairdressing, beauty or nail salons in Friedrichshagen and the competition means the price of a haircut is such that it would feel presumptuous to expect quality as well. Everything's done at top speed and even if it looks reasonable when you leave the shop, the first time you wash your hair, your hairstyle collapses and has a suspicious look of the communist youth movement. And, as a Westerner, it's better not to suggest they could ask two or three times the price for a better cut, one done in less of a rush, taking the customer's shape of head into account, without gaps and visible layers. The decadence people here see in what they feel is vanity is still reflected in venomous or mocking looks. Even for Mrs Seidenkrantz, there are hardly any more variants on her casual 'The usual?' than 'Short' or 'Not too short'—and the latter requires more concentration than she can manage while she's talking. And she does that the whole time since she's found out that he's a writer.

Despite that, he likes going to her. He feels he can see the kind of thing in her face that has struck him about women who spent the years before the end of communism with private reservations about and unspoken opposition to the state—sensitive and non-political in a way he can only describe as existential, she radiates the dignity of those who would never confuse the so-called real world with the truth, under either socialism or capitalism. She always seems a little more timid than she really is and she certainly has a wicked sense of humour. Some of her remarks, as her fingers flit through his hair, have a saucy, subversive spark. However, she rarely smiles. Her delicate face with its pearly complexion, thin but not unsensuous lips and slightly fixed gaze still looks sad or melancholy, even when she's telling a funny story.

Her husband, an engineer who has specialized in tunnel construction, is mostly abroad and she spends all her free time looking after her garden and the verandah full of potted plants. She's even got a pond and, last winter, all the fish in it died. 'Not because it froze over, they would have survived that, but I forgot to rake the dead leaves off the bottom and they made septic gases under the ice so that the fish suffocated. You're more of a monster than you think. But in the spring, I bought some new ones, half a dozen lovely colourful kois, fat as carp. Not the genuine ones from Japan, of course—who can afford those? From the DIY store, sort of cheap replacement parts. And just imagine, the heron's had four already. You just have to accept it. Obviously, you could put a net over the pond but that looks awful. And the plastic dog I stuck by the pond because it's supposed to frighten them off was lying among the lettuces the next day. My son spent a week crouching in the arbour with his air rifle but nothing happened. And shortly afterwards, the beast came for the fifth koi, the biggest, with pink eyes and dark blue and yellow patches. But that one fought back or was simply too heavy for it. Whatever, it dropped it and the poor fish landed on top of the neighbour's garage. It wriggled like hell and the three of us were hopping about on the roofing felt, unable to get hold of it. Only when someone brought a woollen blanket . . .'

While she's talking, she keeps placing her hands on his temples to readjust the position of his head and, quite often, Wolf thinks he can see in her doll-like face, along with her determination to remain calm, an expression which suggests she's making allowances for him when he brings the conversation round to life and conditions in the old GDR. Normally—and perhaps quite rightly—after a couple of questions, his ethnographic interest is felt to be intrusive and only elicits monosyllabic answers. No one likes to be seen as exotic and certainly not as ancient history. People here get in a huff when a West German doesn't know that a 'brigade diary' was a document describing the development of a work team or that 'young people's initiation' was a ceremony at which fourteen-year-olds received adult status, and, of course, here they assume 'confirmation' has something to do with 'firm'. It could be that it's just another expression of the loud-mouthed arrogance they're quick to see in West Germans but, in Wolf's eyes, what strikes him most about older people from the East—the thing that keeps giving a gruff, even aggressive, note to a conversation that is intended to be a friendly effort to obtain information—is their nonsensical feeling of inferiority vis-à-vis Westerners. But Mrs Seidenkrantz doesn't seem to suffer from that at all. She chatters on quite freely about the time before the Wall came down, though, first, she does glance in the mirror at the people waiting by the door.

'Actually, I can't complain,' she says. 'We had everything. Round the lake here, we were in Supply Group A, because of the tourists. We could even get oranges and bananas and things like that. And if something was unavailable, we could always find ways round it. There were a lot of mutual favours, you know. I did everyone's hair. So, the baker would put a white loaf or a cake on one side and, at the weekend in summer, the butcher's wife always had a packet of barbecue meat for me, gratis. I didn't even have to queue, I just went up to the counter, held out my bag and—so long until the next perm. And electric appliances and things like that. I can't remember how many TVs and washing machines we bought on Alexanderplatz to take to our relatives in our Trabant estate car. They live in deepest Saxony, in the Valley of the Clueless where no supplies were sent. Once, when we gave my niece a pair of curling tongs she couldn't get over it for two whole days. Only the opportunity to travel, that was the only thing we missed. You soon got fed up with the Baltic, lake Balaton, the Black Sea. I was always dreaming of London and Paris. Then suddenly the border was open and we stayed here, as if we were stuck fast. I think we were afraid of all the freedom. I really had to give us a kick—me and my husband. Come on, I said, we've been moaning for years and years that we can't go—and now when we can, we don't want to? That would mean it was all wrong, they might as well wall us in again. So we hopped onto a plane to Rome.'

Once, she shows him photos of her husband and her son for whom she asks for a signed copy of a book in the hope that he'll find it more interesting than the computer games he plays all the time and, when Wolf asks her what it was like with the omnipresent Stasi, whether they were aware of the secret police and their network of spies in their everyday life, she shakes her head but suddenly speaks more softly. The fine lines in the slightly sunken skin round her eyes begin to flicker. 'I never met any of them. But then, I was a nobody and I didn't want anything. I mean, if you wanted to get on, to make a career or go abroad, even to communist countries, like my husband with his tunnel construction team, then you were investigated, of course. And you had at least to be cautious about taking advantage of the celebrated helpfulness and solidarity of people over here.

You never really knew who all the guys sitting round the barbecue were. But otherwise . . .'

She grins and glances in the mirror. Two white-haired men are sitting, waiting. 'Though I wouldn't be surprised if there was a file on me. As you know, I collect cactuses, the flowering species, and I got any relatives I could dig up in the West to send me plants. Some even arrived. Then, once a year, there was a suspicious meeting in my greenhouse, by candlelight—there still is. You see, I've got a *Selenicereus grandiflorus*, a Queen of the Night. It's really old and winds up the trellis, it's taller than I am, and it always comes into bloom in July, sometimes in August, when it's really hot, just for a few hours. At first, I often missed it but, in time, you get a sense of when it's going to happen. Towards evening, you can tell that the time will come just before midnight and then I ring up my friends and acquaintances on the estate—there were ten or fifteen of us even then—and we sit there quietly with a glass of wine, waiting. It's like a church service and, when the flowers open and that incredible scent of vanilla or almond spreads, you feel you could cry. At least I've always felt the tears welling up, for thirty years. And this sadness—it sounds odd, I know—is unalloyed happiness. You're oblivious to everything round you, the state and all, despite the shadows in the garden.'

The books are quietly standing in tall bookcases. The books are old. Full of words and full of their own importance, they put on a serious air but, ultimately, they have nothing to say about most things, these little coffins of bliss, not even between the lines. The dust on the gilt edging says more.

Your first crown on a visible tooth, painful wear on the lumbar vertebra, a sudden hearing loss, without tinnitus yet, and suddenly you're buying shoes at eight hundred euros and beginning to acquire complete editions . . . At that age, other men are dreaming of a Porsche or a Swiss tourbillon watch. And already you're hearing of the first acquaintances who, either ill or tired of life, are disposing of libraries they've spent decades putting together and which are valuable in more than a purely monetary sense—their heirs don't read, anyway. And you succumb, succumb to the desire for completeness or even status which the magnificent shelves express. You wall yourself in with all the paper bricks and leaf through prospects and catalogues while, all round, storm-winds are tearing the trees apart. That transience is an essential part of blossoming is a nice phrase but you'd really like to have it bound in leather.

Novalis is all right, but twenty fat volumes of Hermann Hesse—when are you going to read the ten you don't know yet? Jean Paul in buckram, a long row, and you're already weary by the time you reach *Siebenkäs.* A good metre of Wieland, and Heinrich Böll safely gathered in too—a compact reminder to go into him again. But what exactly? And when? Proust in lilac, gold embossed, Proust in a slipcase, and the India paper, as you leaf through the pages, whispering its tender 'Too late . . .'

Still you keep on buying, and the workman who's fitting an extractor hood over the stove points with his hammer drill at the shelves and spines in the living room and asks: 'Are they all genuine?'—No, not really. Essentially they're the same as the fakes he's seen in the furniture warehouse, for decoration only, since whenever you want to look something up, you reach for the tattered and torn paperbacks in the second row. In those you can find any paragraph you want almost with your eyes shut, and all the bus tickets, cigarette papers or sweet wrappers between the pages, the dog ears, the passages marked with your thumbnail or a pencil twenty or thirty years ago, an autumn leaf with only the delicate veins left, the smell of nicotine, or of the heating or mould—in which flat?—at the back of which tenement?—make each of these books more valuable than the new Complete Works, standing neatly next to one another like rows of upmarket townhouses, can ever be.

This or that passage has helped you to live, what's more, it's taught you to be aware of living, thus making it richer and you freer. The best demonstration of the truth of the hoary adage that 'a man who reads gets twice as much out of life' is when you come across one of those marked passages again. The widening of the eyes, the sharp intake of breath down to the most sensitive fibres of your being seems to repeat itself, even when you changed your mind ages ago or think what is said is banal and you're touched by your own naivety. They are phrases round which a shimmer of the astonishment or delight still remains, a reflection of your former purity or youthful ideals, and the way they re-echo within makes you realize how far you have gone and how long it has taken to come to the plain and simple insight that only what is transient can blossom.

The hell of secrecy, the heaven of lies. He's been meeting Charlotte for months now. Because of her, he's bought a cellphone, new underwear and a tangier aftershave, because of her, he's been trimming his pubic hair and, when he can slip away from Friedrichshagen, he rings the bell of her flat at the back of the tenement in Prenzlauer Berg every couple of weeks around eight in the evening. It's on the fifth floor, no lift, with a view of the globe at the top of the television tower, the revolving restaurant. Despite the glass-topped desk, two leather armchairs in the Bauhaus style, a large white sofa and knee-high shelves, the living room seems bare, dominated by the stained pine floor. The brown of the floorboards is dark, like Webster's coat, and when the cleaning woman's polished it, his paws keep slipping.

Everywhere there are angular candles burning, arranged like organ pipes, and on the shelves are old pocket watches that Charlotte collects, dried roses and expensive books of pictures and photographs. In the functional kitchen, everything, even the handle of the washing-up brush, is of stainless steel and, apart from the slatted wardrobes, there is nothing in the bedroom except the wide bed and a lamp, a plastic sphere the size of a football which is on the floor and rolls to and fro when you give it a push. A feathered mask from Venice is hanging from the window catch and on the shelf is a dental night guard in a little blue case that is transparent when you hold it up to the light.

So that his intentions are not too obvious, Wolf has got into the habit of bringing flowers. She loves the big, dramatic ones—Callas, lilies, field-grown roses—and, while she's arranging their splendour in the vase, he, still out of breath from the stairs, slips into the bathroom to give his hands a good wash. He doesn't want her thinking he's breathless with lust, even if that is occasionally the case. There are three toothbrushes in a glass on the shelf, two dry, one wet, and he keeps on noticing different-coloured hair in the drain or in the comb under the mirror. On the edge of the bath, next to the wooden statuette of a Nubian goddess, is a bottle of haircolour for men and, once, his predecessor's condom is floating in the lavatory and refuses to go down even though he flushes it several times.

Charlotte's often wearing a towelling dressing gown when he arrives, a soft, white one that emphasizes her expensive tan. Underneath, she's naked and, at first, she behaves as if she's just got back from the office or the airport and hasn't had time for a quick shower, yet her make-up is fresh. But that doesn't mean he can fall on her straight away, she needs to go through a certain ritual. There's always a bowl of fruit, a jug of water and a bottle of wine or grappa on the low coffee table and they begin by having a drink and talking about the last few days or weeks. As they do so, Charlotte puts her feet in his lap and seldom seems to notice that the belt of her dressing gown is coming undone. She holds her glass in the fingertips of both hands and looks at him while he's talking, but her thoughts are mostly still elsewhere. Sometimes, she clenches her teeth to hold back a yawn or asks him about something he's just told her. Sometimes, she calls him Mark or Urs and enjoys his tender clip round the ear.

She works too hard, too much stress, that's clear to see, despite her exquisite make-up. She needs another glass, 'to wind down', and wearily talks of seminars and conferences and business trips, of the in-fighting among her university colleagues, whom she contemptuously refers to as pen-pushers, and of her desire to leave the narrow-mindedness of academia behind and go into industry. While she talks, she smokes some of the grass a policeman friend brings her back from The Hague and, if out of curiosity he asks about her two men, she doesn't mind talking about them. There's always one of them she's not phoning any more because he's taken one liberty too many. 'Just imagine, I put off important appointments for him and fly to Switzerland and he seriously thinks . . .'

It's always much the same and its purpose is less to impart information than to temper the atmosphere, to harmonize the vibrations through their voices that gradually become deeper as they relax, hoarser too, as if they had slight invisible serrations—like delicate wheels that engage and set clockwork in motion which doesn't show the time but coordinates all the movements spatially so that they make perfect sense. For example, when she pushes a strand of hair back behind his ear and briefly strokes the back of his neck, or when, in a deliberately casual gesture, he places his hand on her thigh, the skin that is incredible, even if you can feel that it's in the final stage of smoothness despite the evenings in the gym. Precisely because you can feel it.

And, while she's playing with his fingers and explaining the difference between Internet and Intranet or telling him about information overload in fully networked companies and the associated psychological problems, he pushes the towelling aside with his other hand and gently plucks at her hair and her strangely long labia which somehow recall the wattles on poultry. If her breathing then changes or she even stops speaking and closes her eyes, he takes his hand away and asks her something else about her field, about the expression 'glass ceiling', for example, or 'female resource', which she answers after swallowing. But, as she does so, she's already leaning forward and undoing his zip, and the soft noise of the slider over the teeth sounds as if, somewhere above them, the next hour is being wound up.

Alina seems to have no suspicion of all this. She even encourages him to take a turn round the houses and go to a cafe, she irons the shirt that Charlotte will unbutton and, when he comes back, more relaxed and particularly tender towards her, she clearly feels confirmed in her belief that a harmonious life together is just a question of getting the balance between closeness and loving distance right. In the early days of his affair, she probably feels that is proved by the fact that hardly is he back home, where he sniffs at his hands in the dark hallway, than he wants to go to bed with her, quickly, right away if possible, for he can still feel the other woman under his skin, savour her aroma, and, given his age and his fear of declining potency, for a few chest-thumping moments, he needs the intoxicating feeling of having satisfied two demanding lovers, one after the other. And since Alina visibly enjoys his fervour more than usual and is delighted at his stamina, he doesn't feel he's abusing her trust. And seen through the prism of his secret activity, she, for her part, becomes more beautiful for him, noble in her innocence and not for one moment does he make a comparison between the two women.

His secret meetings with the other woman are seldom spontaneous. Mostly they're planned well in advance by SMS or brief messages in his mailbox and, as a rule, it's Charlotte who decides on the evening. If, for once, he suggests one, he can be sure she'll have no time or only agree provisionally. Often something crops up, something to do with her work, she claims. As the time approaches, Wolf tries to think up a reason to go into town by himself but he seldom finds anything that sounds plausible. There's very little that can't be bought in nearby Köpenick and going to the city centre for a change is not an argument he'd like to use. Alina spends the whole day at her desk as well and needs a change just as much. He hasn't any friends, he doesn't go to the theatre any more and only rarely to the cinema, the infusions in the Charité Hospital after his hearing loss are a thing of the past and he's already been to his dentist in Kreuzberg three times that year.

He almost holds it against Alina that she assumes his love for her is as exclusive as hers for him, like having the same blood group or favourite food. He has to consciously stop himself from calling it naive, it certainly betokens the depth of her love—but that is precisely what he finds stifling when there's a rendezvous with the other woman in the offing, more and more as the days pass, so that eventually he doesn't really know whether it's being together in the small flat all the time that oppresses him or his guilty conscience. As if there were a chemistry of unfaithfulness which fills the atmosphere with substances which, though tart, keep the worst bitterness away, eventually there's a sudden outburst, a blazing row which takes both of them by surprise and which, as so often, is about nothing—a missing shoelace, a mislaid umbrella—but which, to his mind, gives him the right to storm out, slamming the door, and only come back late at night.

He doesn't want to leave her, that is for sure, he just wants to stay at Alina's side but with a little more freedom. Although, of course, he has no idea how he would react if she had a lover, he has a picture of a life together in which each of them would have space for their own thing, for secrets that would not erode truth but enrich it. He would like to grow old with her without becoming like the Greylings, for, although they are younger than him, he sees their silently celebrated habits, lacking any erotic element, as the secondary tumours of an inertia which suggests the fire has gone out and which, for him, would be the end.

But when, right at the beginning, he tests the water by telling her about Charlotte as an acquaintance from the past, he happened to meet in a cafe and they had a drink and a chat together, she stares at the floor and already looks hurt. Or is that just his imagination? Whatever, she certainly turns pale, which, with her complexion, means white. So, he doesn't go on, he doesn't want to upset her. 'And?' she asks anyway, in an attempt at a lighthearted tone. She's cutting up food for the dog, greyish-yellow tripe. 'Did you end up in bed?'

There's just a moment's pause between the end of her question and his expressionless answer, an apparently composed, 'Nonsense. What makes you say that?' And yet in that brief moment, born of cowardice, he feels caught up in a whole world of half-truths and false notes, a tangle of sad excuses and endless pretences, which even now makes him feel as grey as the evil-smelling entrails on the chopping board. Grey as the stomach of the colour grey.

A letter with an Italian stamp, the sender's name on the back just initials. But even though it's a bit unsteady now, the bold hand, its graphic gesture, still expresses the determined force of character—his former friend and mentor writing from his house in Liguria. A book is enclosed, poems with drawings on Japan paper from a private press, and the letter informs him that he and his partner will be in Berlin in the near future. After an eternity in which they've not been in contact, either by letter or telephone, he wants to 'call on' Wolf in his flat in Friedrichshagen, even suggesting the day and time in a tone the familiarity of which has something disconcerting, even unseemly, about it, since he goes on merrily as if they hadn't parted with ill-feeling, even bitterness, between them. Clearly it never occurs to him—he's over seventy now—that descending on Wolf like this is inappropriate, sensitivity was never one of his strong points. But Wolf thinks he can see a touch of compunction in the fact that he follows his signature, a slightly more angular 'Richard' than previously, with his surname in brackets '(Sander)'. He does, then, think it possible he might be forgotten or confused with someone else and it is this ostensible humility—which simply shows that he naturally assumes Wolf shares his warped sensibility which, anyway, is only switched on in the short periods after he's slept off the effects of the wine—that makes Wolf tear up the letter. He doesn't want to see the man again.

Yet, he thinks of him from time to time. Now he must show he can resist the temptation to pay the older man back for what could be seen as condescending pride, the arrogance of the man who's made it, expressed in a patronizing air and occasional cheques. For there are things he has to thank him for, despite all his reservations—the courage to stick to his own language, for example, and the fact that he can construct a sentence that doesn't collapse at the first questioning frown, that he can distinguish between versification and a gesture and knows how to hold something back so that it shines out. Sander's status helped him stand on his own feet, he gained strength in the shadow of his strength and, for a while, he definitely felt indebted to him, materially as well, even offered his services as secretary at a time when Sander was much in demand, travelling all over Europe. But the day came when his flicker of fame was over, when the silhouette began to crumble, and, even before gratitude began to clog up the metabolism between the disciple and his admired master, the pedestal was empty.

When they got to know one another at the end of the 1970s, Wolf was a little over twenty; he'd just moved to Berlin and found a half-day job in a photocopy shop at Zoo Station. From behind the bars at the other side of the car park you could hear the constant clatter of hooves and the cries and screeching of the animals reminded by spring where they were, for God's sake, and Wolf was filling the paper tray of a printer when the mobile over the door rang and Richard Sander came in. He wanted to have an envelope full of handwritten pages copied, although it was very expensive in that shop, and when Wolf told him that across the road in the Technical University, only a stone's throw away, he could get it done for a fifth of the price, he waved it away. 'I'm in a hurry. After all, it's only money.'

A striking figure, at least in that district of Berlin. His sturdy shoes and his trousers were covered in spots of paint and every button on his checked flannel shirt was a different size. His blue drill jacket seemed to be new, it was usually mechanics or plumbers who wore them, or, as in this case, intellectuals and artists who wanted to look like workers. His long blond hair was combed back and came down just above his shoulders and, although it was raining, he was wearing Ray-Bans. Wolf had seen him quite often on the footpaths round the lake in Grunewald, wearing painted shoes, or in the audience at readings and lectures, which he occasionally went to and at which the man would sit with clear space between himself and all the others. Sometimes, he carried a twisted walking stick and took a mouthful of wine from the bottle sticking out of his coat. Sometimes, he wrote something down.

Not that he stood out as a genuine oddball but the fact that, at forty-five, he obviously wanted to be one was the touching thing about him in a West Berlin where cybernetics was already structuring thinking, where sniffing coke was becoming fashionable and the first restaurants were starting to put white cloths on the tables. But he lacked the often friendly and self-content aura of such guys. His dark spectacles, raised chin and flabby complexion with the wide, distinctly outlined lips, the corners always turned down a bit, gave him a slightly arrogant, almost cold expression and, for a moment, the young Wolf had to resist his negative reaction, automatic for someone with a proletarian or petty-bourgeois background where the odd or unconventional is only accepted insofar as it corresponds to the standard notions of unconventionality or oddity.

He puts the manuscript in the copier. As he does so, reads the man's name and is taken aback and, since he knows poems by him that he finds deeply moving, enchanting drawings full of jumping, flying, falling creatures and impressive short stories, his prejudice gives way to a quiet feeling of shame at not having immediately seen his special quality beneath the aura of a tramp. He thinks he can hear it now, in the man's voice, which doesn't perhaps sound very powerful but which has a fine, silvery edge to it, gleaming with alertness and intelligence, and when the man asks for hundred-gramme paper, to make the thin book look a little more substantial, the look he gives him over the top of his glasses is, for a brief moment at least, not unfriendly.

So, Wolf, facing a writer for the first time in his life, overcomes his inhibitions and tries to put into words how his books appealed to him, how their poetry and insight delighted him, but all that comes out is stammering, as if he were trying to spell out his jubilation. And, as the manuscript is drawn through the machine page by page, the man listens to him attentively but with no sign of vanity, though his expression does suggest mild scepticism and his posture—one elbow on the counter, one hand in his trouser pocket, his eyes on the floor, with the occasional nod—strikes Wolf as intimidatingly professional. Everything about him seems to say, 'OK, that's fine, but keep your wonderfuls for the Bible. There's no point in going into raptures about poems. You have to talk about poems the way you talk about a wobbly chair or a well-built table. Poems equal stamina plus fanciful ideas plus craftsmanship and must be of practical use, that's all. And everyone can be a genius, young man, one way or another. Genius is just small change.'

He takes off his glasses, nibbles at one of the earpieces. His eyes are bright blue, almost aquamarine. He smells of wine, of smoke and turpentine, there's dust from chalk under his fingernails and the sense of freedom about him and the experience of life and the world that shines through every brief comment make Wolf feel his life as a shop assistant as even more cramped, with the result that the words come pouring out all the more breathlessly. Moreover, he wants to atone for his prejudice about the man who seems like a messenger from a sphere he wants to belong to and whom he senses is already showing the first signs of impatience. His jawbones twitch, his eyebrows meet above the bridge of his nose and then he's looking at his watch and taking out his wallet.

Outside, feeding time starts. Half pigs are heaved into wheelbarrows, birds fly up and bounce off the wire netting under the sky, the roar of lions drowns out the station announcements and, as the last scrap of meaning in his words seems to vanish into thin air at the writer's expression, which is cool once more, almost refined, the final page of the manuscript is copied, so that Wolf succumbs to a mild feeling of panic, an internal fluttering and buzzing, and decides to reveal his innermost secret and admit to what he hasn't even told his girlfriend. But the man has long since seen what he's after. 'Yes, yes,' he says, picking up the sheets out of the tray, 'I understand. Send me the things you write, poems I assume. Perhaps I can do something for you.' Then he puts a banknote on the counter, pushes the door open with his shoulder and adds, wagging a finger, 'But only if they're good.'

To be a writer, accountable to no one, to nothing but beauty, to work with poetic licence when and where and how much you want—for Wolf, who, at that point, knew nothing of the inner necessity of a text, the tyranny of the compulsion to create or the viciousness of the literary world, that was much more appealing than the writing itself. Since he was fourteen, he's been working to earn money in various jobs and situations which all had the same message for him: Sorry, you come to work late; Sorry, you lay bricks too slowly; Sorry, you leave too early. As well as that, in the eyes of his instructors and foremen he seldom had his mind on his work, a daydreamer who could trap his fingers just by opening his folding rule; an idiot with his head in the clouds who, during the lunch break, when the others took out their tabloids or porn magazines, had his nose in Reclam paperbacks. But, even if some books had more than seven seals for him and he had to imagine the meaning of some texts, in his youth, literature was the first and only authority to tell him: You're *not* crazy! You're right with your dreams! Life isn't a prefabricated house, life is looking for something unique from you and it's quite OK to embrace a horse or call a tree darling. And that was why he wanted to become a writer.

And now, in Richard Sander, he meets the embodiment of his longing, which is mostly a longing for freedom, for space, and since, for a long time, he remains the only author with whom he's in contact—they're soon meeting regularly whenever Sander's in Berlin—everything he hears and learns from him etches itself more deeply on his mind than its truth deserves. Yet, he would hardly have seen his desire for a book of his own through to the end without Richard's encouragement, without his slightly tipsy but still effective, 'You must write!' Wolf, who even today has no eye for himself or—what in his case comes down to the same thing—too sharp an eye, accepts this lapidary utterance, somewhere between a statement of fact, the finger of fate and a plain imperative, like a shiny, valuable coin he can sew into the lining of his jacket and secretly feel with the tips of his fingers at moments when his confidence is low.

He *wants* to write but keeps feeling he'll never be able to because there's some secret about it from which he is excluded because of his background, his scanty education, which no amount of experience can make up for. What's the point, after all, of having something to tell if you can't give it artistic form? But, alongside his help in matters of the writer's craft, which mostly consists of curing him of his sentimentality, checking for redundant phrases and cutting adjectives, it's mostly the earnest and, at the same time, relaxed way Richard shows him by example that in the end it's all a matter of persistence, literature's a profession like any other, that keeps encouraging him. 'Now we'll go for a meal,' he says after they've talked over Wolf's first poetry collection. 'The mystery will be revealed with the post-prandial schnapps.'

He lives in an upper-middle-class house in Charlottenburg and the hall of his apartment—at least the part you can see from the doorway—is papered right up to the ceiling with posters for his exhibitions, readings and books, which at first Wolf doesn't find suspicious. He imagines it's usual or even required in artistic circles. There's a space where Richard writes and another where he draws, separated from one another by bookshelves full of his own publications, a remarkable number—if they're anthologies, there's a paper marker for his contribution. On the walls of this huge Berlin room are African blankets, carved masks and engravings in silver frames, most by Richard himself. Occasionally, he gives little parties there, with wines from Baden, bowls of stew and meatballs. Or lectures are held and formal discussions where you sit on the parquet floor between the few pieces of furniture, like in the 1960s. Richard, who many say has a gift for friendship but whose embraces with the obligatory 'My dear . . .' also have something proprietary about them, likes to gather young, mostly good-looking poets round him, gaunt lecturers from the Free University, taciturn painters and one or two leading feature writers or text-book authors, and they all, besides their acquaintance with him, seem to have three things in common they desire: undemanding unconventionality, a comfort-zone Bohemia; alcohol till it fills their veins; and women who don't cause problems—teachers of personal and social education with tired, brittle hair in loose-fitting things or jazz fans whose former glow has receded deep into their smoke-filled hearts.

And this is where Wolf gives his first reading—in a feeble voice, quivering to the very corners of the manuscript and, in his shyness, so fast that it sounds as if he's trying to outpace the audience's understanding. Their quiet attention makes him feel more alone than he's ever felt, more distrustful too. Suddenly, all his images seem wooden, every alliteration or assonance shows a glint of his vanity, every special effect is dull because it's trying to be a special effect, and the cultured nods and occasional sighs or clearing of the throat make him feel like a naked nobody showing off his fair-ground tattoos. The silence at the end of the reading yawns like a bottomless pit, the applause begins hesitantly and sounds thinner than for the others, a discussion is abandoned in favour of oxtail soup and, horrified at himself, he decides he will never write another line. In despair, he tears up his manuscript in the loo.

But afterwards, when someone else is reading and he's sitting sweat-soaked in the kitchen, forcing down a piece of cold potato dipped in mayonnaise, a publisher comes up to him.

The summer's coming to an end, their second in Friedrichshagen. The white hydrangeas have turned a dull green with a faint tinge of violet in the side of the clusters facing the light. But it's still warm, the withered foliage still hanging on the trees, and the birds haven't left yet either. Starlings above all are gathering in the evening woods along the riverbanks. You can hear them in the crowns of the oaks and huge pines without seeing much more of them than a yellow beak here and there or a glimpse of their glistening plumage and, if you close your eyes, their constant, bright-faceted chatter, their chirping, twittering and screeching up there seems absolutely magical, as if you were in the cellar of a crystal-cutting workshop.

Then they fall silent so abruptly you feel dazed and they fly up with a rush of wings to catch the last warmth of the setting sun and, presumably, to practise for their long journey south as well, with a few circles, loops and pirouettes spiralling higher and higher. Behind the large flocks, you can just make out the outlines of the dome of the observatory and the jets heading slowly for Schönefeld Airport. If you walk underneath them, the path is darkened, making you think of gossamer material waved in the air, black veils fluttering and billowing, but, from a distance, their formation dances look like exultation, the sky rejoicing.

At the Teufelssee, a small lake in the middle of the woods, there's a former cafe with moss-covered battlements and a tower with a flag advertising Langnese ice cream waving from it. It's a sauna now with a steam bath, a Russian banja and a Turkish bath. Herbal facial packs and shiatsu massage are also offered and there's a children's playground in a fenced lakeside meadow, an aviary full of exotic songbirds and a maze with hedges taller than a man. In the middle, in a spacious pavilion with a glass dome, you can relax by the light of oriental lamps. The drinks machine is beside the door.

Set up quickly and cheaply immediately after the Wall came down, the complex already looks in need of renovation but is still very popular. The woman at the cash desk, an oldish blonde with rhinestone dust on her two-coloured fingernails, hands them keys along with woollen armbands that are still wet. None of the cupboards in the changing room has a door that still fits the way it was made, everywhere there are additional hinges and locks and it's so damp that the chipboard is swollen and the strips of turquoise veneer hang over the corridor like palm leaves.

But the showers work, with a full jet, veiling the mould between the tiles, and the various hot-rooms look the same as they do everywhere. There's a forty-, a sixty- and a ninety-degree sauna, with colourful lighting, and all of them—the jumble of slippers by the doors is a clue—surprisingly full. People move up closer together and it's difficult not to touch the person next to you. Wolf puts his hands on his knees and listens to the birdsong on the tape, fervently hoping that what's running down his back is not the sweat from the man sitting higher up. The firebricks make a cracking sound.

A lot of the people here, if not most of them, seem to be regulars. They greet one another with booming hellos, joke and chat a lot, both in the hot rooms and in the tiled corridors, where people keep looking at him and Alina out of the corners of their eyes, as if they were recognizably Westerners even without clothes—which is probably the case. Their hesitant, slightly coy behaviour in this place they're not familiar with is alien to most of the other customers. Between thirty and sixty, these people wear their nakedness like any other leisure wear and clearly feel comfortable in their bodies, their firm fat indicating a healthy grip on the ground. Some look as if they're working together. An office manager is discussing dispatch problems with his staff.

Two nurses greet a doctor—it's only when he's addressed as 'Doctor' that he appears naked. Laughter rings out over the lake.

After their second spell in the sauna, they go to the ice room. The boxes for spectacles by the door are overflowing there as well, sometimes the frames get caught up with one another. Alina yelps out loud and squeals when he rubs her down with snow which he's scratched off the wall; her buttocks turn red, her lovely shoulders and even her unusually pale cheeks glow. The whites of her eyes are quite clear. When they come out of the ice-room and walk across the meadow moist with evening dew, the air makes their skin tingle, as if they were being sprayed with gossamer mist. It's almost dark under the trees now but there's a fire by the lakeside and the water feels lukewarm and the mud between their toes is like liquid velvet.

They swim out a little way into the falling night, looking in vain for stars. Somewhere nearby, twigs crackle, the rushes whisper and then a bird in the aviary cries. In the maze, that now looks as compact as a building, lamps are flickering close to the ground and people are walking round behind the hedges. Their shadows can only be glimpsed as they flit to and fro, and Wolf can't say why he's whispering as he rubs Alina's back dry. His penis gets longer without going stiff and she rubs him down, very slowly, very thoroughly, even lifting up his testicles. Then she gives a vague smile, with just the one corner of her mouth, wraps the towel round her waist and strides up the meadow with the languid resolution of experienced women. As she goes, she glances round briefly at him.

The paths in the maze are narrow, just wide enough for two to stand beside one another. Moulded by countless naked soles, there's something responsive about the clay ground, despite its hardness, it's almost as if their steps come of their own accord, and the light from the parallel paths makes a filigree pattern of twigs and leaves on their skin. They walk hand in hand, like children in a fairy tale, and listen without hearing much more than the music from the middle of the maze, a song by Karat, and when they turn the first corner they come to an amazed halt. Two men are sitting at a stone table in a niche and, if it wasn't for the swirl of blue smoke from their cigars, with the folds of their towels hanging down and the shadows on their earnest faces, you could have taken them for statues, Roman senators. But they were just silently playing chess.

A wind starts to blow higher up, the tops of the trees rustle, though you can't see them. Along the next path, a man whose muscles have an almost golden gleam is leaning against a tree, looking as if he's waiting for someone or something. All he's wearing is a chain with military identification tags round his neck and his huge penis looks as if it's been oiled. He nods when they greet him and they're almost past when a strong arm comes through the hedge and a hand with liver spots reaches for his backside, a finger disappearing in it as far as the ring. The man seems hardly surprised. He does straighten his back with a soft groan and closes his eyes but doesn't stop chewing his gum.

Before the path ends in the little open space with the loungers and the illuminated pavilion is a turn-off which leads nowhere, a cul-de-sac with tissues and used condoms on the ground. There's no one there and Alina, with a sort of feline glint in her eye, a kind of horrified delight, as on those summer days when they'd slip into the empty back row of a cinema and silently touch one another under their thin clothes, quickly takes his half-erect penis, as she would his forearm or hand, and draws him into the dimness. People are moving behind the hedge, singly or in groups, and their silhouettes rear up and she squats down for what is to come. She goes about it briskly but in a very refined manner, supporting him with just her fingertips, and her shoulders and the curve of her hips shimmer in the light of the red and deep-yellow hanging lamps coming through the hedge.

Wolf throws his head back and digs the fingers of both hands in her hair. Voices can be heard on the other side, the clink of glasses, soft laughter, and while Alina is so aroused she seems to think she's invisible, he keeps looking round out of the corner of his eye. He's really up for it now and can tell he won't take long, assuming they're not disturbed. He tries to pull her up to do it standing up with her but she stays squatting down and rubs her cheek against his tip, kisses away a little drop. 'Tell me, my friend, how are things with us?' She's a little hoarse and the shadows of her eyelashes look like dark rays. 'Do you still love me?' 'Oh God,' he murmurs, 'What's all this about? Are you stupid? Of course I love you. Come on, let's get on with it.'

But Alina, with her elbow stuck out, just makes a few movements with a ring formed by her thumb and forefinger to keep his erection going. There's something so practised about it that it almost makes him come. All the time, she keeps her eyes fixed on him. Her nipples, still swollen at the lake, have gone down again, one so far that it looks like a negative of itself. 'You do?' she says. 'And there was me thinking our dog smells of Chanel. And why do you love me? Come on, tell me.'

Once more the music echoes round the woods, a few women scream, they start clapping in time to the tune and the flickering behind the thin foliage suggests the naked people there are dancing. 'Because I've never asked myself why,' he groans, and that's the truth. It's not the whole truth but a longer explanation at this moment might block his arteries. The thump of the basses makes the soles of his feet tickle and, after pausing a moment for thought, she devotes herself to his arousal again, with abandon, occasionally interrupting her sucking and nibbling to put her head on one side and contemplate his shining penis which, close to orgasm, is still getting bigger, as if it were all her own work. He bends down to kiss her and, if he could speak now, he'd say: I don't love you just because you give me something—I probably only rarely appreciate that as much as you deserve. Rather, I love you because with you as with no one else the little, pitifully little, that *I* am able to give falls on fertile ground and blossoms, in your eyes, your voice, your poetry. And you give it back to me—the gift of your pure enthusiasm, your beauty and intelligence. That makes me strong and, sometimes, I could cry with happiness. And Alina, with a pearly dribble dropping like moonlight from her chin, smiles at him and straightens up. She carefully pulls his foreskin back over the glans and only then wipes herself clean with the back of her hand, passes the tip of her tongue over her lips. Later, they go through the sauna one more time.

Again and again during the early 1980s, Richard Sander invited him to Italy, to his house outside Trioria in Liguria. Often, he would include a cheque to cover the price of his ticket. It's an isolated farmhouse high above the tops of the pines with a view of the little town in the valley and the church beside the river. From morning to evening, goats are grazing on the gentle lower slopes full of vegetable plots and fragrant lime trees, the blackface goats with sawn-off horns from Emilia Romagna. A lot of them also clamber round in the belt of gorse on the edge of the valley and the hollow note of their bells echoes back from the sheer limestone cliffs which have springs bubbling out here and there and which look less like mountains. They're figures from a different age whose looks are not necessarily friendly as they incline their massive brows over the petty affairs of humans.

They often drive in Richard's jeep over the high plateaux from where you can see as far as Piedmont and, if it's clear, on one side Monte Saccarello with the statue of the Redeemer and on the other the sea. There are only shepherds up there, in corrugated iron shacks, and, on summer nights, they sometimes sit round a flickering fire, the flames horizontal in the wind, for a cigarette and a mug of wine from the canister. Richard, who can hold his drink, speaks the hard-lipped Italian of the villagers and peasants and seems to be popular. He lets the neighbours, who look after the house in winter, use his arable land and harvest the walnuts from his trees, otherwise he doesn't try to ingratiate himself with the locals. They wave to him as soon as they see him in the distance and when he says something their mouths often open in a toothless smile.

Wolf can't help it, he has to admire him. In his eyes, Richard's a happy, completely free man, with no material worries and the whole world of culture at his feet, in several languages. The sleeves of his pullover pushed up, a toothpick between his lips, he seems to take life as it comes and even when he stands, legs apart, peeing in the dahlias or pours milk for his cat into his ashtray, it has a certain panache. He's writing and drawing almost uninterruptedly, from dawn to dusk, cooking sumptuous meals at the same time. Not a year passes without at least one or two books, illustrated editions or cycles of graphic works appearing. Every day, mail arrives from galleries, newspapers and publishers, asking for articles, stories, interviews. Admirers passing by place presents on his doorstep, homemade jam and cases of wine, and he wins prizes at home and abroad and has lovers in several cities. He leads a glorious life, almost heroic in his refusal to compromise, never changing his paint-spattered trousers, and the fact that he doesn't seem to care in the least either about his success or carping criticism only doubles the glory for Wolf.

For him, he's a shining light and yet there's something shadowy, joyless about him, something that remains cold that he can't explain and that stands in the way of a truly warm friendship between them. Richard calls everyone who drinks enough wine with him his friend but when Wolf, as the younger man who has opened up to him unreservedly, gratefully, would like, with an almost childlike longing for warmth, to learn something about him and his feelings outside art, he just smiles wearily and slightly absently and, turning out the palm of his hand towards him, says, 'That, my friend, is all in my books.'

Clearly, he's not aware of the hurtful and arrogant nature of his answer, perhaps he's even afraid of losing some admiration if he becomes too intimate. At any rate, he doesn't seem to be interested in a friendship on an equal footing, even after several years. He still wants to read and correct the things Wolf has written but hardly ever lets him look at his own manuscripts, or only when he's convinced they're perfect. If his younger friend, who by now has become more assured in his judgement and has also made his debut with a slim volume of verse, should come across something that needs improving, a hidden cliché perhaps or a wrong note, his reaction is one of consternation, shock and he goes rigid for a few seconds, moving nothing but his eyes—like a man with his back to the wall looking for ways of escape behind his pursuers. Sometimes, he even goes red and says, 'No, no, that's wrong. You haven't read it properly, my friend. If you know world literature—and I do know it—you must see what goes to make this piece. I'll give it to you again, later.'

It is only Wolf's still-respectful bashfulness that stops such formulations leaving him speechless. And, in one way, the arrogance is not so bad in that Richard does indeed have a vast fund of knowledge. His uncle was a writer before him and had a huge library, so there's hardly a classic author he hasn't read—apart from Rilke. But that's part of his programme. He says with a kind of pride, cigarillo between his lips, 'Me, I'm more of a Brecht man.' He's even familiar with out-of-the-way stuff. If, for example, Wolf, full of enthusiasm for a Flemish poet, shows him the translation of his verses he happened upon in a second-hand bookshop, he can be sure Richard has known him for ages, and more—he knows everything about the author's development and has studied the sources of his inspiration in the original language. He really does know them and goes on about them at great length. The assurance that he has read more than anyone else gives him visible satisfaction and even seems to be a comfort to him. But he lacks the sense that flaunting his knowledge damages its true value and feels he can ignore the fact that poetry will have nothing to do with a man who exploits it to show how cultured he is and buries its appeal under piles of books—it will make him turn cold.

One day in early summer, they're sitting on a plateau high above the village. The long grass is bending in the wind and gleaming like bright gold, the birds are quarrelling in the tops of the cherry trees and the warm rocks, shimmering in the sun, are spattered with the juice of fallen fruits. They taste incredibly sweet, they eat them by the handful and spit the stones down into the valley. They're silent, still muzzy from the previous night's wine. When they'd finished the white, Richard had brought a sixty-year-old Bordeaux up from the cellar, a present from a woman who'd supported his work. It was almost black and so full of dubious particles that they'd taken the precaution of decanting it through a coffee filter but it had dripped so very slowly into the glass and since, by that point, they were only interested in the alcohol content, they simply emptied the bottle and then fell into a sleep that was close to a coma.

The next morning, Richard had received among others a letter from some academy, a survey of the way writers saw themselves. He'd stuffed it in his pocket with a mocking grunt and now took it out again under the cherry trees. The sheet of paper crackles in the wind and when he asks Wolf, with a clear note of malice in his voice, what he thinks he should write, the younger man can tell from his didactic undertone that he knows very well and assumes he will give the same answer. Or is ready to teach it to him. Perhaps that's why Wolf shrugs his shoulders. To him, the word 'academy' just suggests something stiff and old-fogeyish, the top hat and tails of a culture he wants nothing to do with, especially not here, in the wind under the clouds. But Richard is clearly determined to spoil the dreamy quality of the day and turn the residual alcohol into ideas. 'Well, it's obvious,' he says. 'I ask you, what more signal task can there be for a writer than enlightenment? It's the essence of all literature. I at least want to enlighten people, you see.'

For all its high-flown rhetoric, that is understandable for a man who went to school during the Nazi period and the war, saw his home go up in flames, scratched round in the ruins for food and found corpses and whose puberty and first attempts at thinking for himself came in the Adenauer period. But it also has a suspicious sound of newsprint, of leading articles in the magazine sections, especially from someone who usually only has disparaging comments about them, and Wolf ascribes it to their hangover that Richard has no eye for its presumptuousness, no ear for its hollow sound. And he himself, whom or what should he be enlightening? That, to his mind, requires an overall picture which he hasn't got, too few things are clear to him for that. He finds it laborious enough to write about himself, his own experiences. For him 'enlightenment' is simply too high-sounding. 'I don't know,' he says, lying down in the warm grass and clasping his hands behind his head. 'Any village idiot could enlighten *me*. But me? I'd probably rather en*chant* people.'

Richard looks up at the sky and laughs, a joyless laugh that doesn't look cold simply because he has such bad teeth, stained yellow. He folds the letter up again. 'Hey, great, man! Listen to the self-taught writer. Are you going to turn out to be a Romantic?'

'A what?' Wolf asks, shaking his head, which hurts. He closes his eyes briefly. 'That doesn't mean a thing to me. Surely Romanticism's mysticism for taxpayers?'

Richard spits. 'Oh-o! And it's the Holy Ghost speaking through you or what?'

Now Wolf is annoyed, naturally. For some time now he's had the feeling that Richard sees something in him that was only partly him and is less and less. As long as, in keeping with his background, he sticks to his woodcut style and writes about building sites, canteen kitchens, cancer wards or dissection rooms in simple sentences, he doesn't have to worry about Richard's approval, sometimes there's even a quiet note of envy of his experiences. If, however, he tries to articulate what is going on behind the expressive images and surface opinions, his least tangible, and therefore probably most truthful, thoughts and feelings, Richard immediately applies the red pencil and, with the years, his shake of the head and 'That isn't you,' more and more sounds to Wolf like, 'What's all this nonsense? Be like me.'

'It's not my hangover talking,' Wolf says, glancing up at the precipitous cliffs with their various rough or smooth strata of limestone or clay full of fossilized shells and snails and fishes' heads looking like grey lines telling of a time when there was only water there, a motionless omnipresence beneath the stars, that knew nothing of mankind. 'But you're right, when it comes down to it, we're more religious than we think.'

That wasn't meant to be anything like as provocative as Richard takes it—or insists on taking it. For the whole morning, some kind of disquiet has been gathering between his eyebrows, he smoked one cigarette after the other and changed gear up or down with a crunch of the gearbox and now he seems almost relieved at this opportunity for an outburst to sweep away his inner fragility. He throws the handful of cherries back under the tree and wipes his fingers on his trousers. 'You know what I think, my friend? What's just become clear to me? You're just a little bit *thick*, aren't you?' And when Wolf, a blade of grass between his lips, closes his eyes again and grins, he gets louder than is right for his voice, it suddenly sounds porous, almost hoarse. 'You've not understood anything about life, anything at all! How can you talk such nonsense! If I hadn't read your poems . . . I mean, you're an arsehole, aren't you? A bloody idiot! You've no idea what you're *saying*!'

The desire to have misheard him is so strong that it delays the more profound effect of Richard's rant. Wolf slowly sits up and looks at his red face, as if darkened by a sudden congestion of blood. For a moment, he hopes the man's already ashamed of his tantrum, which can only have been caused by his poisoned metabolism. Until now, they'd never quarrelled, his profound respect ennobling even Richard's dubious characteristics, and the latter's sensitivity had always been just that bit ahead of his clumsiness. But, when Wolf makes a cautious attempt to tone things down with a reference to the noxious wine and is even prepared, for the sake of harmony, to take back what he said, Richard bawls even louder, telling him he's a numskull, a crack-pot with his Mickey Mouse metaphysics, his hashish spirituality, he's obviously been wrong about him from the beginning, and he accompanies his diatribe with thumps on the bodywork of his jeep that echo back off the rocks. 'Religious!' he roars. 'Religious, when I hear that kind of shit! As if you didn't know what havoc religions have caused! All that nebulous psychobabble . . .'

It's so ludicrous, it seems to Wolf as if he's being auditioned for some kind of theatrical potential. But, since he's always regarded being understood by the older man, understood to the depths of his being, to his most secret thoughts, as one of the greatest gifts in his life, he simply doesn't know what's happening to him. The strength he has so far derived from Richard's encouragement, his expectant affirmation, his example, like a watermark floating inside him, seems for some obscure reason to be sucked out of him. The grass at his feet is flowing in the wind, the clouds racing away towards the sea, and Wolf, who hasn't the faintest idea what he's done wrong and is so bewildered that he even wonders whether Richard, in whom he's occasionally thought he's seen an unacknowledged homoeroticism, is simply just queer and is venting his disappointment at an unsuccessful, since unnoticed, approach, feels his heart sink and fights back the rising tears.

Meanwhile, Richard's malice produces ever more vitriolic curses, as if he were railing against something in himself. At the same time, he seems to be enjoying his rage, finding his utterances to be of substance because they can be bawled out loud. Wolf, on the other hand, begins to suspect that naivety can be hurtful, simplicity taken as an insult. His chin is trembling, the bottom of the valley, the yellow of the gorse blur, and, when they drive back down the hairpin bends to the house in a silence so thick it hurts his throat, he stares fixedly out of the side window at the evening sky so that Richard won't see his moist face. The tears drip down onto the book in his lap.

He has nothing to eat, nothing to drink, goes to bed. It can't be true, is a thought he repeats like a mantra, it's just a bad dream. Yet he clearly feels that the situation isn't solely due to alcohol, that it contains a grain of truth and finality—the effects of which continue in his dreams until daybreak and eventually help to stop him brooding over it. Although the crowing of the cocks sounds like rusty air, to his surprise, he doesn't feel worn out, despite not having slept very much, and not really depressed either. Instead, he feels he has suddenly been relieved, he can breathe more deeply, as if, during the night, something oppressive, something that wasn't really part of him, had fallen away, a painful crust, an alien transplant.

There's loud snoring coming from the neighbouring building and he's still suspicious of this strange freshness. But when, after a shower and a black coffee, the first rays of the sun come shimmering through the olive grove to the east and cast his shadow on the wall, he feels himself clearly released from the outline Richard had destined for him and was hardly closer to his own vision of his future than a quick sketch in the sand is to a living person, and he packs his duffel bag and walks away from the farm. His shirt open-necked, shoes in his hand, he walks barefoot through the wind-twisted trees down the dew-soaked path and, strangely elated at this new freedom, at the prospect of making his way from now on without support, he can't refrain from smiling at the idea that he really has come to his senses.

Subsequently, they see one another now and then, send one another the occasional card, but the magic's gone. Clearly, admiration can easily turn against someone who doesn't tell you to stop it soon enough and enjoys it for too long. Enjoys it at all. With growing distance, the shrewdness and refreshing clear-sightedness with which Richard gave himself the air of a man inspired, were revealed, in the light of the repetitions of which he was unaware and which also appeared in his books, as dreary because it was experience that could be called up at any time, insights from his card index, and Wolf was more and more repelled by the constant drinking, supposedly out of creative necessity, the empty waffle with the grand gestures and the affectation of bohemianism by a man who refuses to accept that he's growing older and who thinks inner freedom is a particular way of throwing your scarf over your shoulder.

And now this letter, the shaky handwriting, the paper smelling of tangy mountain air, or so it seems to him. And when Wolf doesn't respond, there's even a call while he's out, a message on the tape. The voice is strangely diffident but its silvery tone almost unchanged, astonishing in a man who's over seventy. But again there's that impossible word, an old-maidish, prunes-and-prisms word from days long ago—he would like to 'call on' Wolf. That alone makes the hairs on the backs of his fingers stand on end, sounding as it does to him like a sentimental 'Do you remember' round the tea table. Then, he gives his telephone number, is interrupted by a woman's voice in the background, corrects himself and hangs up.

Wolf doesn't ring back, even when Alina asks him to. Possibly he's in the wrong, after all, he does owe the man quite a lot. And he doesn't bear him any grudges. But the fact is that we don't like our patrons, not at every stage in our lives. There's a hint of arrogance in the benevolence which makes us feel justified in our ungratefulness.

4

miscellaneous items from the arts section

Towards the end of winter, the lake freezes over again. The ice is thin and, when a boat crosses the wide expanse or a flock of crows land on it, it begins to vibrate and the air underneath sings as it goes over the pebbles and dead leaves by the bank. Sometimes, he can hear it at night, when he's on the little balcony outside his study. The houses are dark, the streets quiet and the lights of the anti-theft devices flash beneath the miniature snowdrifts on the car windows.

The sound of an almost endless goods train is just fading when a fox trots across the pavement with light, springy steps, a thin beast with a bushy tail that keeps on lifting up its head to sniff the air, the hairs on its pricked-up ears shimmer in the light of the sparse streetlamps. It's already several houses away when Wolf, who has just been reading an SMS, switches off his cellphone and yet it seems to hear the quiet, scarcely audible bleep. As if its fright is tugging at it, the fox takes a sideways step and looks back over its shoulder. But it pulls itself together at once and runs straight into the park. Later, it barks somewhere in the bushes, croaking, plaintive sounds with an aura of the loneliness of the woods to which the dogs behind the curtains and shutters of the surrounding houses respond with wild yapping and howling.

It was after what Alina said about Webster's smell that he first noticed how lovingly she always greeted the dog when he arrived home with him, burying her face caressingly in his hair, which does indeed seem to hold other people's scent or perfume longer than human hair or clothes. Since then, he's stopped taking him when he goes to see Charlotte. Webster's presence always felt like a mute reproach anyway. Since the colour of his coat hardly stood out against the stained floorboards of her flat, he could sometimes see just his amber eyes in the corner, with a look that seemed all the more sad the more abandoned or violent the love they made on the expensive sofa. Even his snorts sounded disapproving and his yawns mocking.

Since, after more than a year of this secrecy, there's still no question of love, they make do with gentle irony. Charlotte at least, after a warm or even breathless greeting, will often—he can almost see her pull herself together—adopt an attitude of smug severity, apparently believing it necessary to make it clear to him, with her raised chin and finely chiselled features, that she's granting him a favour, a gracious favour, for which he has to be grateful. After all, she has appointments and many suitors, her telephone's never silent and even her male students try to chat her up. At the same time she's often wearing the kind of clothes, shoes or too-tight lingerie he's secretly been hoping for and it's less the transparency of her play-acting that irritates him than the brazen way she takes it for granted he won't see through it. Especially since she's hardly ever able to cope with the impetuous frenzy she's trying to coax out of him.

She's going through the menopause and is therefore not always moist, especially when he's in a hurry to get inside her knickers. Sometimes she smells of medicaments and, more recently, she's been asking for a massage first, from her neck to the soles of her feet, a little bottle of lavender oil is always by her bed. He mutely obeys when she reminds him to be less frantic but it's usually not long before his sensitive caresses become insistent and he's digging the limits of his patience into her skin with his fingernails. On some days giving her rough, even crude, treatment, sticking his fingers in her mouth or heaping on her all the abuse his proletarian vocabulary allows, is his revenge for the fact that, in the afterglow of her delusions, all she wants from him is a functioning body.

So as not to give her the opportunity to be condescending, he seldom expresses any wishes but with Charlotte he does the things he wouldn't ask of Alina, either out of embarrassment or delicacy. He lies down in the empty bathtub and gets her to pee on him, slaps her backside until it's bright red, ejaculates in her face or her freshly tinted hair, or sticks his cock into her sphincter without warning—and when he does so, he gets the impression she's enjoying not only the pain but also her own performance as a woman whimpering helplessly. This professor likes being called a lump of shit or a cunt, lets him do everything to her and is open to most suggestions as long as she ends up having her orgasm. And that is, as ever, as red-hot as the fire that in the poem lights candles in the snow.

Then she cuddles up to him, goes on trembling for quite a while and he kisses the tears off her face. Sometimes, there's even a cooing note in her voice. Sometimes, as if in release, she smiles. They lie beside one another, chatting about this and that until the sweat's dry but, when he gets dressed after an hour—he always makes sure he's the first in his jeans—she's mostly monosyllabic and cool, almost formal, again as she says goodbye and, as she does so, she's always correcting documents or typing something on the computer. That, she seems to be saying, was item six on the agenda: Fuck Wolf. Or she's talking to one of her girl friends or one of her other men on the phone and never conceals the fact that he's still there, her pale poet, but is just about to leave, is as good as gone. And she looks at the clock as she says that.

As he goes down the stairs, there's always, almost always, a spring in his step but, even though he has the woman to thank for having one more secret and thus a feeling of a kind of completeness, he often finds it difficult to take her seriously. Despite having had a hard-hearted mother who would beat him until the blood came, he has retained the image of femininity as something bright and gossamer-winged. At times, he can even imagine something with thorns but hardly with a briefcase. There's too much that is unspoken or concealed about her, too much academic self-importance, name-dropping and a tell-tale craving for success. She makes it too clear to him that she can just about put up with him and the confusion he calls poetry within the framework of her professional life, and he's on the edge of events for which he doesn't have the right wardrobe. Yet, despite that, he keeps on ringing the bell of her fifth-floor apartment, with flowers, for it is precisely the way she looks down on him, the way she remains inaccessible, even with her legs spread, that keeps up his addiction to her.

Even if he hopes that the significant birthday he has just reached will be a kind of reconsecration of his life, he has no intention of celebrating his fiftieth with anything other than a cup of tea or a hot dog with curry sauce and chips. He's never had a party, everyday routine is celebration enough for him and he doesn't want to interrupt his work. But Alina keeps going on at him.

She wants at least to go away on a trip with him during these sunny May days, to the seaside, perhaps, or the mountains, to see the chestnut blossom and the lilac. After the Christmas holidays, with all the tinsel and the scent of cinnamon, it's his birthdays that send her into a strange, almost childish fever of excitement because they give her the opportunity to express her affection comprehensively with an armful of elaborately packed and often much-too-expensive gifts. For, more than receiving presents, it's giving them that really makes her happy and she often blushes and even trembles with nervousness whether she's made the right choice—then accepts his pleasure and thanks as if they're a bubbly drink in a cut-glass flute.

But precisely because their so-called milestone birthdays were intended to be such glorious occasions, whenever they tried to give them a special setting they only succeeded in ruining them. On both Alina's thirtieth in London and his fortieth in Barcelona, they had quarrelled bitterly, stamped on the roses and hurled the lovingly chosen presents into the corner. And, when he reminds her of that and even goes so far as to express the wish to spend that weekend alone, wandering round the Oderbruch countryside with Webster, it naturally leads to tears. She insists on doing something special, in a place conducive to happy memories, so he agrees and decides on Paris. Out of laziness, really—the flights are convenient.

He spent a year there once and the city doesn't do anything for him. He's never seen it as beautiful, perhaps because it is always saying how beautiful it is, like an old queen dripping with make-up and glitzy jewellery. It feeds off its own myth too much to be truly alive and, like all metropolises that imagine they're the centre of the world, it's more provincial than it likes to think. But in contrast to Berlin, it does have a memory, so that despite the faster pace of life, you feel slightly less transient. And then, there's the fresh bread . . .

They leave the dog in a kennel and take a cheap flight from Schönefeld. The passengers are divided into groups A, B and C, but hardly have the gates been opened than they all rush across the tarmac, the better-mannered ones camouflaging their pushiness with a faint grin, quotation marks, so to speak, and by the time Alina and he are on board the jet, there are only two seats left, far away from one another. Since the luggage conveyor belt at Orly is out of order, they have to wait almost three hours for their suitcases and thus are tired and weary by the time they reach their hotel, the little Récamier on Place Saint-Sulpice. Wolf has known it for twenty-five years and it never seems to change at all. It still has the heavy front door with the corroded brass trim, the blue glass ball on the first post of the banisters, the pale wallpaper with the Provençal flower pattern coming loose above the cast-iron radiators and the lift with the delicate grille that hardly has room for two. The thin doors have wobbly pottery knobs and the bedspreads and curtains are made of faded corduroy. And, even if there's a design concept behind it which demands as much trouble and expense as constant renovation, you'd rather think that the chairs and kidney-shaped tables from the 1960s, the lampshades with charred spots and the chandeliers that tinkle softly in the draught as well as the massive washbasins with the hairline cracks and the honey-coloured lump of soap on a string have since time immemorial been frozen in the diaphanous present of the high fountain in front of the building, of its insistent drone that can be heard all the time, even when the shutters are closed, and that sounds as if, for some gracious reason, it is taking the passing of time on itself so that everything round can remain unchanged.

It's already getting dark when they check in. The room is small and looks even smaller with the enormous bouquet of roses—forty-nine white and one red—she ordered the previous day. Still clutching her holdall, she looks at him a little anxiously out of the corner of her eye and so as to not disappoint her, Wolf, who's thinking of the expense, chokes back his irritation. He gives her a kiss and comforts her for the porter's uncaring treatment of the flowers: since they clearly didn't have a suitable vase, he's put the roses in two sawn-off Vittel bottles. They have a snack in the Café de la Mairie, take a walk in the bright night, with a warm wind sweeping the browny white chestnut flowers across the pavements, and, at midnight, they have a glass of champagne on a bistro boat by the Pont Neuf, where Wolf suddenly hears an odd noise in his inner ear, probably tinnitus, as if his moss-grown cell-phone were ringing on the bottom of the Seine.

Back at the hotel, he reads a few of the *Duino Elegies* that he almost always takes with him on his travels and, after Alina has brushed her hair and removed her make-up, she hums as she oils his cock and turns her back to him so that he can slip into her. They move slowly, almost somnambulistically, Alina also stimulating herself with her fingers, and it's only a matter of minutes before she comes, panting softly. She goes to sleep at once and while he's lying awake for a while and looking at the roses in the light of the bedside lamp, their shadows going up to the ceiling, the fountain outside, its insis-tent noise, stops and, in the silence, the room suddenly seems to shift. It's as if things abruptly hold their breath and, all at once, they're so close and sharp-edged all round him that his heart stands still and it's only when a horn sounds somewhere out in the square that Wolf gets his breath back with a gasp. Then he turns over on his side and goes to sleep as well.

It's only a light sleep and yet he doesn't notice Alina getting up at some point during the night to put a little package wrapped in gold paper underneath the flowers. It looks as if it's a dull day, at least that's what the light coming in through the gaps in the metal shutters suggests, and, although it's very early, there's already the smell of coffee and croissants in the hotel. The door to the little bathroom is open and, besides the drip in the bidet and the glug-glug in the pipes, he can hear voices in the ventilation shaft, the cries and laughter of the African chambermaids. The wide wardrobe on the other side of the bed has sliding doors with mirrors and Wolf sits up a bit, resting his head on one hand, and looks at himself from head to toe.

It's OK, OK. It could be more sobering. Still a full head of hair, no wrinkled, flaccid neck and no belly, of course, thanks to his exercises, a mixture of yoga and gymnastics, it's firmer than in his younger days. But his skin, on which the flattened hair is just standing up again, making him feel as if insects were crawling over it, does seem pale to him in this light, dull, almost drained, and there are signs of tiredness in his face, too, which have nothing to do with his lack of sleep. The shadows under his eyes, the deepening lines running down from the side of his nose, the corners of his mouth that are more and more often turned down, the lips that are getting thinner seem to stress that his body is beginning to fight, with dogged determination, against the increasingly downward slope of his life while the physiognomy of his inner being is becoming apparent, a being which—to go by the dull sheen of his forehead and his big, at first sight brown, often greenish and mostly somewhat restless, eyes—is still dominated by fear, fear of everything and everyone, and which does not believe its own wisdom.

As if his page in the book of the universe were the only one without a watermark, he still suspects he hasn't understood the essential meaning of life. At weak moments, especially with other people, he feels he's fundamentally insecure, without a clear profile, and perhaps that's one reason why he always takes everyday business more seriously and sometimes even allows his thought and speech to be distorted by a noise in the background that he's always found off-putting, even repulsive in others, the creak of a standpoint. The more foreseeable his future becomes the more preoccupied he is with concern about it and he profanes every happy moment with the petty wish for a more beautiful one to follow. While he's eating, he's already thinking about what he's going to cook the next day.

Despite that, shouldn't he be content? He has a wonderful partner, a splendid lover, he's healthy and comfortably off, he still enjoys his work and, yes, recently, he's even had some success. He ought to get a desk diary and a tax consultant, and his bank keeps sending him brochures about annuities and unit trusts. He shouldn't complain. But, to be semi-secure and heading for middle-class respectability—which he would perhaps treat ironically but live out in all seriousness—when the sky's the limit, somehow leaves a flat taste in the mouth. As if you were eating your own wings. And to accept the recognition of a society he has rejected for decades or only put up with under protest and to have success in the arts is as sad as finding money on the seashore.

When he raises his arm to push his hair back from his face, he notices that the part below the biceps seems to be a little flabbier than the rest of his body and, as he feels it, he can't help thinking of the body of a well-fleshed but no-longer-quite-fresh fish only slowly filling out again in the places where it's been held. It gets lighter and the furred feeling inside his mouth gets worse. He'd like to clean his teeth but daren't get up. Behind him, he can hear Alina breathing in that calm rhythm he's always taken as an expression of profound trust, of the assurance that she will be cared for, something he's never possessed. He can't remember a single day when she didn't smile at least once. But then, she gives a short, softly plaintive sigh, her voice like a shimmer of something silver beneath the surface of her sleep.

It has the sound of a young girl, a child even, and he automatically wonders how long she's been under his shadow and when the time will come when he's too old at her side. The age gap between them comes out even more clearly in the fact that the odd wrinkle and occasional white hair make him more attractive to her than ever. And he sort of believes her, given that he feels the same when he thinks of the ageing Charlotte. Her tired cheeks, her scrawny neck, her wrinkled throat, like a dried-up river delta, though still with the swell of perfect breasts below, her slackening bottom and the creased skin on the backs of her thighs from all those visits to the solarium turn him on like nobody's business. It may be a trick of nature, but Charlotte's attractiveness certainly also has something to do with the aplomb with which she carries herself and her body despite everything. But a straight back like that, like a plumb line exuding self-confidence, emphasizing achievement, success, is precisely what he hasn't got. Will never have.

The little bell of Saint-Sulpice strikes seven and when the fountain suddenly starts up again and a door slams, making the thin walls shake, he thinks for one frightening moment that the silvering of the mirror is starting to flow; he puts a hand behind him, touches her hip, presses one leg against hers to feel her body warmth, now almost amused at his fear. At the same time, however, it becomes plain to him—never before has he seen it so clearly—that it is precisely that fear which is the most unmistakable, the most genuine thing about him. And that makes it a gift . . . Alina moves, wakes up, her tousled mop of red hair appears over his shoulder, her clear forehead, and now he, who only a moment ago thought he could taste his own ashes, can breathe deeply again. As if the sight of her features had lightened his grey aura, he feels a kind of confidence and new heart and as she looks at him from the mirror with her shrewd eyes and wraps her freckled arms round him with an unrestrained yawn, the world is back in order again.

'I don't think much of you as a fifty-year-old,' she'd said on the bistro boat. 'You'd make a decent forty-year-old now.'

That morning, he decides to tell her the truth. They have breakfast in their room, go back to sleep again and it's twelve o'clock by the time they go out into the street. The great bells boom out, the metal pots on the waiters' tray sparkle in the sun, the green of the chestnut trees seems to flow over the windscreens. Alina's present was a camera, a clever little thing with which you can even make short films, which they proceeded to do, in all positions and with sound. The reproduction on the display was brilliant, which was perhaps why everything was so disappointing, so crude, even if he secretly congratulated himself on his equipment. And he'd never before realized how red his face is when he's doing it.

As for Alina, here, in front of the drifting cascades of the fountain, it's the same as always—whenever you point a lens at her, the magic and almost everything that makes her unique in his eyes disappears from her face. She hates being photographed and goes so tense until the click of the shutter—there's hardly a picture of her where you can see her true nature. It infuriates him that the atmosphere of trust in which her charm blossoms is destroyed by the glass eye even when he's the one taking the picture. At first he suspected she was less beautiful than the way he sees her. Actually, however, it's the fact that she has one decisive dimension too many that makes most pictures of her unsatisfactory. Only shallow, superficial people, whose inner being lacks radiance, can be reproduced as they are, at least in this medium. For the others are subject to the truth in the Indian books of his childhood—a flash robs the person being photographed of their soul.

They wander slowly round the Jardin du Luxembourg, where the lilac blossom is already over. They eat something in the Select and drink a beer on the glassed-in verandah. With a mute gesture, Alina indicates the waiter's waistcoat buttons, little metal dogs' heads. They don't talk much, they just watch the boulevard where a few people are crammed together waiting on a traffic island and scraps of paper and plastic bags go swirling higher and higher in the updraught from the cars in a strange dance choreographed by the unceasing stream of traffic in both directions—as if they were the cuffs of ghosts gesticulating wildly or conducting a furioso such as only exists in unwritten symphonies.

Then the lights turn red and, in the moment of deafening silence, a man gets off the bus carrying a hat in his hand—it's full to overflowing with mushrooms. For a while, Wolf tries in vain to photograph the glints of colour in the little oil and vinegar bottles on the table or the shadows of passers-by. The place is almost empty, the wicker chairs creak in the sun, the napkins folded into cones on the next table slowly open. In tiny reflections, the traffic flits round the lower curves of their glasses. Alina leans her head back and closes her eyes, and Wolf, softened by a gentleness that makes him undecided, keeps putting off the opening words.

The green material of the door curtain drags heavily across the floor. Time passes with the quivering of the white and pale-yellow rings of light meshing like wafer-thin cogwheels on the panes and, finally, he takes a deep breath and, as she is pushing her chair back, having just paid, places a hand on her shoulder. She sinks down onto her chair again and turns to him with a cheerful, expectant look. It reminds him that only a few weeks ago, they'd once more indulged in fantasies about getting married, almost smirking, given their ages, with his fiftieth birthday as a possible date. But then, they'd found that too sentimental.

His elbows resting on the arms of the cane chair, his hands clasped in front of his mouth, he clears his throat and begins to speak, avoiding looking directly at Alina. It has little to do with feeling ashamed, it's just that he doesn't want to be diverted from the truth by the crinkling of her brow, her open mouth or increasing paleness, which he can already see out of the corner of his eye, or even to go easy on her if she should cry. But she remains composed, at least outwardly. For passers-by, they are just another couple having an ordinary, everyday conversation. She folds her napkin in her lap, crosses her legs and jiggles her foot. Once, she even leans forward and picks something off his collar.

But, as usually happens when she's anxious or uneasy, she starts to swallow, again and again, and then her eyelids start to move as if she'd got something in her eye. The rapid flutter of her mascaraed lashes on the edge of his field of vision gradually makes him feel that he's being hurtful with what he's saying, causing damage, irrevocable damage, and he feels choked with quiet pity. Yet, he goes on speaking, he wants to, he's determined to tell her everything, to purify their friendship, which he no longer wants to see overshadowed by something that only becomes important because of the secrecy. For the way he sees it, his connection with Charlotte is no more threat to their life together than a walk in the woods or a visit to the sauna. It's healthy exercise, promoting relaxation, giving him strength, that's all. Why then go along with the ubiquitous culture of unfaithfulness and debase Alina by making her into a woman who's been wronged—that would be to misrepresent not only her life but also his. For, if love means anything to him, then it's trust. More than that. If, in the past, love was often only a word for him and thus contained all possibilities of misunderstanding, trust has always been crystal clear, like taking a deep breath.

Alina closes her eyes, gnaws at her lower lip and, while he remains amazed at the way something that has been causing him pangs of conscience for ages can be put into so few words, she says nothing. For an anxious minute, he recalls how, when they lived in Kreuzberg, they'd once talked, as a kind of game, about the possibility of being unfaithful. At the time, he'd been annoyed by her categorical 'That will never happen to me,' and not just because it smacked of the sour moralizing of women's magazines. Of course, by that she was just saying that he was the one man in her life, but, by shutting herself off with such certainty from the imponderables and possible passions of existence, by telling him he could be sure of her, her image lost its enigmatic shimmer, her look its profundity, at least for the moment. But when he'd asked her what she would do if he suddenly acquired a lover, if only for sex, she immediately froze, seemed to listen to the question for a few seconds more intently than it warranted and whispered anxiously: 'Have you?' And when he, who didn't have a lover at the time, shook his head, she leant back against him again and said, 'Thank God for that. Otherwise, I'd have been over the hills and far away.'

That was a long time ago, at least ten years, and yet that threat delivered with a smile—like one of those homoeopathic medicines you've long since forgotten taking but that continues to have an effect because the doctor occasionally expresses his reservations about it—is one of the reasons why he's been keeping the truth from her since his first meeting with Charlotte. She's crying now, just a little, but her mascara's starting to run already and, as he usually does, he wipes it away with the tip of his thumb, then wipes his thumb on his jeans. Only then does he search for a handkerchief.

'And there was me thinking we'd get through a significant birthday with no disasters,' is the first thing Alina says, her voice almost inaudible. He's almost relieved at the gentle irony, seeing it as a sign that she's taking the matter the way he'd hoped, like a good sport. And, when she goes on to say she'd long since suspected it, not least because she'd occasionally noticed a tinted hair on his clothes and the dog had always given off the same scent after his excursions into town, he even smirks. Chanel No. 5.

But then she sits up straight, pulling in her chin, and, at the very moment in which he realizes that it's less his lover that hurts her than his lack of openness, all those months of secrecy, she gives him a look full of fury and contempt, which he doesn't immediately recognize because even now he can't believe her capable of having and showing such feelings. Even as the victim of his unfaithfulness, he can only see her as above all that. She screws up her eyes and a further tear wells out, leaving a blackish trail down her cheek, and suddenly, he has to swallow and finds it difficult to breathe. Passers-by look at them as he holds out the handkerchief to her, intently, as if there were nothing more important at the moment, and she knocks his hand away and stands up so abruptly that if he hadn't stretched out his arm the chair would have fallen over.

He glances round surreptitiously at the other customers, at the waiters with the gilt bottle-openers in their waistcoat pockets who made it clear they had not noticed anything, the woman at the cash desk, motionless as a wax figure. In the past, he'd been very quickly cowed by histrionic scenes played out in public by this or that woman who felt hurt. The explosion of bitterness in which they ignored the general curiosity and frowns and took him to task, as if they were still concerned with matters of substance when, in fact, they were taking revenge on him and his stiff sense of form, embarrassed him as much as if they had opened up their shared bedroom to all those sitting round. Here, too, he's already beginning to feel pressurized at the prospect of a loud outburst and silently wishes he could take something back or retract it. He, who professionally has no problem speaking freely before a large audience, comes out in a cold sweat at the thought of drawing attention to himself in a restaurant or some other public place and wishes he were even more rimless than his spectacles. But what's said is said and Alina shakes her head when he gently pushes the edge of her chair against the back of her knees. She doesn't want to sit down, she wants an answer to her question—which he didn't hear.

'Do you *love* her?' she repeats, more clearly this time, as a few tears drip onto her white blouse, giving a hint of the delicate lace of her lingerie and perhaps he's been staring at it too long. As if these leaden minutes were already dissolving into thin air, as if the grey drops were making not only the material more transparent but also the present moment, he suddenly sees what is at the heart of the situation and realizes that he has never been closer to Alina than now, in the shadow of her grief. That his own mystery speaks to him through this woman, the source of his strength, and that her whole being is a refuge for him, a gift from somewhere or other. Of course he's hurt her but that's part of her life as well and, as surely as the pain will pass, their shared joy must return, for they were made for nothing else. It's the delicate mainspring driving even their dark times and, confused by this certainty, he can't find anything to say for the moment, so that Alina perhaps assumes he's hesitating because he has to think her question over. Whatever the case, she throws the starched napkin she used to wipe her face down onto the table and now a glass does fall over, shattering on the ashtray, and she whispers, 'Oh, to hell with it . . . You never do know what you feel!' Then, she turns round and goes out.

A distinctly too-dramatic exit and he stays there defiantly and orders another coffee and an expensive cigarillo, which, however, he doesn't take out of the foil wrapper. He finds a moment's comfort and support in the waiter's almost imperceptible smile, in the understanding and worldly wisdom he thinks he sees in it, and he leaves a generous tip beside the splinters of glass. Then, he goes along the rue Delambre to the market beside the cemetery, buys a white gladiola and places it on the grave of Soutine, who's long been his favourite painter. And, as so often before, he looks in vain for that of César Vallejo among the close-standing monuments, which are dominated by the obscenely tall one of a literary critic, so he acknowledges him with a nod in the general direction.

In the German bookshop beside the Closerie des Lilas, he leafs through a few recent publications but doesn't buy anything. Back in the park, he passes the merry-go-round with the old wooden animals that have been painted again and again and that—you only notice after a while—revolves without any music at all. He watches the children who've put their colourful laptops and other electronic toys on the chairs to push the little boats that have been for hire here since time immemorial, across the water in the fountain with bamboo sticks. Gusts of wind keep swirling up clouds of dust between the people taking a walk and he sits to listen to the brass band, where the sheets of music are fluttering on the stands, and lights a match. And as he feels, the first time in ages, the taste of tobacco on his tongue, its empty earnestness, he can't get Alina's question out of his mind, the one about the other woman and his feelings for her.

Love, such a radiant star—how infinitely grey and dreary it can be as you stumble across its surface. Since his experiences almost never came close to the splendour and passion of his idea of it and since he, whenever he surrendered to it unreservedly, never had long to wait for the kick in the teeth, from very early on, he had resisted love's pretension to be an absolute phenomenon and had, in moments of particularly intense longing, even derided it in cynical terms. But even if it's true that love's dictate is nothing but a biological stratagem guaranteeing the matching or complementing of genetic characteristics and that, at its most intoxicating, it produces precisely the lack of inhibition necessary to release the instinct to carry on the species, which often runs counter to reason and our desire for freedom, it is surely clear that that hardly touches on what is at its heart. Love presumably needs less to be felt than to be lived out—the very thought that the dust you're stumbling through belongs to a star increases its radiance.

As for Charlotte, only recently she'd wanted to know how he sees their affair, their occasional fuck, and he'd suddenly found the expectant silence that filled the room, as if made for declarations of principle, disturbing. His shoes were in the hall, his trousers on the floor in the farthest corner of the room, and he desperately sought some offhand response that would disguise the fact that the situation was threatening to get serious. But she already shook her head, picked a bit of fluff out of his navel, some dried sperm, and said, 'We're good for one another, aren't we?' Relieved, he took a sip of wine.

When he gets back to the hotel, Alina has gone. Apart from his poplin raincoat, the only thing in the wardrobe is the scarf he once gave her, and the tickets and some dental floss are on the glass table in the bathroom. He dials her number but her cellphone's switched off, all he gets is her recorded voice, and now he's worried, though he doesn't manage to say more than, 'It's me. Where are you?' Then he sits in silence for a while, staring at the roses, a few already drooping in the warm room, and it's so quiet he realizes that he can't hear the fountain any more. The water's been let out and some men in green overalls are in the marble basin sweeping up cigarette ends, coins and paper.

A Brecht Evening at the German Embassy, invited guests only. Moonlight on the limousines as they slowly process up the gravel drive. The cultural attaché is wearing a dinner jacket and not as a joke either. Apart from a delegation of East German theatre folk, slightly crumpled in their ghetto, two of whom are even wearing jaunty caps and smoking cigars, the other guests are exquisitely dressed—the smart men with their perfectly constructed sentences and their fair-haired wives who, of course, are not blondes. Brecht goes Armani.

Real candlelight sparkles on the crystal of the chandeliers. Representatives of industry and culture sip their champagne with exchange students and officials of the Goethe-Institut while the reliable actress, totally immersed in her seriousness and dressed in flowing silk, tosses her fiery-red hair, rolls her theatrically underlined eyes and holds up her hands with their blood-red nails like claws. That Baal, he was a bad man. Later on, he'll reappear in French.

The pianist's wearing a dinner jacket too and, while people are walking round eating nibbles or earnestly scooping up caviar, he plays a few unknown pieces by Kurt Weill, what else. The mostly male diplomatic staff can be recognized by their perfect haircuts and the refined manner by which they conceal, with a high degree of credibility, the fact that they'd really rather be somewhere else—at their computers, for example. But their boss has commanded their presence at this shindig, together with their better halves, and so they make conversation, keeping their eyes fixed on a point half an inch above the head of the person they're talking to, as if they don't want anything to disturb their concentration, all the while gently waving their hands to and fro in manicured gesticulation. Their wives, many of them in backless dresses in the spring warmth and festooned with long pearl necklaces, stand just the right distance away, nodding now and then or throwing in a word that no one can argue with and that is acknowledged with gratitude, adding, as it does, a touch of freshness to an often strained atmosphere tainted with a whiff of halitosis. They are the garnish for this evening, the parsley, which is OK since they're aware of it, go along with it. Brecht is men's business and not only in the smoking room full of grained-leather armchairs where Wolf is drinking a whisky.

Then, the ambassador arrives, takes up position beside the piano, taps a glass with his signet ring and apologizes for the delay—an important dinner with the president of the Republic where, among other things, culture, in particular music, had been one of the topics discussed. The president was profoundly knowledgeable about German classicism and, after all, the bicentenary of Mozart's death was at hand . . . At this point, he pauses but no one laughs or even whispers and the silver-haired diplomat, visibly enjoying having his guests and subordinates on tenterhooks, takes a drink of mineral water. A man of his experience is not one to let a joke fall flat, so much is clear, but, although the silence is a bottomless pit, one of the Berlin theatre folk cannot resist reviving the spirit of rebellion which, with his black suit, open-necked white shirt, designer bald head with earring, he has long since made into a fashion item. 'Was Mozart,' he asks, 'not Austrian?'

Naturally, he wants to be rewarded for that and the ambassador gives him a grateful nod, with a tinge of melancholy to his smile, as if he's thinking: We can still rely on you lefties. With a wink, he turns back to his audience and his junior colleagues in particular give an audible sigh of relief when he replies, 'The president pointed that out as well, young man. And what could I say? Of course, Mozart was Austrian and the age of annexations is past. But his origins, the source of his skill, his father, that is, Leopold Mozart, came from the fair city of Augsburg—from the same city, by the way, as dear old Brecht. Which brings us back to the subject of tonight's celebration. We are a land of classics! And, even if we do not hear a magic flute this evening, I'm sure there's a message that will be drummed into us . . . So, without further ado—'

And the prima donna returns, appearing from behind the life-size photo of Brecht. She's changed in the meantime, everything about her is purple now, including the broad velvet choker round her neck. She waves the blazing torch of her hair, lashes out at the smoke with her claws, threatens with her fists and rolls her *r*'s like the cooper of Augsburg rolling his barrels down to the River Lech. The shark has pretty teeth and Mack a very dangerous knife, and that has to be grated into our consciousness with a saw-edged voice so that we don't start singing along or—God forbid!—get the idea that presenting Brecht and his songs of poverty in the cold world has become a cynical piece of business. Though perhaps one can do that with them, Wolf thinks when he's on the Métro again, trying Alina's number in vain, because Brecht himself wasn't really serious about his sympathy, because he, in his cheerful astuteness and his flirting with power, avoided the claims of the absolute and exploited the political zeitgeist—the entertainer in overalls. And whom the zeitgeist is now serving up as a relish to go with caviar canapés.

They're due to fly back the next evening and, since he doesn't manage to get through to her during the day, Wolf eventually goes out to Orly. He waits there until all the passengers have checked in but Alina doesn't turn up. There's just one latecomer, a woman with a cello case, who hurries up and is dealt with, and he's just drinking a coffee at a bar near the check-in when they're called. The loudspeaker is directly above him and his name, spoken by a German voice, startles him like a voice of thunder from high. He almost ducks at the sound, which, simply because of the volume, has something of a reproach. The announcer herself seems to be surprised at the sensitivity of the microphone and to draw back a little, for Alina's name sounds quieter and at the second call, the last, is spoken almost as an aside, as if even the airport staff no longer expect her to turn up. Wolf goes out and hails a taxi.

On his way to the city centre, he tries to call her again and, even though she doesn't respond, he realizes from the time it goes on ringing until he gets the mailbox that she's switched on her cellphone. The traffic is slow-moving, the setting sun is reflected in the windows of the skyscrapers and makes the aerials gleam and the cheerful driver, an Algerian, turns the music up and sometimes brakes so hard that Wolf makes a mistake as he types. 'Another evening,' he writes, 'when the mere thought of you gilds the tips of my antlers . . .'

Since he knows she likes sentences like that, he sends the message and, while the driver's trying to find a way round the traffic jams and getting into narrower and narrower side streets, Wolf is reminded of the diplomats' wives at the embassy, of their long necks and sharply outlined profiles, of the conversations full of undertones and how aggressive they were in their desire to be proud of their husbands. They looked impressive and yet so sad in their efforts to match up to an idea of greatness through which they will never really find their own because it is a stupid and cold-hearted ignoring of the truth to imagine that waiting for every person is a form of perfection that is just right for them. To understand that, to see what life demands from us and to develop accordingly is a prerequisite for greatness and he has never wondered whether Alina feels that need—to be proud of him. It is more likely that she is concerned by the fact that he doesn't like himself a bit more and isn't a bit happier with what he's doing. And that makes her great for him, always will, and he catches his breath when he feels the quiet vibration near his heart and she replies, though only with one word, and that not a particularly friendly one. And yet it seems to him to contain a hint of reconciliation, a smile amid tears. 'Arsehole,' it says, nothing more.

A little later, they're stuck, the roads are blocked in all directions and after a quarter of an hour he pays off the driver, slings his bag over his shoulder and wanders along the Seine towards Notre Dame with the flocks of pigeons circling its towers. Since none of the drivers held up in the traffic jam switches off their engine, the air's almost unbreathable. In addition, it's getting more and more difficult to make progress on foot because of all the tourists. So, on boulevard Saint-Michel, he goes down to the Métro and decides to go to Montparnasse, where it's less crowded, and eat something there. Again he calls Alina. Again there's no reply.

In the white-tiled passages of the huge interchange station the ticket machines are clicking and the compressed air of the gates hissing in a rhythm that recalls old films and what the director imagined as futuristic factories with dramatic lighting in which tins are filled with silence or eternity cut up into individual portions, and a few people in a hurry jump down several steps at once to get on the waiting train. Although the signals are already red and the buzzer before the doors close is sounding, Wolf tries to get on as well but he's held by a beggar who's grabbed his sleeve, a man with a sad smile and an accordion slung over his shoulder, so he steps back from the edge of the platform and gives him a few coins. And, after the train has disappeared in the tunnel and the rails on their oily sleepers, with swarms of mice between them, once more reflect the overhead lights, he sees her on the other side.

Just as abruptly as she left him in the Select, she reappears in her thin coat and hesitantly raises one hand, as if to make him aware of her in the throng. But then she presumably finds that too conciliatory and turns her gesture into a movement to brush back her hair. As if Paris were a village, he is not at first surprised that they should see one another again, there in the catacombs of a station he chose by chance with trains passing through in all directions every minute, not having made any arrangement. He would never allow that to happen in one of his books, it wouldn't be believable, would make the fatefulness of the moment too obvious. But that only occurs to him much later. For the moment, he is simply relieved, takes a deep breath, being careful not to smile too obviously as he makes his way up the long stairway and across the bridge to the other platform and approaches Alina's silhouette, the shadow of her thin shoulders on the wall. And, as he puts his bag down beside hers and stands so close that their coat buttons are touching, he thinks he can read in the gentle seriousness of her gaze and the calm composure of her expression that she would hardly be surprised if, on the day after he'd died, he continued to live with her quite normally, giving her breakfast in bed, buttering her toast, pouring her coffee. Seen in the light of her love, it can be no other way, for, ultimately, the logic of poetry is always more precise than any other.

The birds, that she feeds every day with a handful of sunflower seeds, have become accustomed to Webster's silhouette behind the tinted glass of the balcony doors. At least they show no fear as they eat. Sitting on his haunches, he's almost motionless as he watches their fluttering and pecking on the terracotta tiles, as if the constantly changing patterns formed by the ceaseless hopping to and fro of all the sparrows, tits, greenfinches and nuthatches were something he could read, a secret script whose meaning is never exhausted. Only when they quarrel and the feathers fly does he become restless and whines softly. The brightly coloured nut-hatches, especially treat the others brutally and if the fight lasts too long, he even barks—the glass by his muzzle mists over and the flock flies off to the lime tree.

In the house across the road, Mr Greyling, half hidden behind the curtains of his west windows, is photographing the work on the neighbouring property where the kindergarten is to open soon. They're concreting the base of the slide, making a sandpit and a tree-house in the yew. He has a balcony on that side, too, and could take his photos out in the open but he stays inside and pulls the tulle of his blinds right round his body so that presumably only his lens can be seen from outside, if anything at all.

Wolf, who's just making a camomile tea for Alina, can't believe it. Since they moved into this district, the way young people, made for wide-open spaces and rebellion, settle down here, comfortable within their own four walls, has struck him as eerie, even threatening, not least because there are expressions and voices connected with it in which narrow-mindedness struts about as if it were smart. In a similar way, the hairs on his arms now stand on end at the thought that a man there is not, as he might be, gathering evidence against the owners of a possibly rather noisy or chaotic kindergarten but is himself proof that the polished veneer covering this way of life, for all its seals and insurance stamps, is extremely thin and, underneath it, the essence of their history is still seething—a hell of spying on people, betrayal and self-righteousness.

For all that, he feels a little too happy with his disparagement not to have doubts about it. Presumably, the good fellow across the road is just afraid his property might drop in value or is documenting something for a possible court case. Yet, Wolf finds him so depressing that he can't bring himself to get his new camera out and take a picture of him at his observation post. He peels an apple, cuts it up into bite-sized pieces, sprinkles it with cinnamon, sweetens the tea with honey and, so as not to appear at Alina's sickbed looking too gloomy, cheers himself up with the glimmer of hope he can see in the fact that Mr Greyling seems not to have realized that he can be observed spying through his south-facing window.

Wolf says nothing of this to her. She has a bit of a temperature, a cold and a sore throat, she's wheezing and he helps her out of bed so she can sit in the armchair while he changes the sheet. In Paris, cold sores suddenly appeared on her upper lip and she began to sweat and shiver on the plane, her teeth chattering. And when Wolf put his hand on her forehead, she closed her eyes and said quietly, 'Will you do me a favour?' Her voice was quite different, hoarse and weak, and, assuming she was going to ask him for a drink of water or an aspirin, he just nodded and leant down so his ear was close to her mouth. She swallowed several times, cleared her throat, clasped her fingers, then unclasped them and fiddled with her ring. 'Will you promise not to kiss me straight away after you've slept with her?'

In the first week after their trip, he sleeps in his study and as long as Alina's ill, they don't talk about Charlotte. They don't say much to one another at all, what is left unsaid is forceful enough. He goes to the chemist's for medicine, makes hot-water bottles and compresses for her legs, pulls her sweat-soaked T-shirt off over her head and gives her one of his own clean ones, the favourite one she uses instead of pyjamas. He rubs camphor ointment over her chest and back, buys newspapers and magazines, though she hardly touches them, and sits on the edge of her mattress to feed her spoonfuls of homemade chicken soup. Every time she takes one, her eyes, red with crying, stare right past him at the empty corner of the room, her fingers gently fondling Webster, who's sitting close by the bed, on the back of his neck.

She rarely ever gets up when Wolf's in the attic part of the flat, at most she goes to the loo once. But hardly has he said goodnight and lain on the sofa bed beside his desk to read than he hears her taking a shower upstairs or gargling, opening drawers, rummaging round in the fridge, switching on the radio or talking to Webster, affectionate noises, and when it's quiet again, the only sound the rustle of the chestnut trees outside the house, Wolf imagines he can clearly feel her pain, like an invisible edge in the air. Its cold geometry seems to make the room larger, the corners more acute, the darkness more serious and gives her a nobility, in the light of which he finds himself more and more dubious and his need to make a clean breast of things suspicious. Was he really concerned about her dignity in Paris or did he just want to make things a bit easier for himself, because he had become too lazy or too weak for the effort secrecy demanded? Must she not even take his confession as a form of contempt?

On the other hand, he believes that with time his continuing masquerade has undermined their relationship and, like an insidious poison, eroded his respect for Alina. Now that she seems to be asleep, he goes up the stairs barefoot to get a glass of water. But, when he opens to door of the living room, illuminated with moonlight, she's sitting on the sofa eating ice cream and gawping at the television. It's playing without sound and when he asks how she is, she gives an almost imperceptible nod. The dog is lying among the cushions as well, which is not normally allowed, so that there's no room for Wolf and he sits on a chair at the other end of the room. Alina's fingernails with their neutral varnish are shining in the bluish flicker of the screen, the thin shadow of a palm leaf is quivering on her shoulder and after she's spent some time scraping out the cardboard tub, she holds out the spoon with the last blob of stracciatella to Webster and switches on a standard lamp.

She's become a little thinner in the last few days, she looks hollow-cheeked, her nose is still red, but her eyes are clear and she's washed her hair again. She's clearly got over the flu and perhaps even more—she is so beautifully relaxed, so warm as she stretches out, that she gives Wolf the impression of someone who, although she's been through something she never thought would happen to her, has found her strength renewed by it and that puts her in a conciliatory mood. At least there's no trace of bitterness, of reproach in her looks any more and she folds her arms across her breast so that her sweatshirt shifts, revealing one strap of her bra. 'I've been thinking it over,' she says, taking a deep breath that still sounds a bit quivery. 'I don't think we should get caught up in petty details.'

He doesn't ask what she means by that. He leans back, waiting for what's to come next, and crosses his legs, shivering slightly in his shorts. The dog yawns and turns over on its back and she strokes its stomach, apparently searching for the right words. She begins to speak several times, her lips moving without sound, and, when she finally swallows and asks whether there have been other women, whether he's been unfaithful to her more than once over the years, he's secretly glad that the lamplight only comes as far as his toes. Reaching over to the table, he takes a sip of her herbal tea, which is already cold, and stares at the rim of the cup as if in it he'd find an answer that would spare her feelings. She then squeezes a pastille out of the pack and adds that she's not talking about his one-night stands or visits to brothels, she doesn't care about those.

She shows no reaction at all to his look of astonishment. Sucking her throat pastille, she pushes her feet in their white woollen socks under the dog that has fallen asleep again and is groaning contentedly. What she wants to know, she says, is whether he's had *lovers*, women who've become the objects of his longing, who've been able to give him something she hasn't got, women of his dreams, if you like. And when, after a deep breath, he denies it, irritated by his hoarseness, his scratchy voice, and tells her with a clear conscience that he's loved no one but her for a good twenty years and can't imagine that ever changing, she stares at the TV screen, shaking her head almost imperceptibly, and slowly runs her fingers through her hair with a look of almost happy amazement on her face, as if she genuinely wasn't expecting that.

Time stretches in her long silence and he has to pull himself together to stop himself going on, even rambling on with unnecessary assurances. Her trusting belief has always been a space in which every wrong or merely misjudged note sounds like a profound untruth. The silence between them is sometimes more precise than any discussion, it clears the air better too, as if it contained a moment of transformation which only requires patience to bring back the magic and complete the healing process. Webster at least jerks his head up and looks from her to him, twisting his neck, and Alina scrapes some dead skin off her upper lip and briefly closes her eyes.

It's a clear night outside the windows that reach right up to the ceiling, with almost no wind and stars glittering above the huge lime tree, which has recently been declared a 'natural monument', with an official plaque on the trunk, and Wolf can see a deer in the gardens behind it, its cautious, slightly stiff-legged gait between the bushes, the light escutcheon under its tail. It's almost white round its shiny nose as well. Twisting its ears in the light of the half moon, it nibbles the rosebuds and this or that flower and finally Alina switches the television off, in an oddly abrupt way, as it seems to him. 'As for me, I still love your arse,' she says as she passes him, almost licking the spoon she'd just held out to the dog. But she stops herself and adds, halfway into her room, 'From behind and from the front.'

Then, she closes the door and, after he's seen to Webster and put out all the lights, Wolf follows her. She's just taking her tracksuit bottoms off, looks up at him with a frown and he, ignoring her soft 'Push off,' goes up so close to her that she has to hold on to him to stop herself falling over. Hands on his shoulders, she jiggles the trousers off her legs, leans her trunk back and turns her head away. Her mount of Venus is a firm bulge under her burgundy panties and she gives him a push with it, presumably still to ward him off. But he forces her back against the wall and, as he sniffs her and they kiss, more tentatively than they have done for ages, he undoes her bra, the straps of which are already hanging over her shoulders, with one tug and touches her breasts as if it were the first time. She keeps looking at him, as if she still has something to sort out inside herself, but her breathing is more audible and, eventually, she finds it impossible to resist the new innocence between them and shoves the flat of her hand as far up under the bottom of his shorts as her pearl ring allows. Then she closes her eyes.

When he comes back from the lake with the dog the next morning, there's a little basket on his desk—cherries from the Green Man. It's a farewell gift, the old villa with the overgrown garden has been sold to a man from the West, a politician, and is to be restored in the summer. Only recently, one of the violent storms, that have been occurring more and more often of late, blew off half the roof and the hermit covered over the damage with a heavy plastic sheet that billows and crackles in the wind. It's an old cinema advert and now a gigantic Spiderman is crawling over the roof-ridge.

It's the last grey house in the street. The variously sized stones in the mortar of the roughcast, only cursorily smoothed out and typical of the GDR, have created structures which look deliberate but are presumably simply due to a lack of sifted sand and, on some days, countless sparrows and tits cling to it, fluttering their wings as they pick insects or their larvae out of the holes. There's even moss growing on the side exposed to the weather, a shimmer of brown like an animal's coat.

The day before he leaves, Alina takes the man a bottle of champagne and chats with him for a while over the garden fence. He's found somewhere to live, a flat in one of the GDR high-rise settlements in Marzahn, about ten kilometres to the north, and, after he's loaded two suitcases, a foam mattress, a few pans and a standard lamp in a little trailer, he waves to them and gets into a Trabant driven by a woman. From the cap on her greying hair it seems she's a nurse and she bursts into a ringing laugh when the engine stalls as she lets in the clutch. But then, the two-stroke chugs off over the cobbles with its rattling load and Wolf breathes in the special smell of the bluish smoke that hangs in the air for a while. Usually, he abhors it but now it makes him almost melancholy, as if it's something precious, the essence of a story that accompanied his own for a short stretch. 'A nice man,' Alina says, taking his hand. 'He thinks we're a happy couple.'

He's just preparing a new manuscript for the publishers when scaffolding is erected across the road and the house is cleared out. They use electric hammer chisels, the rubble clatters down the tube-like slides into the skips, sending up clouds of dust, and, if for once they're not milling, grinding or knocking holes, pop music comes booming out of the building site from the workers' radios. Wolf stuffs cotton wool in his ears and, one day, he's standing at the window dabbing some Tipp-Ex on a page while one of the men is throwing the glazed firebricks from a stove down from the balcony, carefully, he's presumably going to reuse them—they fall onto a pile of soft topsoil and one of his mates cleans them up with a paintbrush before stowing them in his van. 'Stove-fitter', another word, like 'hot-metal compositor' or 'collotype printer' that soon won't exist any more.

Wolf goes back to work with a bounce in his step, the sight of the building workers has given him just the kind of boost he needs for a manuscript to round itself off for him. His doubts about whether he's managed to produce anything of significance are seldom dispelled by his publisher's or editor's encouragement, by positive reviews or good sales. That can so easily be undermined by his scepticism—the publisher wants to sell books, reviewers can't read, which you can see from how often they quote you wrongly, and good sales could always be better. If he were to attach importance to all that, it would be a sure sign that he'd lost sight of the essential part. But there have always been unmistakable signs that have guarded him against that.

It's a delicate topic, really far too personal to talk about. When he once tried to, years ago, after a reading, the response was uncomprehending frowns, even the accusation that he was just trying to draw attention to himself and his writing in order to increase sales. Mystic marketing. Since then, he's preferred to keep quiet about poems and stories that have come to him in a dream, about events he's thought up that have later happened or about characters or animals he's already described appearing in the park—and about the soft toy he found on Fontanepromenade just after he'd sent off his first novel in which a white rabbit kept lolloping across the pages.

Glazed tiles are still being thrown down from the balcony, once even an ash-can, in elaborately wrought iron, and, as he watches the workers ,Wolf sends mute thanks off into the unknown. In the volume of short stories he's just completed, there's one, the last, in which a young girl and an older man cure their boredom during a train journey with word play. Both have the tendency not to look at things or listen to people properly, they read humour instead of tumour, ketchup instead of kitchen, urological instead of zoological. But for all its amusing opening, it's a story in which the boundaries between life and death are slowly blurred.

The man is almost run over by a lorry outside the station and, for a moment, he thinks he reads the word 'demise' on the side of the vehicle. All it says, however, is 'demolition' and, as the worker across the road lets down the gilded coping tile of the stove on a rope and his mate cleans it and stows it in the back of the van, Wolf puts his imprimatur on the manuscript and takes it to the post office.

Is it a sign of approaching old age when you suddenly start spelling words correctly that you often used to get wrong. Rheumatism, for example, or haemorrhoids? Oh, the erotic attraction of check-ups—the orthopaedic X-ray under your arm, the plaster-of-Paris impression of your teeth in your pocket, the eye specialist's optometer, bristling with little screws and wheels, on your nose and the urologist's rubber finger up your arse—a man who'd make a cancer mountain out of a mole.

The pain is often unbearable, household remedies, diet, homeopathic medicines have all failed, with the result that Wolf fears the worst, stomach ulcers or Crohn's disease, when he finally makes an appointment with the specialist. She's a technically sound body mechanic, trained in the old GDR, who clearly assumes he's from the East too, at least during the preliminary examination in the crowded practice, echoing with the ringing of telephones, the clatter of clogs and the whine of some kind of centrifuge, she breaks off palpating his stomach to say, 'You wouldn't believe how many still carry the old state round inside them—in the form of cancers . . .'

There are knick-knacks everywhere on the cupboards and side-tables. A gilt gondola, a silver Eiffel Tower, a crystal Statue of Liberty. There's a row of soft toys, animals arranged in order of size on a shelf. She talks in a loud voice, almost bawling, and when she hears that he's a writer, she raises one eyebrow, has a quick glance at his health insurance and leans back again. She read *War and Peace* when she was young, she says, in Russian, and she cried all the time. 'That Tolstoy,' she says, 'he was quite a guy, wasn't he? Ugly as a scarecrow but, then, full of beautiful ideals. And he wrote that scene where Levin and Kitty find one another—or was that in *Anna Karenina*? What do you think he would say to our world? It's all babble nowadays, isn't it? I just want to watch a football match on television but, first of all, I have to sit through an hour of people yattering on, then finally the game gets going but during half-time its talk, talk, talk, by supposed experts who have problems with elementary grammar. And the ref's hardly blown the final whistle when the manager joins them and they all go on at great length telling me what I've just seen on the screen. I'm not blind, am I?—Right then, we'll do a sonography for you. No, no, I mean a gastroscopy. It'll be OK.'

He spends two days taking nothing but laxatives and riding the lavatory pan through the lowlands of his depression, with Alina making him cups of herbal tea, until his intestines are rinsed out and can be viewed. On the early morning of his appointment, the clinic is very quiet. There's a vase of fresh flowers on the reception desk, a lighted candle on the glass table covered in magazines and brochures containing full-colour information about all kinds of diseases and, beside a bowl of biscuits—only to be eaten after the examination—a pot of tea is steaming on a warmer. Soft, soothing music comes from the loudspeakers below the cornice and the staff too seem to be on tiptoe and they talk in whispers, as if the waiting room had suddenly become a sacred place, a place of humility. All the patients—apart from Wolf there are two white-haired men and a woman of Alina's age waiting for their endoscopies—are carrying a plastic bag with the tissues and the pair of extra thick socks they were asked to bring and no one is talking or reading or leafing through a magazine. Weakened by the days without food and the laxatives, they're dozing or staring at the walls, the landscape watercolours in silver frames, and, just now and then, one of them can be heard swallowing or clearing their throat and the candle-flame flickers when someone lets out a sigh.

Wolf's legs had felt heavy even in the vestibule of the fine old building and he'd turned round to look at the sky through the glass panes in the door. He couldn't stop himself feeling that the next time he was looking at that blue it could be as a doomed man. And, as far as so-called positive thinking was concerned, the effort of will it requires has always made him feel pessimistic. But then, he remembers the walk they had together the previous day.

It had been rainy by the lake, deserted, and Webster was trotting through the bushes off the lead. Wolf felt light after his fast, not properly earthed, and had taken Alina's arm when, silently and too quick for alarm, a bird landed on the path, a young great tit. It came so close to their feet that they automatically stopped and stared at it, as if it were some miracle. They could have bent down to pick it up and, as it pecked at this or that on the path, it kept looking up at them with no fear at all. It must have been hungry and was hoping from some crumbs but all they had was some chewing gum.

Despite that, it stayed close to them and didn't even fly off when they eventually took a few cautious steps to leave. It hopped just far enough in front of them to preserve its initial distance and kept doing that for several minutes, giving little sharp cheeps now and then. 'Well, my darling?' Alina asked him, not taking her eye off it, 'What does that tell you?' But he, stuck in his gloomy mood, completely preoccupied with the pain, the endoscopy the following day and the possible diagnosis, just shrugged his shoulders. What should it tell him? She gave a broad smile. 'Isn't it obvious? *Don't be afraid*,' she whispered and the bird suddenly flew away.

The high-ceilinged examination room, where the doctor talked to him about literature and football, is full of scratched white furniture and all sorts of technical equipment and monitors. The blinds are drawn and the only light is from a little lamp on the desk that makes the blade of a paper knife gleam. While the assistant's hanging a pair of paper boxer shorts up in the changing cubicle—gap at the back—her look is so gentle and friendly that his hands go moist with sweat. At the same time, he's grateful for this unexpected consideration for his embarrassment, and even if the light-blue paper is so thin he can see the time on his watch through it, it's with a sense of relief that he puts on the hygienic shorts and spreads his towel over the couch. The tubes they're going to stick into his body are already hanging on the stand—a short, thin one for his stomach, a wider, longer one for his intestine, and, as the nurse is checking the lights at the ends, the very bright beam that sends the shadows of the soft toys shooting up the wall, the doctor comes in.

She's wearing a mask over her mouth, a white rubber apron and gloves that come up over her elbows that she's adjusting as she sits on the swivel chair. 'We're out of coffee filter papers,' she mutters as she leafs through his records. 'Has he been sedated?' Her assistant shakes her head, he didn't want any anaesthetic, and the woman gives him a wink, sprays his throat with lubricant, sticks a teething ring between his teeth and switches the monitor on. 'So now we're going to have a look deep inside you, Mr Writer. Perhaps we'll find a few sonnets. Keep breathing normally.'

The gastroscopy isn't as uncomfortable as he feared. He just retches once as the tube goes down his throat, after that the feeling under his breastbone just like you get when you've swallowed a piece of food that's too big and too hard, perhaps even slightly angular. After a few seconds, he hardly notices it. His nasal passages have been squeezed and he pants a little as he breathes in and out past all the plastic in his mouth and is fascinated by the sight of his illuminated organs—the lengthways folds of his gullet, the pulsating cardiac opening, his grotto-like stomach. With its uneven surface pattern, it looks like the reverse image of a strange planet and the smooth mucous membrane, which he imagined would be a yellowish grey, like the velvety lights they get for the dog, and which is an amazingly delicate shade of pink, looking in every sense more pure than he ever was. He stares at the doctor to see if he can read anything in her expression.

'It's OK,' she says from behind her mask, the tissue of which moves slightly. 'Almost like a textbook illustration. No ulcer, no scar, nothing. You've probably got a *Helicobacter pylori* infection, it's a bacterium that's very fashionable at the moment among people of your age. Every second person has it. Some don't notice it at all, others go almost out of their minds with the pain.' When she takes a tissue sample with the pointed pincers, tiny as a tit's beak, that shoot out of the endoscope, he feels a dull pain again, and then the assistant wheels the shiny tube out of the room. Crouched in a slightly foetal position, he doesn't feel much at all during the subsequent enteroscopy and, one hand under his cheek, a peppermint in his mouth, he's spellbound by the images on the monitor. By his absence in his own insides.

He'd been prepared for anything, blood and mucus and streaks of shit, festering ulcers and polyps. And now this. As strong as the horror that makes you go pale the first time you hear your own voice on tape, he's overcome, after a brief shock at the sight of the enlargement of his hairy sphincter on the screen, with sudden delight at the poetry of the invisible—the endless hollows and the calm contractions of his colon, whose crescent-shaped annular folds have a symmetry he wouldn't have believed possible inside himself. The pink mucous membranes have a delicate purplish tinge along the grooves and with their branching veins disappearing into the shadows and the light-yellow flecks of foam left over from the laxative, his bowels are like a scene from the depths of the sea, a reef never before seen. In the mirror opposite he can see a point of light under his abdominal wall and the doctor seems to be smiling behind her mask, on which a patch of condensation has appeared, and briefly lowers her eyelids. 'Amazing, isn't it? Man's a romantic system of tubes.'

Amazing's putting it mildly. That things in a realm beyond, whatever its nature, could be not just unimaginable but perhaps even unimaginably beautiful—that is what a silent voice is suggesting here. Until now, for him, everything within, whether physical or mental, was synonymous with chaos, transience and dark seethings. But this stunning cosmos, so delicately formed, elegant down to its tiniest twists and turns, is the expression of a profound order that visibly goes further than his own body, a perceptible benevolence that he finds devastating because, among other things, it makes him aware how unworthy of it he's been so far, how badly he's abused it. How little faith he had. He takes a deep breath as he goes out through the glass door, he feels a great sense of relief. The smell of fresh rolls wafts across from the bakery. Police cars drive through the park beside the surgery, blue light flickering beneath a blue sky.

'What would you have done if they'd found something bad, something terminal?' he asks Alina a few days later when the comforting results arrive and she shrugs her shoulders. While he almost always gets in a state when she has a mere cold or headache, immediately goes out and buys anything that might help and makes her suffering even worse by tormenting her with his impatience, she mostly remains calm. 'Then, we'd just have had to live with your illness,' she replies. And when he laughs at her pragmatism and says he's really looking forward to some future date when he can wipe the porridge off her chin, sit her on the bedpan and suck out her throat tube, she gently shakes her head. 'Oh, no, sweetheart, it'll never come to that. Not with us.'

Woe betide anyone who doesn't grow old within the haven of love.

Where the rusty kennels used to be, a long row for the East German police dogs, they're now roughcasting private houses. And the first thing the people will put up in their new homes will be shelves for their files.

She wants to see a photo of the other woman, wants to be able to imagine her, and he gives her two—the official one that's on the website of her faculty and in which she looks like a senior executive, kindly but always decisive, and, at first sight, the hint of melancholy, condensed from unfulfilled longing, blurs the clear aura that gives her an air of competence but when you look again it emphasizes it; and one from the previous year in which she's standing in her bedroom doorway, in a dark trouser suit, a frilly blouse with a plunging neckline and, as always, pointed shoes, looking at the camera with a strangely embarrassed air, despite the radiant smile that is presumably intended to conceal the fact that she wasn't feeling well at the time. She looks as if she's lost weight, though that doesn't stop her making her silhouette more alluring by swivelling one hip forward, and Alina looks at the picture for a long time, then says, 'Impressive. She suits you. I can understand the pair of you.'

Nothing much has changed since his confession. Every two weeks—an interval that has gradually been determined by their desire—he goes to see Charlotte and even if a meeting has been arranged for some time, to make it easier for Alina, he only tells her on the day, after breakfast, for example, or he just mentions it casually while they're washing up after lunch. They're in the habit of drinking their second cup of tea or coffee in the morning on the sofa, leaning back against one another, staring dreamily up at the sky over their south-facing balcony and listening to music, sometimes talking about their work, giving one another advice.

He finds it difficult to feel at home in her subject or to be comfortable with the language of the secondary literature, and he's always amazed at Alina's ability to assimilate his concerns and to see the essence of his writing without losing sight of its finer ramifications. She has an unerring instinct for quality; she develops plot lines, suggests titles, advises him who to write to or telephone, and, while she's speaking, he listens to the mood behind what she's saying until he's sure that the pointed casualness of his quiet announcement beginning with a 'By the way . . .' will not, in fact, give it greater emphasis and, perhaps, lead to an argument or tears. For the fact that she's decided to accept the affair does not mean it's easy for her when he goes to see his other woman. Her sudden sleeplessness, the new seriousness in her eyes, the traces of vomit in the bathroom all speak for themselves.

At least when he says, 'I'm going out later on' or 'I probably won't be in this evening,' she doesn't let her disappointment show, she gives an almost imperceptible nod, perhaps asks him if he wants to eat first or needs a shirt ironed, and warns him not to wear the same suede or baggy corduroy jacket all the time when he goes to see his lover, after all he's got such lovely suits. And when the time approaches and he showers, shaves and rubs cream into the tired-looking skin of his backside and puts on clean underwear, she stays in her room with Webster, working or listening to quiet music, mostly Mozart or Haydn. He can't bring himself to say goodbye. Whatever her expression, he would only see the hurt in it or her attempt to hide her sadness from him. Without a word, he goes down the stairs, closing the door softly behind him.

And just as, when he'd broken up with someone in the past, he couldn't believe that after all the passion and despair, after the battles and tears and thoughts of suicide, they would end up arguing about a toaster, a set of eggcups or an unpaid electricity bill, now he can't understand that this new situation only leads to discord or even a proper row at times when, before going to see Charlotte, he hasn't slept with Alina for a while, thus appearing to prefer the other woman—which is naturally not the case. He has to fit in with all Charlotte's engagements and she's very busy. But his partner couldn't care less about that and once he's seen the importance of the sequence, he makes sure, not without a certain smugness, that he sticks to the somehow zoological-seeming ritual and goes to bed with her first. And because he doesn't want her to feel she's been in any way downgraded, he's more affectionate than ever—which appears to be confirmed by her cries, the reddened skin between her breasts and the unusual violence of her movements. As if his guilty conscience were the sulphur that turns the whole business into a firework display.

In those first weeks after his confession, however, he expects more of himself than he can manage. Euphoric at his sudden freedom and relieved of the need to put on a pretence, he is as if reinvigorated and, given Alina's changed attractiveness, clearly as a response to the shadow of the other woman, he comes to believe his own cliché of virility. Her tight-fitting silk dress, her fishnet tights with the hole in the heel, and the magnificently vulgar blue of her eyelids—sometimes she corners him shortly before it's time for his train in order to suck him dry, which he's happy to accept because it gives him a feeling of strength, of exceptional strength, and not just the desire for strength.

Which is what it actually is. Then he flops, drained, onto Charlotte's sofa, where they get undressed but have to watch a porn film on her laptop and then wait for his prick to wake from its snail-like sleep. She has a whole selection of DVDs with titles such as *Boobwatch*, *Blowing in Style* or *Anal Attack*. The producers, to whom she sent requests on headed notepaper from the University, provided them for a study on the psychological profile of consumers of porn films commissioned by a feminist periodical. Their favourite is a lesbian one in which two full-bosomed women rub their cunts against one another like half fruits, endlessly, and the soft noise it causes seems to him like the acoustic representation of sweetness, pure sweetness.

Even before their general availability on the Internet, he found it difficult to resist the mildly hypnotic effect of such performances. In hotels with that kind of TV channel, he often lay watching the screen until the early hours—without it leaving him with the misgivings that come after hours staring at the series and chat shows of the supposedly chaste channels. For, while the latter set firm limits to our natural voyeurism and only have substitutes with artificial colours and flavour enhancers to offer our life-giving interest and pleasure in lust, they are the truly obscene ones—the only thing they leave you with is the feeling of shame at once more having been too weak to switch off and having wasted valuable time. Watching porn films, on the other hand, quickly brings a new strength and drive that goes beyond the purely sexual and dispels depression.

Towards the end of his Catholic childhood, when the words chaste and unchaste could be heard more and more often, and, with every month as he grew older, something unspoken seemed to be condensing round him, when there were suddenly particles in the air he could taste on his tongue—something bitter-sweet that kept making him swallow and his little cock stand up—it had struck him like a revelation when he had found a packet of black-and-white pornographic photographs in his father's bedside cabinet. Private photos, by all appearances, the people in masks and carnival hats were no longer young, the men showing signs of hard work and alcohol, the women of caesarians and long periods of breastfeeding, and yet, he found them indescribably beautiful simply because of what they were doing. The very existence of such a possibility he found as devastating and wonderful as the Sermon on the Mount or the music of the Beatles and it opened up heavens inside his head; the two or three couples on the carpet seemed to him transfigured by the permissiveness which, at least to his mind, is part of being grown up beyond worries and resentment and which he had unconsciously been longing for all the time. So this all-encompassing love did exist, this smiling goodwill with a prick in every hand, and this promise was so exhilarating he could scarcely bear it and, at first at least, he pushed it away with an outraged 'They do it! They really do it! The dirty, unchaste sods . . .' And, with tears of joy, he started to wank, taking care not to soil the bedclothes. And never went to church again.

Midnight-blue satin. The concluding music with wild French horns and dramatic violins surges to a climax at which the main character bares his teeth before the little bit of what Charlotte calls 'liquid male' spurts over the sheet like a shooting star. Another DVD glides into the player. 'You have precisely the profile that keeps the industry going,' she says, fondling Wolf's balls—recently shaven but already showing stubble again. 'You don't really believe in taboos any more but you refuse to forgo the pleasure of breaking some. That's the last little remnant of anarchy and brings the money rolling in. Oh, look, he's waking up . . .' And while, on the screen, limousine doors open, champagne is poured into a shoe and expensive lingerie falls to the floor in slow motion, she lies on her stomach over the arm of the sofa so that he can impale her the way the muscular black did to the blonde in *Dripping Animals,* though even more violently—which doesn't prevent her later from trying to discuss with him what misogynistic attitudes such films display, they're clearly ineradicable, she says—but he's already looking at his watch and wondering whether to phone Alina to keep dinner waiting until he gets back.

She just can't take things easy. She doesn't want a cleaning woman for their small apartment and she won't allow him to take any of the housework off her apart from the cooking. She's tireless and he seems to be the only one who's worried by her recent dizzy turns, her sudden mental blanks. Alina explains them with the strain of her dissertation and the low blood pressure that she's always had since she was young and which drops even more on warm days. 'I'm getting on,' she says and laughs. She's obviously astonished herself that she'll soon be forty. But you couldn't tell by looking at her that she's at an age that is problematic for a woman, especially one with no children. Her body's magnificent, her blue eyes clear, she has dreams, especially ones of trips and long stays abroad, still believes the possibilities are endless and loves her head-in-the-clouds existence, as she calls it. And when she says she believes that in a family she would have an established routine, in many ways determined, even dictated, by others, whereas in a life such as they lead they have the chance of going beyond that, she's not making the best of a bad lot, she's genuinely saying what she feels—his instinct here is unerring. But where or what could 'going beyond that' be?

Richard Sander is sweating. The blue of his blue eyes, which are closer together than they used to be, has become a bit lighter—or the shadows at the corners of his eyes darker—the beautifully curved furrows on his high forehead look more clearly defined, the skin on his neck is somewhat slack, otherwise he's hardly changed at all. He's over seventy but could easily pass for someone in his late fifties. Even his voice still has the shimmer that gives it a suggestion of youthfulness beneath the gloss of slightly bloated manliness, if not the hint of a feminine quality. His mouth, too, still looks as sensuous as ever, his almost colourless lips are astonishingly full, so that, at first, you don't notice the scepticism or even bitterness in the way they are turned down at the corners. His look is expressionless, almost fixed, and grey hairs stick out of his nostrils.

He has his arm round the shoulders of his girlfriend or wife, a gaunt woman in flowing clothes holding a rolled-up music score. She could well be the age he looks and, even when Wolf invites them in, Richard doesn't smile. The sun is glinting on the windows behind the trees and he looks at him calmly as the sweat runs down his temples and the sides of his neck. Clearly not sure himself what form the greeting should take after so many years, he scrutinizes him openly from head to toe, a touch of amusement playing round his features, presumably directed at Wolf's ironed shirt and polished shoes. With his bushy eyebrows, damp at the edges, it seems to him, for a moment, as if there's something horned about Richard's look.

The most striking change is in his hair, no longer curly but still wavy, its former light, almost corn-yellow blond is now a dull, greasy slate colour—possibly because it needs a wash—scurf can be seen between the strands. His chin is bristly, his fingernails dirty and, in general, he looks more like a tramp than a well-off writer. He came by rail but, as Wolf has heard from a gossipy woman bookseller he knows, he has a car and owns a house in Berlin as well as the house in Liguria, which has been greatly extended, and he's just rented another place in the Allgäu. But his down-at-heel walking shoes, his crumpled flannel trousers, far too thick for the early summer heat, the sweatshirt of fleecy polyester and a check lumberjack shirt, with the threads of the quilting hanging, make him look as if he's just emerged from underneath the arch of a bridge.

The hessian bag, in which he carries a bottle of water and a few books, goes with that, but it's not his grubby and slightly rancid-smelling presence that makes Wolf stretch out his hand towards him, as if measuring the distance. He simply wants to avoid being drawn into one of those embraces that even in the old days were of a dubious warmth. Since Richard is impressively tall and towers above most people, his tact ought to tell him not to smother everyone in his shoulders. But, just as he would drive anyone who was flaunting his knowledge of literature into a corner with his superior knowledge and lay down the law at the top of his voice, he also used most embraces to emphasize the pecking order. After it, you always felt a little smaller than you were. So, Wolf just shakes his hand, at which a petulant look passes briefly across his face, like a cat when a mouse has just escaped.

He's afraid of dogs, always has been—he's been bitten several times by the large, shaggy ones the farmers on the high plateaux round Monte Saccarello keep to guard their sheep and Wolf locks the growling Webster in the study. Alina, who's had to go to Tübingen for discussions with the second examiner of her thesis and is then going to visit a friend in Zurich, tidied everything up before she left, polished the floors with scented wax and even cleaned the large glass walls giving on to the south-facing balcony and it was only with difficulty that Wolf stopped her baking a *tarte au citron* as well. He's put wine to cool, dry white wine, and a bottle of schnapps, just in case, but Richard, breathless from the stairs, flops into the first chair he comes across without waiting to be invited and, like his wife, only wants water.

She waits for Wolf to offer her a chair, a straight-backed one, clasps her hands in her lap and says nothing for the moment. She has a soft smile on her thin lips, the look in her brown eyes with the shading of fine lines round them is serious, slightly melancholy. She has tied her long hair, which is dyed dark, in a bun which she somehow manages to keep together with two varnished chopsticks and, to go with her white blouse, pinned at the neck with an amber brooch, she's wearing a linen skirt, also white, that comes down to her ankles. She's clearly waiting to see how the mood between the two men will develop, she's making an effort to keep her expression neutral and, as he examines her silhouette out of the corner of his eye, Wolf is astonished at how different she is from what he has always thought of as Richard's kind of woman. Like an engraving after a pastose oil painting.

When they were still associating with one another, Richard changed his lovers almost every quarter, which the younger Wolf observed not without envy from the dungeon of his shyness. Richard was one of those classic ladies' men who, despite the stuffy moral atmosphere of the time, had no problem with the word seduction and could make elegant compliments to a woman like a baker putting icing on a cake. Without ever really succumbing to passion, he produced love poems by the dozen and was convinced that all that was needed for an efficient seduction was a bottle of wine, candlelight and an open fire. The main prerequisite, however, was a woman with large, best of all huge, breasts. She could have a nasty look, a false smile, she could be calculating or money-grabbing, her backside might not live up to the promise of her hips but woe betide her if the shadow of her bust didn't stretch as far as his glass. Her silhouette was the acme of his longing and it didn't matter even if his fair lady didn't have a brain in her head—he would stuff flowers, silk scarves and chocolates into the gaping hole and urge her towards the bed with a unceasing stream of honeyed words. He was one of those men who idolized women and put them on a pedestal so that they didn't keep getting in the way.

Hannelore is the name of his delicate, totally flat-chested partner who has lovely long hands and is just taking a sip of her water so that a couple of enlarged hairs on her chin can be seen through the prism of the glass. She rang Wolf a few days previously and, after a few pleasantries, asked him straight out whether he would be prepared to make a speech at the celebration planned by Richard's hometown in northern Germany, including a survey of his life and work. In alarm, Wolf had begun to stammer and not only because it would mean an interruption to his own work. It was ages since he'd seen a picture or read almost anything by the man he used to admire, the man who had helped him in so many ways and now, clearly, wanted to collect his debts. That seemed all the more petty to Wolf in that Richard was hiding behind his wife, but he felt he was in a situation where he couldn't refuse without afterwards looking—at the very least—unsupportive of a colleague. And as he saw, in his mind's eye, an unbearably formal celebration full of local worthies and flowers and well-meaning voices clouding the general unction in the flat-roofed hall of some town surrounded by cows grazing the meadows, he did just that. He took a deep breath and, for some reason or other, refused. The brief silence at the other end was presumably meant as a reproach but he was listening to the music in his room, 'Karma Police' by Radiohead. When, however, despite everything, she expressed a wish to 'call on' them in Friedrichshagen, he didn't dare say no. Even though he found the obstinacy with which this request, which had been made for months now, more and more suspicious, he agreed to see them that afternoon.

He's more than glad Alina's not there. Her friendly acceptance of their guests would have made him waver in his reserve, left him more open to attack. But he's determined to be on his guard against a man who thinks he knows him because he once knew him, and now they're sitting with their glasses of water, talking about the weather, about the unusual heat, and it's

Richard Sander who shows signs of some impatience, as if he were the one whose time is being taken up, the one who's being pestered even. He makes the fact that he avoids looking at the bookshelves all too obvious and the way he ignores conventional politeness and doesn't say a word about the picturesque district, the tree-lined avenue, the unusual plan of the apartment and the fresh flowers on the light-coloured furniture is presumably deliberate and, at the same time, the expression of a grumpiness that only increases the longer it goes without the younger man addressing a word to him.

Of course, he wouldn't give a true answer to an inquiry after his health but that's not the point. He wants to be asked the question and, as punishment for not being allowed to preen himself as he sets out on one of those protracted answers that usually begin with 'Listen, my friend . . .', he jiggles his foot, stares at the sky above the lime tree or pushes his thumbnail through the spaces between his grey, visibly dead teeth—while Wolf pours some more water for his partner and learns from her what precisely a music therapist is and how, above all, by playing the harp, which she teaches, autistic children are released from their encapsulation. She keeps glancing over at her partner, at which a painfully soft expression appears on her face, as if she were silently begging his forgiveness that the conversation is about her and her banal affairs. And Richard jiggles his foot even more.

Now it becomes clear to Wolf that he's meant to notice something that he's naturally long since seen but not asked about. In the side of the leather uppers of one of Richard's walking shoes there's a large round hole, obviously cut with scissors or a knife, with part of his instep, a ganglion covered by a blue sock, sticking out. It happens, especially in people who are getting old, and even now he ignores it and, instead, asks whether they would take some wine after all, he's put it on ice. They both say no and, for a while, all three seem to be listening to two magpies squabbling, the cackling in the treetops. Hannelore feels the material of a cushion with her fingers, Wolf turns the winder of his watch, as if it were wound up by hand, and finally Richard clears his throat, licks the sweat off his upper lip and says, 'In summer these attic flats really are too much . . . And you, my friend? How are you? How are things going? Are you working a lot?' And when Wolf raises his eyebrows in surprise and, after briefly considering the question to see if it has any potholes, shakes his head, he says, 'Oh come on, of course you are. A book every other year for twenty years . . . You really are ambitious, aren't you?'

So there it is, the first kick in the balls, with a ganglion. Wolf gives a mild snort, takes a sip of water. He couldn't care less whether the man thinks his smug grin is vain, as if he felt flattered. In fact, he's just pleased that one of the blessings of growing older is that you find it easier to see through people. Richard himself has always exhibited a serious work ethic and even if, seen from a distance, there was something of an act, even a confidence trick about it, measured by the results, for a long time, Wolf was impressed by it. 'I have to work!'—above all, that meant that he *could* work, while Wolf often heard the faint crack as the point of his pencil broke before it touched the paper. Richard's whole life seemed to be determined by work, he didn't simply go on a cruise—he worked on board. He didn't just go to Provence or some other beautiful area—he rented a house in order to work. Even the gallons of wine he drank were for his work, to stimulate him, as he said, and the woman he happened to be living with at the time, often an artist, too—'a great, a very great artist' as long as they were together, 'only superficially talented, tragic' after they'd split up—would put callers off, telling them, 'He can't come to the phone just now. We have to work.' And, if they met in Berlin, he would roll up his sleeves to show Wolf the sores on his forearms from the acid baths for his etchings or tell him how many prints there were in his graphic cycles or chapters in his trilogy—which made the younger Wolf doubt his own powers more and more. But, if the years working at his so-called profession had taught him one thing, it was that people who keep on stressing or even complaining about how much they've done have never worked enough, despite their obvious exhaustion, all they are saying is that they are busy, like everyone else, and, moreover, give rise to the suspicion that their occupation is too demanding for them. Should not the aim of an artist, or perhaps of everyone, be to *embody* their work? Then it's no longer necessary to trumpet one's keenness abroad. Then there can be no too much or too little.

When he says that, Richard doesn't seem to be listening, he scratches the part of his foot sticking out of his shoe and sucks in air though the gaps in his teeth, at which a look of alarm appears on Hannelore's face. But he shakes his head briefly, which is presumably meant to reassure her, and while Wolf pours them more water, he stretches out his leg and places his foot on a small pile of books on the floor. 'Hey, the district's really come up in the world. I used to come out here to the lake sometimes, in the 1960s, even before the Wall was built. It was all crumbling then. Despite that, it was a privilege to live in Friedrichshagen. Only well-behaved citizens and Stasi officials were allowed to live out here. Or loyal artists—sculptors who could carve Marx's beard with their eyes shut, painters with dark-red palettes or nature poets.'

'More Stasi collaborators, that is,' his partner says, and the way they bare their teeth in a silent laugh as they look first at one another and then at Wolf has such a crude inclusive assumption of his agreement that he shows no response. Moreover he's outraged at the way

Richard rests his foot in his old shoe on the books, either because he wants to attract attention to it or because it's hurting—whatever, he feels it takes far too much for granted and he lowers his eyes and stares at his glass, as if someone had spat in his water. Probably all that Richard wants is for him to voice some objection, thus revealing himself as the petty-minded bourgeois he is—what are books anyway, especially for someone who writes them? But Wolf goes into the kitchen and opens a bottle of wine.

One of the last publications by Richard Sander that he's read was a newspaper article about a colleague from East Berlin who had been revealed as a Stasi collaborator—a nice guy, a great translator, and it was an open question whether he had actually harmed anyone, many of his reports were pure fiction, and you got the impression that the storm it had set off in the press had been so furious simply because the revelation came so late, all the other prominent authors or artists had long since been exposed and people clearly felt it was doubly shameful that the man, who had always been seen as quiet and upright, had not made a voluntary confession. Richard—his observations revealed his pure delight that his opinion on current events was in demand while other, more competent commentators had long since tired of the topic—also took that line and did so with precisely the relentless self-righteousness, the inquisitorial rigour which has ever been the sign of a related disposition. He took uninhibited advantage of the opportunity of finally being in the right, on the side of the morally pure, and even appended a poem entitled 'Mud for Sale'. When you looked more closely, you could see that every sentence wore braid and epaulettes, every paragraph stood to attention and the fact that he did not even hint between the lines that he might have behaved in the same way in a historically comparable situation was the secret stamp on a file you'd prefer never to have to handle.

Mrs Seidenkrantz, the hairdresser, also knows the man. Like her, he lives in Schöneiche. 'He's finished,' she said the last time he had his hair cut. 'Every day, he shuffles round the town with his Zimmer frame, waiting for death. And he only did it for his little daughter. She would have died without the expensive medicine from the West. She constantly needed a new supply and that was only available through the authorities. He had no choice but to let his arm be twisted. Wouldn't you have done the same?'

When Wolf comes back into the room with the opened bottle, Hannelore breaks off whispering and Richard, clearly having been reprimanded, takes his foot off the pile of books, twitching the corner of his mouth as if to say: OK then, if you're all going to be so pernickety . . . And then, he does have some wine after all, pours it onto the ice in his glass and, for the next half hour, they talk of stuff that could perhaps best be described as shop, though its real function is to allow them to avoid any topic that would demand even the hint of an opinion that you couldn't contradict without offending the other person or couldn't endorse without betraying your own beliefs. The pauses between remarks, accompanied by the quiet crackle of ice cubes, are still furtively watchful but, while both Richard and Wolf allow the conversation about publishers, book covers, reading tours or advances to run on as harmlessly as possible, they are communicating their covert conviction that the other isn't worth the effort or the passion required for an exchange of opinions that were more than empty air. But it's no use, this deliberate avoidance only makes the pair of them grit their teeth even more and the woman's occasional interventions and waving of her bell sleeves are an additional irritation, with the result that the surliness etches itself deeper and deeper on Richard's face and Wolf has to keep a tight hold on himself not to ask the question that is floating under the surface: Why on earth has Richard come to 'call on' him—what the hell does this poseur poet want from him?

In the hope that a medical turn might give the conversation at least the appearance of substance, Wolf is about to bring up his somewhat histrionically displayed ganglion when Richard clears his throat and remarks in a voice which sounds as if he were speaking through a thin piece of paper, which, in the past, used to betray his embarrassment or nervousness while his bored tone was intended to suggest that basically he was above what he was saying: 'By the way, I've just remembered, last year I read an article about you in the paper, though I don't know now whether it was in one of the nationals or some rag from the backwoods of the Allgäu. It dealt with other writers as well—to be precise, there were only four lines about you—but some clever dick was saying that recently something like a spiritual undercurrent could be perceived in your work and that there was the occasional allusion to the Bible. I was rather taken aback by that, wasn't I, my love? Could my friend have turned religious in his old age?'

Both give him an expectant look and, while Wolf feels sudden relief that Richard clearly hasn't read anything by him since they parted (he probably thinks that hinting at this *en passant* is being subtle), at the same time, he has to keep himself under control so as not to show his amazement at this sly forgetfulness. For a moment, he thinks he can see something of the vitality of his earlier years in his face, his intellectual aggressiveness, armed with cultural knowledge which even then had something forced about it because it wasn't really him, it demanded a particular effort from his languid hedonism. But his elegantly formulated scepticism towards everything, whoever it was expressed by, was not just a pose, it sprang from the rationalist author's fear of having to see that the world would be irretrievably lost without our sense of awe—a realization that demands precisely the kind of humility of which an egocentric or a freethinker, who confuses it with submission, is incapable. The tip of his tongue is on his lower lip, his eyebrows raised, his look has something piercing about it and, while he waits for an answer, he looks just as sad to Wolf as those who make a point of showing an interest or being full of the joys of life and take active steps to combat ageing in walking groups, cholesterol courses or senior citizens' discos. 'No, no,' he says, putting his foot on the pile of books himself, 'They can write what they want. Of course, I'm not religious, just like any angel. It's only the godless who pray.'

Richard is taken aback and, in the laughter that follows—his laboured, as he surveys Wolf out of narrowed eyes, hers delighted, almost childlike—the tension in the room relaxes and, although the windows have been open since the visitors arrived, only now do they sense the fresh air. It is, as all three feel, the one moment that will make the memory of that afternoon tolerable, possibly even cheerful, and when Wolf looks at his watch, Richard gets up, finishes his wine and crunches a piece of ice.

'Well, my friend, we'll be off then. We wasted enough time by the lake. Still things to do.' Handing him his glass, he examines the spines of the books on his shelves and if he's disappointed to see only Shakespeare under S, he doesn't show it. He takes out a volume of

Novalis, an edition from the 1920s, strokes the pale-blue leather and points at his shoe, his ganglion, with it. 'Since we're in the metaphysical realm, do you know what that is? A cloven hoof.'

But no one laughs any more. Hannelore puts her music in his cloth bag and Wolf opens the door to the study a crack to calm down Webster, who's whimpering. There's a bowl of apricots on a shelf in the hall and Richard sticks a little one in his mouth before going down the stairs to the front door, step by step, slightly shakily. Wolf, who suddenly finds his shoulders touchingly narrow, sees them out to the street, opens the garden gate for them and Richard looks him up and down again while Hannelore bends over their neighbour's peonies. They're burgundy, delicate pink and also white and, in full bloom, they look like plumage on the stalk.

She breathes in the scent and Richard spits out the kernel on the grass. 'D'you remember when we used to go up the valleys and over the plateaux round Trioria? Those incredible skies, the grass flowing in the wind, the wild cherries—we really stuffed ourselves, didn't we? I sometimes remember the day it made you cry.' Hannelore looks up, comes over, curious, and he puts his arm round her shoulders and says, 'Just imagine, the tears really did come to his eyes. As a townee, he couldn't believe there were no fences anywhere, that you could just climb up a cherry tree by the track and eat those incredibly sweet fruits, without asking anyone's permission. It must have been a foretaste of paradise. He cried like a little child.' His partner seems moved and he gives a wistful smile, comes back to the fence and holds out one hand so that Wolf, who's so amazed he's forgotten his caution, abruptly tenses, which looks rather brusque. But Richard isn't going to embrace him, he just pats his cheek and repeats, a little more softly, 'Like a little child . . .'

Then, the pair of them say goodbye, the shadows of the trees flow over their clothes and as they take the sharp turn into the next street, Wolf can see their faces again, the customary discontent in them, the lifelessness. The woman is walking, upright and slightly stiff, two steps in front of the man with the slight limp, the cloth bag over his shoulder, and the fact that even now, when they could see him on the steps out of the corner of their eyes, they don't give one last farewell wave, as most people do when they leave, doesn't just strike him as deliberate rudeness—it contains the real truth about the visit.

He can perhaps understand this man he used to admire, respect him within limits, but certainly not love him and that harms him, he can feel it clearly, like a dose of bitter radiation. He locks the door from inside, sits down at his desk and, on one starless night towards the end of summer, while his thoughts are still revolving round him and he goes out onto the balcony to sharpen his pencil and wonders what the point of the visit was, the brief answer, that will shame him for a long time to come, is being printed for the morning paper, under 'Miscellaneous' in the arts section. Richard Sander is dead.

5
the morning after death

Autumn is taking its time arriving. The trees are still green and there's not a breath of air on the roof terrace, the hair Wolf combs out of the brush stays on the tiles and the heat of the day hardly diminishes during the night. It's only in the city centre, where the tram rails are becoming warped in the soft asphalt and the slats of the ventilation shafts over the restaurant doors clatter constantly, that a few lime trees are already bare and all the lighter and darker shades of grey, that, during the last few weeks, merged seamlessly under the shimmering dust of summer, are again becoming more distinct from one another.

There are Sunday afternoons when the city looks as if someone had lost it at poker. Hardly anyone in the streets, not much traffic, here and there a dog. He accompanies Alina, who has to go to Tübingen again, to the station and then goes on to Prenzlauer Berg, taking no flowers. Charlotte is sitting at the computer in her slip, scrolling through a text, and although she likes it when he smells sweaty, especially round his balls, he goes to have a shower. There's a new dressing gown hanging on the bathroom door, dark blue with a coat of arms on the breast pocket and the same aftershave as he uses is on the cupboard with the mirror. He just gives himself a quick dry with the towel and, as he massages her gently, the water from his hair drips on her shoulders and she moans with pleasure, though without taking her eyes off the screen. 'I'll be finished in a moment,' she says as he moves closer to her so that she can feel everything and puts his hand inside her slip to stroke the trail of sweat between her breasts. 'You can pamper me in a minute.'

Her mouth has recently been freshened up, discreet permanent make-up applied with a fine tattooing needle making it look younger than her face, which gives it a hint of the macabre. A new mouth for nine hundred euros. She reminds him of the beauties of the later 1960s with their fashionable heroin-addict look and, while she can once more give her kiss, despite her stale office-breath, the consistency of very runny honey, she pulls down the lid of her Notebook without looking at it as she loosens the towel round his hips. Then she lies down on the desk and he sits down in front of her on the chair, pushes the satin of her slip up above her navel and starts to examine her, the way she likes it—'like a piece of meat.' He dribbles the juice of squashed grapes over her and takes a sip of wine now and then.

They're in no hurry. Because they're no longer seeing one another in secret, their meetings have naturally lost the thrill of concealment, what you might call their whispering quality, and there's less of a build-up of tormenting arousal caused by their uncertainty. On the other hand, there's now a matter-of-factness between them which is equally exciting as they calmly try out everything their good fortune has in store for their bodies, and since there are no time limits set any more, apart from the last train perhaps, no end of a supposed visit to the cinema or theatre to take into account, they can lie for hours on the wide sofa, just like a married couple. They even watch TV and on that Sunday evening, as a gentle breeze makes the curtains billow and Charlotte is dreamily playing with his cock, it's suddenly there, the silent spasm under the breastbone, the sweet ache they both feel at the same time as, with a quiet 'Come' that is little more than a breath, she puts her arms round his neck and pulls him, who has suddenly gained new strength, back inside her, into the warm semen that's already there. And he bites her neck and comes again.

'Oh God,' she groans a little later. 'You're almost the only one I have an orgasm with at the same time.' Immediately he feels put out and looks for his boxer shorts. That she, a trained psychologist, cannot refrain from such crude stratagems, even at moments like that, suddenly strikes him as pitiful and unsavoury as well. It makes him think of athlete's foot in high heels. His jealousy would be the preserving, even rejuvenating, gloss on what she can see in the mirror on the wall over there and he can readily appreciate that, but ultimately he's more than happy about the existence of her other men since it spares him more explicit claims, even demands on him, which he'd have to reject for lack of time, if nothing else. So, he ignores what she's said and goes and gets some Camembert from the kitchen.

Charlotte, who likes to boast about her flirtations while she's away on business and, therefore, probably more likely gets by without one-night stands, shows great intelligence in the way she manages her three official twosomes. For Urs, the Swiss nuclear physicist, she has a restlessly caring, almost maternal love; the man with the full beard, who looks very striking in his photos, seems to have immense difficulty organizing his everyday life, so that for fifteen years now she's been getting lawyers, estate agents, accountants and tradesmen for him, correcting his letters, reminding him to take exercise. And, whenever Urs interrupts their moments of mute understanding with an expression of pain or a slight cough, she cancels her appointments. She uses role-playing to rehearse important discussions the shy man is due to have with his superiors or the authorities and, if she can't fly to Switzerland to check up on his apartment—he keeps manuscripts in the frying pan!—she buys him two dozen pairs of boxer shorts from an organic mail-order firm and sends them freshly washed to him by express delivery. They meet every few weeks and they spend their holidays and more important festivals at his sister's stud farm on Lake

Biel, where they spend half the day poring over their academic books, eat by the open fire in the evening and lie quietly beside one another during the night with no sex at all. That, she once said, had gone out of the window right at the beginning of their relationship, the poor chap clearly found her femininity too much for him. But she loved him very much.

Since it's almost impossible to entice Urs away from his formulae and theories, she needs a man for what she understands by an active metropolitan life. For that, there is Mark, the government official, married, two almost grown-up children. He, who has the problem of a wife who drinks, idolizes Charlotte and willingly trails after her to the Philharmonic, to cinema or theatre premieres, to the latest clubs, restaurants or galleries. This stocky man with thick, curly hair, tinted, whose voice, refined by all the talking he has to do and which she sometimes goes into raptures about, you almost feel you can see in his photos, is one of the old 1968 revolutionaries for whom their strategy of conquering the institutions has become his goal in life and his imminent pension the ultimate utopia. She's spent the odd weekend in Brittany with him, eating oysters, or on a gastronomic tour of the south where the olive trees grow, and the fact that, like many of his generation, he never talks about his feelings, is incapable of it, so taken up he is with the politics of the day, is clearly not a disadvantage. It's enough for her that he desires her—

even if it's just so that she can keep him on short commons. That, at least, is how she once put it and when Wolf accused her of being cold, she said, 'No, no, not at all. I like sleeping with him.'

He had to laugh. It made it sound like: 'Barley soup's not that bad at all,' and she shrugged her shoulders. 'Of course, compared with you, it's like the difference between day and night.' So, he's the Latin lover in this quartet, a role he's happy with because it saves him having to talk too much. It's not really him but the slight thrill that she might be asking too much of him gives him that extra bit of strength and means that having lived up to her demands gives him profound satisfaction. But even if, like Charlotte, he sees the almost purely physical nature of their relationship—from a certain distance, there is a great attraction in it, from too close, a certain revulsion—he sometimes wishes there were more attention and exclusive abandon than he dares to say out loud, even if only that tiny bit that would get her to take her watch off in bed and not check the display on the telephone as it rings when he's already penetrating her, that she'd give him a massage for once as well or make him come without expecting the same for herself in return and ask him in a tender whisper not to go, not yet. But so far, she's never done that. Part of their Sunday ritual is to watch an episode of a TV crime series, *Tatort*, after sex.

On that quiet evening, too, when their brief closeness would probably have been too much for her without something to distract from it, she's looking under the pillows for the remote control even before he's picked up his socks. It's in the fruit bowl. 'You just can't give,' he says with a grin as he does up his belt, the clinking buckle, and puts on his shirt. Her body is striped with the shadows of the blind, there's late-evening light on her hip and her breast, red from his bites, and she's stuck a Kleenex in her slit and behaves as if she hasn't heard. She can't get the TV to work. 'You can only take,' he goes on, plucking a few grapes off the bunch. 'But in a way that makes us happy.'

He turns to go and he's almost out of the door when he hears a faint, soft noise, one that is difficult to imagine in the bare walls and Bauhaus furniture, as if it comes from the depths of childhood, and the weight of the following silence draws him back into the room. The sun has sunk below the roofs, the shadows have merged in a general greyness that is a relief for the eyes and Charlotte is crying. She's put her arm over her face, her nose is running, her lips quivering, and because he immediately thinks she's putting on an act whenever she whispers words from the heart or gives him tender glances in bed or just before, he can tell she's not pretending. Apart from moments of intense physical pleasure, he's never seen tears on her cheeks and he's slightly embarrassed as he perches on the edge of the sofa, clasps his hands in his lap and waits. The sky above the courtyard is still red but it's quickly getting dark in the room.

Charlotte says nothing, he can hardly hear her breathing, just the second hand on her wrist, but that gives her sorrow a seriousness he finds more and more intimidating. It also makes him feel helpless as he asks himself what can have been so hurtful about his casual comment. Its echo seems almost flattering to him, at least the poetry of his remark is a gift, he thinks, a gift not every lover gets. And anyway, there have been more hurtful things said between them, and that only recently. After an argument over some minor matter, Alina had said, 'Boy, you really are screwed up, you'd better go and see your Charlotte again.' And when he told her that, with a kind of smug grin but still proud and full of admiration for such detachment, she had shown no reaction, she stared out of the window, took a sip of her Scotch and eventually muttered, 'She must think of me as a high-class tart.' And, since he felt it was not her place to criticize Alina, he unscrewed the tube of lubricant, casually remarking, 'What do you mean, high-class?'

But then, Charlotte had just hurled a few cushions and a book—his last novel—at him. Now, she's still crying and, when he pats her shoulder and strokes her hair, she gives a loud sob, rolls over and puts her head on his knee. The suspicion that he's touched a hidden sore place grows stronger and, once more, he's aware of how little he knows about her—and that not because she doesn't tell him things but because he's so impatient, horny or tired that he hardly ever listens. Her cold-hearted parents, her nasty brothers and sisters, her difficult childhood marked by illness, the time she spent in a Catholic boarding school, the way she used to masturbate every day from the age of nine, the compulsion to be the best everywhere and at everything which was only bearable if she told herself that was what she wanted, her unfulfilled longing for a woman, and all the weird men, the depressives, the schizophrenics, the stammerers with moist hands, that she has been drawn to since her teens—there's clearly a nerve in the dark recesses of her past which only someone who can take her sorrow is allowed to touch. A loving friend, perhaps, but certainly not a lover. Wolf, anyway, finds it easier to tell himself that, by now, she's not suffering so much, and therefore in need of comfort, as enjoying crying—taking a bath in warm tears, which he can feel through the material. So he says, in a deliberately joking tone, 'Oh God, I'm surrounded by wailing women. Try not to drip on my trousers. What's wrong?'

Slowly, she sits up and he hands her the box of tissues. But, she picks up her panties from the floor and blows her nose on the cotton cloth. Then, she lights a cigarette from the packet someone or other's left there, the lighter has the logo of a computer firm. She has hollow cheeks when she sucks on the filter, the lines on her upper lip deepen. She stares into space, her eyes narrowed, blowing out the smoke through her nose, and the longer she stays without saying anything, the more severe her profile seems to him. For the first time, he is made aware that she's an educator and he can imagine the respect in which she's held by her colleagues in the research groups.

'I give you a lot,' she finally says, swallowing, her voice sounds croaky, almost old. 'I give you more than you realize, you selfish swine.' She has to cough and stubs her cigarette out, her fingers are trembling. She crosses her arms over her chest. 'Without me, your life would be missing the element that saves you from dull resignation, from becoming an old fogey. You see, I'm the shaft of light in your narrow little existence. Without me, your nice home would be nothing, the mere shadow of nothing, if you see what I mean.' And, when he defiantly rejects this, raising his chin and asking her not to overestimate her importance in his life, she becomes more vehement. 'Without our hidey-hole here, you would have long since wasted away in your narrow-minded suburb full of ex-GDR idiots and eco-friendly furniture. You would have hidden away behind what is necessary because you're afraid of what is possible. I swallow your semen but, in truth, all you ejaculate is tears. I'm the one who fires up your sex drive so that you can write sentences people can read without dislocating their jaws yawning. I stick my arse up for you and without the variety I offer, without the underwear I let you tear and the filthy things I let you do to me, you would have long since lost any desire for your oh-so-understanding little woman at home and she'd be vegetating in front of the telly like all the others. I keep your relationship alive, just you remember that, my friend. And now, I'd like to be alone.'

She wipes the tears from her eyes with the back of her fingers. On her face, almost white with bitterness, her mouth looks as if it's painted on. She pulls a blanket up under her chin, presses the button on the remote control and switches on *Tatort*. And, instead of treading quietly, as he usually does, he stomps across the parquet floor, takes his jacket off the hook and opens the door to the landing wide so that he can slam it shut. But then he closes it softly.

The hissing of the swans on the lake—as if the skin were being stripped off the silence.

A writer's deadly sin—to write about Mozart.

The journey through the warm night is far too short. The line runs straight as an arrow between the trees. Twigs scrape against the windows and the light from the juddering carriage shows bushes full of velvety blue or red berries. There are high stacks of wood along the tracks which show up bright from the sawdust, here and there is a house.

The seats in the old GDR tram are insultingly small. Wolf imagines he can feel the dictates of the obsolete state, the ordained moderation, in his back. Alina, who's been suffering from a headache all day, leans her cheek against his shoulder and closes her eyes. The pupils under her eyelids are twitching nervously, sometimes vertical furrows appear between her brows and he can see the vein in her neck beating—too quickly, he thinks. He doesn't say anything but clearly she can sense that he's concerned and pats his hand reassuringly. The dog places his head on her knee.

The journey through the nocturnal woods lasts just ten minutes and they get off at Pyramidenplatz. Despite the roads radiating from the castle park, Schöneiche, just outside Berlin, is a pleasantly irregular settlement. It's somewhat spread out and, if you're initially inclined to regard it as a village, your weary legs soon correct that impression. The separate districts go deep into the hilly fields and woods which cast their shadows even on the car parks of the discount warehouses where raccoons rummage in the rubbish bins, snuffling eagerly. At the time of the old empire, the side streets were paved with undressed stones, many of the fences are made of wire mesh and the people who live there carefully rake the footpaths of bare earth edged with grass.

The beautiful, mostly very plain houses on the large plots are surrounded by pine trees and are far enough away from one another to exclude any discord, one would think, and allow peace and quiet to reign. From Schönefeld Airport, you hardly even notice the planes flying high above the town.

Famous GDR actors used to live here and, in one or other of the villas, the Stasi trained their collaborators or put up guests it was better to keep hidden—exposed Nazis whose collaboration they still needed or young terrorists wanted for murders in West Germany who ate Thuringian sausages and drank the excellent Radeberger Pilsener while they waited for new passports or air tickets to Lebanon.

It's just ten o'clock but most of the houses are already dark. Alina and Wolf automatically lower their voices and put the dog, who seems nervous, on the lead. In contrast to the private properties, the little Goethe Park, beside which Mrs Seidenkranz lives, is not particularly well-kept. The rotting benches are surrounded by clumps of nettles, wild corn is growing among the acacias, their beards glinting in the light of the few lamps whose bulbs haven't been smashed and, when Webster suddenly halts, raises one paw and stretches his head forwards, his whole body quivering, a wild pig bursts out of the undergrowth, a slim, slightly long-legged sow, and runs off, the bristles on the back of its neck standing on end. The clatter of its hooves on the road sounds as if it's running on bakelite.

Mrs Seidenkrantz greets them with a radiant smile and opens the door wide. She's wearing a starched white apron with lacy straps over her dress and a cream blouse and, since Wolf has to keep a hold on Webster, who's growling and almost dragging him off the steps, Alina hands her the flowers. She claps her hands together in delight and her soft, almost whispering tones are certainly meant to express breathless joy, yet it seems to him as if she doesn't want to attract the neighbours' attention unnecessarily. Despite the smell of freshly baked cake in the rooms, he thinks he can detect a faint touch of alcohol on her breath and a certain liqueur-happy look in her eye. He thanks her for the call and the invitation and she closes the door, saying, 'Well, I hope you're not going to be disappointed. I've just made meatballs and defrosted an *apfelstrudel*.'

The unremarkable detached house turns out to be very spacious. The living room, lit only by a standard lamp and an aquarium, full of nooks and crannies with potted palms, leather armchairs and sofas, looks as if it's been extended several times, using different materials on each occasion. There are different floor levels and cloth-covered, wood-panelled or white-brick walls with plates, barometers and clocks hung on them and, when Wolf expresses his amazement at its gallery-like proportions, Mrs Seidenkrantz says, 'Yes, you just try and keep that clean. But my husband's in the trade—if he's not bricklaying, he's sawing wood in every free moment he has. You can hardly see the house for all the extensions. The neighbours are already asking when he's going to roof over the cemetery next door. But, for the moment, he's in Bulgaria.'

She opens a door and leads them along a narrow corridor with windows, lit only by the moon and full of shelves with cactuses on them. Some are as tiny as thimbles, others as fat as cucumbers or even pumpkins and, here and there, a delicate pink, yellow or bright-red flower can be seen—they're arranged in species and the species according to size, so that the impression is one of an archive, despite the weird or even obscene shapes. Occasionally, one of the spines has a slip of paper stuck to it. 'Sometimes you can hear them grow,' she says. 'It's as if they were whispering.'

There are lights behind a semi-transparent plastic sheet, an old shower curtain. Mrs Seidenkrantz draws it aside and ushers them in. The actual conservatory is a glassed-in oval with a pointed cupola, full of citrus trees, camellias and fern-like plants whose shadows start to sway as the flames of the candles suddenly flicker, making the people—two women and one man—sitting at the round table in silence seem all the more motionless. Their hands on the arms of the white plastic chairs, they look up at them with curiosity and, although one of the women is smoking, an intensive smell pervades the air which reminds Wolf vaguely of a sweet from his childhood days but he can't remember its name.

Mrs Seidenkrantz does the introductions. The Mauchs, slightly older than him, live across the road and probably don't originally come from Berlin or Brandenburg—at least the way the man in the blue shirt speaks when he springs up from his chair sounds as if he comes from somewhere further south. He stands up, his shoes neatly side by side, and bends his head with the precise parting as he shakes Alina's hand, adding a crisp 'Egbert' to his surname. His wife, who stays seated, smiles as if asking them to make allowances for him—with a black flannel dress with a little white collar, she's wearing stockings with a lozenge pattern and warm slippers—and strokes the panting Webster.

Their hostess turns to the other woman, a deli-cate old lady with a bun and a cigarette between her fingers—her aunt. There are bluish shadows round her large, grey, slightly roguish eyes and, since she's pouring herself a stiff drink—Russian vodka—she just greets them with a nod. Mrs Seidenkrantz frowns. 'Good heavens, I don't believe it! Do you have to drink that stuff neat? You should think of your heart.' But her aunt just takes a drag on her untipped cigarette, plucks something invisible off her blouse and says, more with the smoke than her voice, 'I don't have to do anything,

Erika. But you know I'd do anything for you if I had an ashtray.'

With a resigned smile, her niece puts a little crystal bowl down in front of her, then takes Wolf and Alina to a trellis a bit like the wall bars in a gymnasium. Right up to the glass ceiling, its horizontal struts are so thickly entwined with the arms of a clearly very old cactus that you can hardly see the wood. It looks like a not very fat, pockmarked snake tangled up in itself. Here and there on the dark-green surface are scars and, in one place, it's been cut back, presumably where an arm had tried to wind itself round a window catch. It's a tall plant, taller than either of them, the curved upper sides look like shoulders armoured with spikes and the fact that they have to look up to see the single, lotus-like bloom with the pointed sepals and pure-white corona gives the plant a regal air and makes Mrs Seidenkrantz's quiet reverence seem appropriate when she whispers, as if she'd just drawn back a curtain with an embroidered coat of arms, 'So there she is, our queen of the night.'

There's something breathtaking in the intensity of the exquisitely fresh scent coming from the custard-yellow shimmer on the base of the petals. It seems entirely familiar and, at the same time, something never before experienced. Just as a starry sky is more than a sky full of stars, it has a quality which goes distinctly beyond the biological—if only because as a lure it testifies to the astonishing level and refinement of the creatures that it is to attract and that surpass humans, as far as taste and elegance are concerned, in the depths of their echo chambers, even if they're only moths. The longer you look at the flower, the darker its surroundings become, and it is presumably the sun-like corona that increases the impression that this stylish desert plant, that only opens for a few hours during one night of the year, it is not so much blooming as shining—a light with tiny insects twitching round it.

Mrs Seidenkrantz points to another part of the trellis. Arranged in bunches, the growths, bigger than a man's fist, distinctly heavy and full, surrounded by a swirl of sharp sepals, look like fruits, old rose and light yellow. In fact, they're buds. 'And I was thinking they weren't going to bother this year. Normally, they would have appeared six weeks ago but they know the seasons better than we do. Because of the lasting warmth they took their time. If things go well, they'll all bloom tonight. But you never know. Sometimes it only takes the hint of a change in the weather or one candle too many and they give it a miss. Or cigar smoke too. Then we have to wait another year.' Hands on her hips, she turned round to face her aunt. 'Did you hear, Gerda love?'

But she shakes her head, making her flabby earlobes wobble. 'No, my child, I'm afraid I have to disappoint you. I was just listening to Mr and Mrs Mauch, they had something very interesting to say. Something rude from their club. I'll tell you, if I remember . . .'

Mrs Seidenkrantz sighs and indicates the two empty plastic chairs. They have cushions in crocheted covers and after the aunt has poured them beer in slim glasses with red hearts printed on them, she leans towards Wolf and says, 'So you're the writer? We can be glad you've still got such a good head of hair and need Erika's services now and then, can't we? Otherwise we'd hardly have met. I live over there, in Heinrich-Mann-Straße—do you know him? I much prefer him to his starchy brother, he wasn't such a tight-arsed goody-goody, he enjoyed life to the full and he was the greater author anyway. I once heard that as a young man in Lübeck he was always in a dilemma when he had money. Should I buy myself some marzipan or go and see the girls? he wondered. That would naturally be a sin but if I remain chaste and eat marzipan, I'll get stomachache and that will make Mama and Papa worried. So it'll be better if I don't get sick and go to the brothel—that's the kind of man he was.'

Mr Mauch, who is nibbling at nuts out of a bowl, gives a snort and shakes his head and even her niece put her hand over her mouth, in a shocked gesture, but there's a smile on her face behind her fingers. Aunt Gerda stares at her glass. 'But if you're a writer you've got to have ideas all the time, mustn't you? I imagine that must be pretty difficult. Do things occur to you?'

Wolf takes a sip of his beer, which is almost black. 'God, I don't think I'm particularly imaginative.'

'There you are! Nothing occurs to me either, hasn't done for ages. And whenever I read something, I have the feeling I know it already. But why should I feel differently about novels than about people. In the past, they often used to say that the worst thing about getting old was that you stay young and, for a time, I'd have gone along with that, one hundred per cent. It was only other people who had a lot of wrinkles. But do you know what's really horrible? That it lasts so long. That death's such a slowcoach. Who keeps fin-ishing off my drink? You, Mr Mauch? Isn't that something stuck on your lip?'

Screwing a digital camera onto a stand, Mr Mauch takes a deep intake of breath, as if he's about to protest, but then he reaches over and pours her some more vodka. With a lopsided grin, his wife, who's pulled two candles over beside her and is leafing through a fashion magazine, says, 'I used to be in one of those district poetry groups. The things you did when you couldn't get Western TV. "Be the cultural lung of the nation," they always used to say, even at work. They organized writing competitions with themes such as "Tell us your experience of everyday life in the GDR, how you help to mould it, how you continue the work of the fathers of the revolution, what makes our society worth defending?" and so on. And I wrote, "We are the cultural dung of the nation." A typo, of course, I come from farming stock. Despite that, I was out on my ear.'

Laughing louder than all the rest, she reveals a distinctive gap between her two front teeth and, in order to divert attention away from himself and his activities, Wolf asks Mr Mauch about his work. Apparently taken aback at being addressed at all, he swallows on the cashew nuts and places a hand on his chest. 'Oh,' he says quietly, 'I was just a waiter. In Leipzig, Hotel Mercure. "A happy guest is what we like best." After the Wall came down, we inherited the house here.'

Without looking up from her magazine, his wife tut-tuts in irritation and, when she quietly corrects him—he was a *head* waiter—he smiles vaguely and replies, obviously for the benefit of Wolf and Alina, 'But, dearest, we were all equal then, don't you remember? True, I was a leader with section responsibility, though only for the coffee bar. Even there you could be rushed off your feet. We were constantly running out of whipped cream and then there was trouble because our folk felt they were being treated as second-class citizens. I had to deal with hundreds of calls and letters of complaint because, supposedly, we gave the Western visitors to the Trade Fair preferential treatment, for the sake of the hard currency.'

Aunt Gerda yawns. 'Well, wasn't that true?' she murmurs picking up the crumpled cigarette packet.

The gouty joints in her fingers gleam, as if they were bursting with pain, as if even the candlelight hurt her. 'I even used to do that when I was a loo attendant. One cubicle was always kept free.'

The man nods very slowly. 'That is correct, you could say that, Madam. But it wasn't official. The accounts had to be reconciled, with fraternal greet-ings. There were abuses but never without a receipt.'

His giggle sounds like quiet bleating and Mrs Seidenkrantz, who probably finds the conversation embarrassing, places a hand on Alina's shoulder and points to the trellis where, at that moment, two buds are opening, almost unnoticeably at first. Some pure white can be seen between the points of the salmon-pink sepals, tiny frills which don't change at all for a long time—as if the abrupt silence and expectant attention in the room constituted a resistance the flowers did not yet dare break through. One could almost believe it was out of modesty. Mr Mauch sets his camera going and slowly the pointed sepals, straw-coloured on the inside and twisted in a spiral round the buds, loosen and bend back to make room for what is to come.

'With fraternal greetings!' the old woman says with a sarcastic grunt. She points the dead match at Wolf. 'Do you know what was at the bottom of my first letter from my later husband? "I love you always. Heil Hitler! Ever yours, Kurt." Funny, don't you think? He was one of those ultra-dashing types. I hate to think what he got up to then. And thirty years, four children and two miscarriages later, after he'd slipped off to the Polish side of the Baltic with his new piece, it was, "I hope we can still remain friends. With fraternal greetings, your old man, K." The history of the last fifty years in a nutshell. Where's my ashtray?'

Now enough of the coronas has appeared to make you think of old costumes, of lace cuffs coming out of dark velvet sleeves. The scent, its abrupt sweetness, seems to make the greenhouse swell, insects flutter against the glass and Wolf pushes the crystal bowl over to the woman. She drops the match in it, subjecting his hands to a brief inspection as she does so, and, when she raises her tired eyelids, there's something roguish in her look, a gleam from the past. The lipstick she put on at some point during the last few minutes goes a little over the edge of her mouth and she twists a few hairs, as fine as gossamer, round her shaking finger. There are two wedding rings gleaming on it.

The woman is grey to her very pores, to her eyelashes, the skin on her neck hangs loose, but the dreamy and slightly sad serenity of her expression, quite clearly brought on by her memories of love, make her more beautiful than she suspects. Fascinated by her bright eyes, expressive, like the surprisingly clear handwriting of some old people, of both longing and composure, Wolf probably looks at her for too long, too intently as well, and suddenly feels tactless with his virility. He does up one button of his shirt. And when, as a diversionary tactic, he asks her where Heinrich-Mann-Straße is, she sips her vodka and takes a deep breath before pointing at the window with her cigarette at a few pine trees on the edge of the lawn. 'Why do you ask? Do you want to come round and see me? The key's always under the steps.'

The white house among the trees is very small. It has a five-sided mansard roof with a dormer window, a semi-circular balcony sitting on slim pillars on the first floor and high lattice windows on the garden side, where there's a terrace and a pond ringed by rushes. The worn steps leading up to the entrance are in the shadow of a canopy made of wooden beams and shingles; there are empty milk bottles underneath it. An old house of the kind no one can build any more today; from its light-looking yet solid form, its intellectually satisfying but not purely abstract proportions, it must have been built in the 1820s and, despite the closed windows and doors, gives the impression of offering everyone a friendly welcome. The edge of the woods can just be made out beyond the roof and Alina leans forward, moves the branch of a camellia to one side and whispers, 'Wow, that really is beautiful.'

The windowpanes gleam in the moonlight and the old woman looks across the lawn with them. 'Do you think so? I don't see it any more, of course. I'm hardly ever here anyway. At least it's dry and warm. You can buy it if you want. It's not expensive. Two rooms downstairs, two upstairs, ideal for a couple. I have another in Rahnsdorf, right on the lake. But I'll probably go to the old folks' home anyway, to join my daughter. She'll soon be sixty-five.'

Mrs Seidenkrantz puts bowls with meatballs and potato salad on the table, hands out plates and cutlery and opens a bottle of Rotkäppchen champagne. After that, there's *apfelstrudel* with vanilla ice cream and whipped cream as well as freshly made coffee and, as he's pouring it into his cup, Wolf examines the mat that goes with the pot as unobtrusively as possible. It's a brown plastic plate with a layer of foam rubber to catch the drips and it's attached to the pot by two green elastic bands stretched tight over the white porcelain and a brass chain on the lid. In addition, the spout has a foam-rubber sleeve and tin angel's wings with 'VEB Doppeladler' printed on them. Fascinated by the fact that there was obviously a whole factory devoted to protecting the citizens of the socialist republic and their tablecloths from coffee drips, for a moment, he's not sure whether to see the state that's disappeared as poetic or monstrous.

Whilst Aunt Gerda pours a slug of vodka into her cup and, without a word, stares at the queen of the night, Alina chats to their hostess and Mrs Mauch about special places to buy things in Friedrichshagen and the surrounding area. She stores telephone numbers on her cellphone and takes the opportunity to show them a few photos—her brother's newly born twins. Since they don't want to disturb the eloquent silence of the plant nor the rapt attention of those observing it, they mostly whisper and, yet again, Wolf is struck by how his partner's posture and aura change as soon as she's with other people. Her contours seem more delicate, her look more radiant. As if liberated from his exclusive presence and the fine dust of togetherness, in the company of others, her features come out clearer and fresher, in a different interplay of forces her charm expresses itself in a new way.

Her hair has a copper gleam and her teeth, when she smiles, shine pure white, which makes her look younger, like a girl—but it is this glow that brings out alien shadows. For a few weeks now, he believes he can see a new melancholy in her face as she stares into space, lost in thought, deeper furrows on her brow, and he anxiously hopes it's not sadness about his relationship with his other woman or the bitter lees of all their major and minor quarrels that has deposited itself over the years. She often looks tired, exhausted, and his words only seem to reach her from a distance—which she mostly explains as being a result of her concentration on her work. But, if she makes a show of cheerfulness, he feels it's an act. Whatever it is, there's something different about her and, sometimes, he finds her just as mysterious as in the early days when they lived at the Südstern and her cautious crossing of his threshold looked so indescribably noble, as if she were stepping onto the delicate edges of her future, and he saw her mute shyness as hidden wisdom, which it probably was. For, unlike him, she was blessed with that bright seriousness directed towards love which only truly strong people, truly free people can summon up. And while he was in the men's toilet, still worrying about his unmade bed and wrestling with a condom machine that was stuck, she had long since realized how unique their encounter was and, when he eventually came back to the table covered in empty glasses, there was something in her eyes he can see in them now—pure affirmation, despite her vague fear, and the readiness to face up to everything, even suffering.

True, after so many years, after everything she's had to put up with because of his inconsiderate sensitivity, which is mostly only about him and his work, he can hardly assume hers is a love without reservations. And yet, he harbours a faint hope that, on good days, whatever it is she sees in him affects her like some music which, at first hearing, might seem incomplete but, in fact, just demands patience—like those songs or pieces which affect us so much, indeed move us deeply, because they don't quite satisfy our desire for a sweet resolution, because they don't fill out the inner curve of our hearts flawlessly, so that we ourselves have to supply, with the vibrations of our soul, what is lacking And that would be a higher perfection.

He shifts his chair closer to hers. It seems to be getting brighter and brighter in the room. Whole bunches of blooms are hanging from the spiny arms of the plant and, while Mr Mauch is fast-forwarding on his display through the two hours of the blossoming—from the hesitant opening of the buds and the sepals radiating out from their spiral arrangement and then, as if their momentum were too much for them, springing back a little, to the flowers appearing in a flurry of brush-shaped pistils, like birds ruffling their feathers—Wolf and Alina, who's playing with his fingers, keep looking across at the slanting shadows of the conifers on the lawn and the gleaming milk bottles by the door of the house that has long been a dream: a little house with big windows, close to the woods. A magpie hops across the roof. A cat disappears under the stairs.

Time passes, Mrs Mauch has fallen asleep and their hostess, who has put a blanket over her yawning knees, has long since stopped counting flowers, she's counting the buds that are left. The heavy scent in the room does get tiring but the windows have to stay closed because of the insects, moths and bats that keep flying into the glass in a pitter-patter that's making Webster increasingly restless, he hides under the table. The full moon goes down behind the trees, the jagged line of tops, a glimmer of dawn can be seen in the east and finally all the flowers have opened, some have even died back already. Here and there, the remains of the covering sepals are hanging, limp and reddish grey, and, when Mrs Seidenkrantz tells them they used to make pills for the heart out of them, at the same time giving her aunt a very stern look, the latter defiantly lights another cigarette. 'Yes, yes,' she mutters, shoving the packet back into her skirt pocket. 'In our next life, we'll only do spiritual things, drink holy water, that sort of stuff . . .'

She stands up laboriously, she's surprisingly tall, pulls a knitted shawl round her shoulders and shakes hands with Wolf and Alina. 'Right, then. The house is number twenty-three. You know where the key is, have a look at it when you've got time. I'll give you a good price. I don't want to make anything out of it. The main thing is that my niece should have nice neighbours. And that's it for me, children. Enough poetry for a faded rose. I'm off to bed, at least I can smoke in peace there.'

There were only brief obituaries, in some papers none at all, as if they wanted to punish Richard Sander for his lack of taste in not dying until he'd outlived his fame. Young reviewers stressed his ability as a stylist in a style that was obviously a result of their computers' style-checker or their glances at the clock. At least the local paper from his home town on the east coast of

Schleswig-Holstein printed a prose poem by him, his last—'Hymn of the Ashes'. Hannelore sent Wolf a copy. He left it among the chaos on his desk for a while until, one day, he couldn't find it any more. Written in a defiantly laconic style by a man who could already feel the presence of the angel, the short text was a lament about everything that slips through our fingers in the course of our lives and had an unforgettable conclusion: 'The despair at being nothing but ashes,' it said, 'that is the fire. And the despair at being bankrupt, that is life. But be not afraid, you've not invested a cent in God.'

When Wolf comes back from seeing Charlotte on one of the following days, Alina is sitting reading on the couch and, since she only replies to his greeting with a nod, he switches the ceiling light on and sees that she's been crying. Her lashes are almost colourless, which gives her eyes a somewhat unprotected look and the sides of her nose are red. The tears on her cheeks have dried but hardly has he sat down beside her than they well up again. Her forehead feels hot, as if she had a temperature, but she denies that, she's just got a bit of a headache, she says, snuggling up to his chest with her face so he can't see it.

She's been reading the Bible, the Psalms, and he turns his head away, looks out of the window. His visit to his other woman was not a success. Charlotte, beside herself with rage at a colleague with whom she was editing a collection of articles and who insisted on being named first on the book cover because of his greater involvement, had got drunk. Going by alphabetical order, that was her place. Wolf, for his part, was saddened to see two adults with teaching responsibilities get into a bitter argument about something like that and even take one another to the senior administration of the university—he could not help but be disappointed with Charlotte. They did go to bed together, without getting particularly aroused. He politely licked her, she took ages to come and then with strange groans, as she were clenching her teeth, and, since he wanted to leave as quickly as possible, he'd forgotten to have a wash. On the train, he noticed that he smelt of her round his mouth and so as to have a reason for letting go of Alina, he stands up with a mocking comment about Charlotte.

'No, no,' she says, sniffing. 'I don't want you to stop seeing her. I can see that it does you good. Perhaps we really are thrown back on one another a bit too much here. But I wouldn't say it's a matter of complete indifference to me. I'd feel it was odd if it meant nothing at all to me. D'you want something to eat?'

The money's out of the question. They've no savings, no insurance policies and no savings contract with a building society—no way!—and a bank giving a writer with what you might call a poetic income a loan to buy a house is something that doesn't even occur in novels. Alina's not earning anything either, which only leaves his publisher who, in the past, has always shown friendly concern about his circumstances and to whom Wolf, after a further trip to Schöneiche to view the house—it has an interior spiral staircase and cherrywood panelling and its rooms are just the size that doesn't make you feel small—writes a letter. But he doesn't feel happy about it, keeps making new versions and trying to give his handwriting the boldness he lacks.

Until now, out of a mixture of instinct and calculation, he's avoided tying himself to his publishing house. He's convinced that the slightest restriction on his freedom would be harmful to his work, turn his visions into 'projects', stop his failures enriching his experience, deprive his language of its fluid quality. He's never demanded advances for unwritten books and, for completed ones, only asked for as much as would come in from the foreseeable sales, the lowest imaginable. To present that as proof of his creditworthiness seems so naive that, even while composing the initial drafts, he's worried about losing the respect of the man he's writing to.

While it's true that his distinguished publisher is often much more than just a businessman, he is still never less than that and there are limits to his sense of humour which are expressed in figures. Moreover, a refusal would not only mean they couldn't afford the house, even though the price is more than reasonable. He could accept that. It would, above all, mean they no longer believed their author, who was now fifty, had the potential to write the books that would pay off the loan. And even if what his publisher calls the influx of expectation is something he has so far assumed rather than felt, the very idea of having to live without it, without even its hypothetical existence, is already draining him of energy. But, he eventually manages to overcome his scruples and posts the letter.

The reply is a long time, many days, coming. He sees it as a reply itself, an icy one. He can't work, is irritable, has stomach pains again and doesn't sleep well. He takes the dog out for walks in the dark of the early morning, when you can't see the ground mist but can feel its coolness about your knees, through the woods to Grünau or even Kuhle Wampe. He's bought himself a small pair of binoculars and likes watching the deer, the silent movement from one square section of woodland to another. On the morning of the day when everything was to be decided, he goes to the lake.

Somewhere, a pygmy owl calls, its melodious whistling cry fades in the distance. There's a rustling in the reeds, a gurgling of water, then it's quiet again if you don't count the midges which attack him all the more furiously the nearer he gets to the muddy pool where the wild pigs wallow. You can smell the resin, the marshy ground is springy under his steps and, when he stops, he hears a few bubbles burst and the soft hissing noise you get when water gathers in a footprint. Reaching the top of a little hummock, he looks down at the clearing, the delta of a shallow stream. The mist has gathered over the watercourse and the lakeside, the hidden bay where the animals come to drink, but it's not dense. The tops of individual fir trees stick out, a few hazels and, farther east, where the beech trees meet the conifer forest, the gnarled Scots pines, it's already beginning to lift and drifting up the slope in wisps. It slowly gets light.

There's a click in the stream, very quiet, as if the current had turned over a flat stone, the treetops above the hide are already turning pink and Wolf orders the obedient dog to stay by the ladder, hangs his binoculars over his back and climbs the rungs. Some of them are new, the resin from the spruce wood the forester used is still sticky. The door to the platform is only held shut with a sliver of wood, there are crown corks and cigarette ends on the floor, scraps of paper from a magazine, and the sill is full of notches, each one a death. He sits down on the smooth bench and feels in his jacket for the cigarettes; he found them on a cafe table not long ago, a French brand, and sometimes he takes a few puffs again.

But then there's movement among the trees and he picks up his binoculars. Although they're plastic, the eyepieces feel like cold metal. A few deer are slowly approaching the water but still staying under cover, their shadows shift between the trunks. Only one old doe, already rather thin round the loin and with scars on her flanks, ventures out of the copse and goes down the slope, step by step, turning her ears nervously and stopping again and again to look up and down the valley. Her mouth moves as she chews, one stalk of grass sticking out, her breath can be seen in the cool air down below. She keeps her hindquarters, half concealed by the grass, almost sideways-on to the way she's going, ready to take flight, and, after she's checked the bay, black nose twitching, for any possible threat, she goes into the lake with her forefeet and starts to drink. Only now do the other deer come down the slope, a small group of does and kids, their coats still flecked with white. Their slim backs seem to glide through the grass.

Just one roebuck stays on the hill. A delicate yearling with a light coat, he stalks up and down in front of the spruce and keeps hitting his horns against the trunks, making little scraps of bark fly off, or he throws up moss and twigs with his forefeet and charges mist-shrouded bushes as if they were rivals. The stench of urine from his resting place is pungent, his flanks are covered in dung. It's obviously his first rut, frothy saliva drips from his mouth and waves of excitement ripple across his coat. But, when he tries to approach the animals that are drinking and grazing, the kids slip behind their mothers and the old doe goes for him. Her neck stretching forward almost horizontally, her knees at a sharp angle, she even pursues him a short way into the woods and his outraged scream, a throaty bleat, is still sounding from the thicket when the herd has long since gone on.

After he's smoked one of the strong cigarettes, which gives him a pleasantly dizzy feeling, Wolf packs up the binoculars and opens the door with the silent leather hinges. The sun is rising, there are flashes of early rays of red between the tree trunks and he climbs down the ladder through strands of warm air. He's halfway down when he sees the roebuck again. It's alone, striding through the shallow water by the shore. It stops, has a drink and looks across the lake, with its quivering reflection, and now, Wolf can see that it's injured. There's a long, dark-red tear across its left side, with flies buzzing round it and a rib sticking out, and when it turns its head and sees him on the ladder, it doesn't start in fright. It looks at him for a while with dull eyes, its tongue throbbing in its open mouth, scrapes the gravel briefly, has another drink and then goes off unhurriedly in the tall reeds that close up silently behind it.

Somewhere pigeons are cooing and, for a brief moment, the brightness of their wings and bellies can be seen among the treetops. The cones sway but none fall down. The space beside the bottom rung is empty, the grass the dog was lying on is already straightening up again. Puzzled, Wolf looks round and clicks his tongue, to which Webster usually responds, but he doesn't appear. A woodpecker is drumming and it sounds as if the trees were hollow.

A few paw-prints can be seen in the mud but the trail vanishes in the undergrowth. Wolf calls and whistles. He scours the lakeside and goes back and forth through the forest, snapping his fingers, and if he reproaches himself for not having tied Webster up, it's only out of concern for Alina, her dismay, her sadness. By the steps to the echoing tunnel under the Spree, he jingles the spring-clip on the lead and, for all his impatience, he's astonished at his composure, which isn't an expression of lack of concern or indifference but derives from a certainty, which he hasn't felt until that moment, that an animal can't get lost.

So Webster, the dog to whom he owes so much, has even taught him something by disappearing. Since he's been living with them, he's felt stronger, healthier. His tail-wagging excitement calms him and his calm takes away some of his uncertainty. Everything round him seems more alive simply because the dog won't allow it to be irrelevant and, often at night, when the windows in the street are dark and Wolf is staring at his writing in his little room, the panting under his desk seems like the pulse of the air. The animal will probably find its own way home without him, he thinks. Moreover, he remembers a conversation between Alina and the local forester, a man with a bushy beard who's stuck his decorations and crosses of merit from the communist period on the interior mirror of his jeep—if a dog runs away, you should note the time and be at the place where you lost it at the same time. Eventually, it'll come bursting out of the undergrowth again. He drapes the lead round his neck goes home.

'Fear is man's best friend.'You live with it, it's always there.You tend it and cultivate it precisely when you've nothing to fear and, although it's a kind of quivering, dazed state, it makes you more alert, more ready to defend yourself. For the feeling that there's someone protecting you, guiding you or that the creation reaches perfection in you—all this humbug from a huckster peddling muesli metaphysics collapses with the intake of breath as you feel a lump under your collarbone or see a smear of blood in your stools or read the farewell letter out of the blue. 'Catastrophes,' a tipsy executive once said in the train on which Wolf was going to a reading—he doesn't like the atmosphere in the first class, the over-earnest grey of the faces, the deliberately unobtrusive sidelong glances appraising shoes and suitcase brands and the self-important telephone calls in businesslike tones. He even loathes this world where it's only figures that makes them behave as if they weren't dealing in half measures, as we are everywhere.

But he loves the individual seats—'Catastrophes, there's only one way to protect yourself from them: be afraid of them.'

Although the post can't have come yet, he has a look in the letterbox. Alina's not at home. She's probably gone to the bakery or the supermarket, which has recently begun to be open twenty-four hours a day, and he lays the breakfast table, squeezes a few oranges and lies on the bed that's already been made, where he goes to sleep and doesn't wake up for ages, till just before midday. He dreams of his parents, who are dead—they're living in New Orleans, in a district called Moneygarden. He dreams of the dog, his barking that sounds like steps going down the stairs. Then he feels the sun on his face, opens his eyes and at first can't make out what's going on. He's hungry and calls Alina but gets no answer, looks round, takes an apple out of the bowl beside the bed and calls louder, which just seems to intensify the silence in the flat and, when he sits up, pulls the telephone over by its lead and dials her number, her cell phone rings in the desk drawer.

The rooms are the same and they're not the same. The bits of fluff under the bed and the cupboards move almost imperceptibly and the late-September light looks as if it's been spilt over the floor that creaks softly in the heat, while the outlines of the objects become more and more distinct, more and more definite, shelf marks of memory. A fly's swimming in the orange juice.

Time contracts, the last chestnuts fall onto the car roofs and the next time he looks up the trees are bare, the nights unspeakably empty and the soft patter of the raindrops on the sloping windowpanes reminds him that she once did compare their love to a church, somewhere by the sea round Brittany, a lonely church where you could hear the seagulls' cries. It was in Saint Malo, he suspects, as the reflections of the blue, yellow and green New Year's rockets flit through the darkened flat and he sits motionless in the silence, amid the flickering shadows. Or was it outside Brest? There was a huge mirror hanging on the bare masonry, a rust-stained thing with a golden frame in which they could see themselves, shoulder to shoulder on the bench—an image in which the one colour brought out the other and the two of them made a third, unnamable, never seen, not really visible and yet strangely lingering.

Time expands, even the light off the snow in March seems wasted on the man who's waiting for a call, a word of release, while his pulse throbs in his ear, systole, diastole, and his eyes smart from lack of sleep. While new shoots appear on the withered pot plants, birds begin building their nests and pick up hairs from the roof terrace, black and faintly gleaming red ones off the moss in the joins between the tiles.

Ever convinced that an author must have beautiful things to write with, things he likes the feel of in his hand or that inspire him, Alina has given him, over the years, along with high-quality paper and leather-bound notebooks, an expensive Montblanc pen with a gold nib, a heavy tortoiseshell ballpoint and elegant propelling pencils, and, of course, he uses these things now and then. But what he likes best is cheap stuff from the Kaufhaus store, faintly lined spiral-bound jotters with fibrous paper, creaking felt tips or pencils smelling of cedarwood, and he likes pushing a new ink cartridge into the old Geha school fountain pen that's been mended with sticky tape and writes so easily and smoothly that if you're not careful it takes you over the edge of the paper. And if something works, then he's pleased at his ink-stained fingers just as he was at his first cracks and calluses when he was an apprentice on building sites—they tore the girls' stockings but, for his parents and his friends, they were proof that he'd done some 'proper' work.

When the door clicked shut, she got up, he writes and immediately corrects it: . . . she rose. Although she knew he didn't really like lying in bed that way, she'd snuggled up to him all night. But it was not her closeness that had woken him, it was the quarrelling cats in the garden, their warlike cries, whereupon she quickly closed her eyes and now it was so quiet that she heard not only her partner's departure, his calm steps in his heavy boots, but also the soft scratching of the dog's paws on the road. The sky she could see through the open window was almost starless but the moon must be shining somewhere behind the house. The shadow of the gable fell across the courtyard and the moss on the top of the shed there was gleaming as if there was a film of silver over it. She looked at the clock, put on a T-shirt, jeans and a thick pullover, and ran her fingers through her hair. She didn't put on any make-up, not even round her eyes, ate nothing, just took a drink of soda water from a little, half-full plastic bottle and stuck it in the pocket of her parka. Then she put the bedspread on the bed, watered the plants, scattered a handful of sunflower seeds on the balcony and checked the contents of her desk drawer again. Finally, she kissed the little icon on the wall, the Virgin and Child with St Anne, switched off the light and went slowly down the stairs.

The smooth wood where the banister turns, the creaking bottom step. The old corduroy jacket on the hook. She'd used up all her tears, those of hope as well, gone through every despair and, yet, it still brought a lump to her throat when she went into his study. The much-too-small table, originally for the kitchen, the piles of manuscripts on the floor, the dusty guitar, the wardrobe that smelt of lavender, the leather sofa and the wobbly standard lamp—all that had never seemed so serious and so characteristic, like hieroglyphs of a happy time when they romped round on the cushions, talked about novels and poems as if they were the world and drank tea on the little balcony. Her picture, the only one in the room if you ignored a few postcards, hung in a silver frame between the packed bookcases and she could never understand why that was his favourite photo of her. Probably because she'd been unaware she was being photographed and thus looked completely relaxed. It was just a head-and-shoulders picture. Twenty years old and still with a shock of curly hair, she had her head slightly on one side so that the flash made her hair seem almost white and gave her forehead an unusual sheen, something of the purity of a madonna. And she'd been frying fish fingers.

She took the letter out of the pocket of her parka and placed it in front of his laptop, which had little yellow Post-it notes stuck to it. She'd read it again and again, and she smoothed out the envelope and wrote 'My Dearest' on it in pencil. Her fingers were trembling so much, she had to press harder to finish the word and the lead broke as she underlined it. The crack as it suddenly snapped startled her and made her heart stand still for a moment and she briefly closed her eyes. The gap in the line was tiny, as if there'd been a hair lying on the paper, and yet for a moment she read her whole story in it. She broke out in a sweat and had to sit. The leather of the couch was pleasantly cool. An insect was buzzing behind the curtain. Then, she put her key beside the envelope and went out of the room and across the hall without looking into the mirror again. She closed the door to the apartment from outside.

The few lamps among the houses spread a hazy orange light. Dewdrops glittered on the metal fences, with the plant motifs welded on, that shut off the front gardens there. Not a person in the street and the soft soles of her boots made hardly any noise. Since she knew her partner, as almost always, was by the lake with the dog, she took the opposite direction, went under the brick bridge at the station and past the taxis with their sleeping drivers. There was a thin mist, ankle-deep, on the grass in the park. A siren could be heard in the distance, then the clatter of a train going into town, the morning star glittered above the poplars and, quickly passing the allotments behind the tennis courts, she turned onto the footpath beside the mill-stream. The banks were strengthened with wicker-work and the clear water gurgled softly. A heron was standing there in the half-light.

At what used to be the forester's lodge, a half-timbered house with pointed gables, she crossed the road with its bumpy surface of undressed stone. So far, the narrow path had run along the allotments, the out-buildings of an old folks' home and the paddocks of a stables but now the completely undeveloped valley of the Erpe lay before her, a wild tract of marshland surrounded by oakwoods and thickets of acacia, stretching out to the east with its ferns, rushes and knotgrass under an apparently endless sky. There was a strange metallic smell here, of soil with a high mineral content or excessive acidity, and, since such an expanse of open countryside was completely unexpected in Berlin, she had always felt there was something unreal about the area, like a false promise or a cleverly contrived theatre backdrop—and that impression was intensified by the way the occasional tree, losing its hold on the ground during the recent storms or lightning strikes, thrust a dramatic, splintered trunk up into the sky or the pollarded willows growing along the path would quiver to the tips of the leaves if you trod firmly on the ground.

It was getting lighter, a plane was heading for Schönefeld Airport and she saw an animal some distance away, a brown dog she thought at first. It was going along the same path as she was, trotting at a brisk but relaxed pace towards the horizon and occasionally looking back at her. As the light got better she could see it was a fox, very thin and slightly tousled, and, when she came to a muddy stretch, she stopped for a moment and watched the dead straight line of paw prints slowly fill with water. There was a touch of red on it, though the sun couldn't be seen yet, a shimmer of copper which suddenly blurred and she closed her eyes to resist the dizzy spell, took a deep breath, and stumbled as she went off the path. The fox had gone. In the forest a barn owl screeched.

The mill-stream was foaming over a weir, there were brownish flecks on the rushes and the branches of the weeping willows and when the abandoned mill came in sight, a simple brick building that had long since lost its wheel, she looked back at the open expanse that was now behind her. In the half-timbered cottage with the smoking chimney, a window was opened and a potted plant put out on the sill. The brake light of a moped jolted across the cobbled bridge and she pulled up the zip of her parka and turned off along a narrow, hardly discernible path between nettles, sorrel and dew-damp plantains—a faint animal track that became clearer in the moss between the occasional oaks, more branching, too, until it disappeared in almost impenetrable thickets on the other side of a forestry road.

Although the sky above the treetops was turning grey, it was still almost dark there and she switched on the pocket torch she'd brought with her, put one arm over her face and made her laborious way under the low-hanging branches and the jumble of spruce trees that had fallen across one another. Twigs, some dead and brittle and sharp, stuck in her clothes, her hair, her feet kept sinking into rabbit warrens and sometimes she heard the soft splat of the cap when she trod on a mushroom. A puff of peppery dust came out of some. This whole section of forest was left to run wild, presumably because it was almost inaccessible to forestry vehicles, consisting, as it did, of bomb craters from the last war, some deeper than others but all covered in a tangle of thick undergrowth. In daylight, you could see the remains of bunkers here and there, and everywhere were notices forbidding entry and warning of the dangers of live ammunition.

In order not to lose her way, she took a rough bearing from the occasional jet passing high above her. She could see the signal lights of some but mostly she just heard the jets. Schönefeld was to the south. She stumbled down a hollow and sank into the mud almost to the top of her boots, pulled herself up the nearest slope on the withered broom and other bushes and paused for a moment among some thin birches. Her heart was pounding and she switched off her torch and fought against the sudden feeling of nausea. There was a musty smell, a smell of decay, of dung, and the forest was so silent it seemed to her as if it were holding its breath, pausing in expectation, before she suddenly heard the crack of wood splintering nearby.

It must have been a heavy animal dashing off through the tangle of spruce. The ground covered in pine needles seemed to bounce under its weight, the more delicate treetops waved. For a moment, there was a shower of dew and again she crossed a crater full of brushwood. The ground made slurping noises under her old boots that were no longer waterproof. She stumbled over lumps of moss-covered concrete, tore her jeans on the reinforcing iron rods and kept slipping back down an oily, glistening shale slope. She had to move more quickly as the thin slivers of stone crumbled and was panting with the effort. She grabbed at plants but they came out together with their roots, the sweat was making her eyes smart and the damp wool of her roll-neck sweater was itching, but suddenly she was in a clearing full of knotgrass that came up to her hips and the sky above was almost blue already.

She wiped her hands on her parka. Only people gathering mushrooms chanced on this place, or dog-owners following their pets as they nosed through the undergrowth, that was how she had discovered the pond behind the beech trees, an oval pool half surrounded by rushes and with prints of lots of large and small animals in the muddy bank. The huge trees with letters, cyrillic letters, still visible up to head-height and higher in the silver-grey trunks, radiated a feeling of seriousness which struck her as kind, even wise, despite the fact that the larches among them looked more as if they were merely tolerated, half starved because of the lack of light that trickled down to them, their needles were already turning yellow.

There was a hollow under one of them where Webster had once hidden, a bleeding dormouse in his mouth, and she spread out her parka there, sat down on it and looked across at the pool where the grass was still flattened from the animals that had settled there for the night. Further into the forest, she could see a licking stone on a wooden post, a round lump, bright blue, the salt crystals gleaming like hoar frost in the early light. A bird cried behind the rushes and seemed to be beating the water with its wings, then it was quiet again and she unscrewed the little bottle, had a drink, savoured the flavour and then went through her arrangements once more, point by point.

The letter to Wolf she knew by heart, as she did the ones to her parents and her brother. She'd torn up the one to the other woman and sent her an SMS with his address, just 'Please ring me.' In her desk drawer, underneath her cellphone, were the documents and powers of attorney, handwritten, as well as the X-rays, body-section photos and all the diagnoses, the first from the Charité Hospital in Berlin as well as the subsequent ones from Tübingen University Hospital and the final one from the Cantonal Hospital in Zurich. She had highlighted the key phrases with marker pen and, as if the very thought of them had concrete substance, she felt the pressure on her optic nerve, breathed deeply and took Wolf's watch out of her pocket, his old self-winding one with the balance wheel that hummed softly as she put it round her wrist. Half past seven.

She untied her bootlaces, felt the leather. For a while she sat there motionless watching two squirrels chasing one another spirally up the trunk of a pine tree and, once they reached the highest branches, launching themselves from one treetop to another, claws outspread. Cones fell onto the muddy shore of the pool, a very pale, almost transparent cabbage white fluttered up from the grass and suddenly the silence sounded different. She pushed a few twigs aside, screwed up her eyes, but couldn't see anything, at least not clearly. Shadows, as if born of fear and sadness, were moving between the bushes and trees, spectres, not even a rustling could be heard. It was probably a deer that wanted to drink but didn't dare leave cover. The watch glass steamed up.

The first sunbeams came slanting through the tall trunks—hazy, softly moving shafts of light, in which the spiders' threads on the ferns stood out more clearly. Some of the clumps, already brown, were completely enveloped in them. The gossamer nets, with insects' wings sticking out, billowed and then shrank again in a breath of wind. Wood pigeons were cooing somewhere, the flawless morning sky was mirrored in the water, suggesting that it wasn't going to get any cooler that day either, on the contrary. Despite the early hour you could already smell the resin of the conifers, a warm scent, and on some trunks was the glitter of the drops that had just emerged, still completely clear, like crystal.

They looked as if they were spraying light round, the finest possible rays, with delicate rainbow colours here and there and, now, she couldn't repress a smile. This morning before her death was, she felt, already the morning after death and it relieved her and gave her the calm she had hoped for, took away the fear of the moment and stopped her trembling as she unwrapped the ampoule from her handkerchief, broke off the glass neck and tipped the solution, that had no name, only a bar code, into the half-full plastic bottle. It clouded briefly, a milky mist, which quickly cleared so that, after a few seconds, nothing but water could be seen once more, pure water. The purest.

It's not clear whether she was still alive when the dog found her. There were a few of his hairs stuck in the clasp of her wristwatch. Two mushroom gatherers, who were in the area where the pond was, heard his barking and yowling but at first ignored it. They were looking for russulas and bay boletes and it was only after a good half hour, when the barking didn't stop, that they ventured closer, their knives at the ready. It was a brown, very slim labrador, a gentle male, that lay down flat and wagged its tail joyfully, and when one of the men put his basket down and bent to stroke the dog on its head, it licked his hand and rolled over on its back. It had a licence disc on its collar and one of those little capsules with the name and address of the owner. There were two muddy boots in the grass with an empty water bottle in one of them and when the man went closer, took a piece of bread out of his anorak and held it out to the dog, he saw the red hair and the indescribably pale face of the woman behind the branches of the larch hanging over the hollow, some animal's resting place. Hands flat on her solar plexus, she lay there as if in bed and despite the half-light, in which an earring shimmered, her motionless profile with the curve of the chin and the straight nose, with a slight depression at the bridge, stood out clearly, as if the lines had been emphasized by a seriousness which left little room for doubt. Her fingernails looked waxy, there was no pulse at her wrist. Her eyes with the light lashes were closed, her mouth slightly open, a few withered pine needles were sticking to her temples and while the man took out his cellphone, the dog ran down to the pond, had a drink, snapped playfully at a white moth and then disappeared into the forest.

On the cover of her half-finished thesis is a quotation from Meister Eckhart that can still be read, a possible epigraph, written in pencil and then lightly rubbed out: 'Truly, my soul is as young as the day it was created, indeed, much younger!' it says. 'And truly, I would not be surprised if tomorrow it were even younger than today!'